THE WORM OF DEATH
NICHOLAS BLAKE

"Mr. Blake tirelessly and entertainingly baffles the reader, bringing in lots of sharply distinguished characters, all seen in the light of humour. . . ."
— *Times* (London) *Literary Supplement*

"For some years Nicholas Blake has been turning out some of the most exciting suspense yarns in the business."
— *Richmond Times Dispatch*

"I've just finished *The Worm of Death* and I was sorry to come to the end. It is one of Blake's very best—and his best is better than almost anyone's. His quiet but convincing Nigel Strangeways takes his place alongside such masters of deduction as the literary Lord Peter Wimsey, the cynical-sentimental Hercule Poirot, and the sedentary Nero Wolfe. . . . More crimes and a long life to him." — Louis Untermeyer

THE
WORM
OF
DEATH

NICHOLAS BLAKE

Harper & Row, Publishers
New York, Cambridge, Philadelphia, San Francisco
London, Mexico City, São Paulo, Singapore, Sydney

A hardcover edition of this book was originally published in 1961 by Harper & Row Publishers, Inc. It is here reprinted by arrangement with the Estate of C. Day Lewis.

First PERENNIAL LIBRARY edition published 1976. Reissued in 1986.

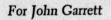
For John Garrett

Note to the Reader: I have taken three liberties in this book: (a) to alter the weather of February, 1960; (b) to build a house where no house is—on a certain quay in East Greenwich; and (c) to install Dr. Piers Loudron, his daughter, and two of his sons in my own house at Greenwich.

N.B.

THE WORM OF DEATH

1.

Dinner at the Doctor's

Nigel Strangeways and Clare were strolling down the hill past the Park. It was foggy, this February night, and the six-o'clock news had promised worse fog to come. From the Thames a hoarse bellowing broke out, and, like the pandemonium in a jungle when one great animal roars, it was followed by a series of hoots, yelps, bronchitic snorts, and breathy howls as the river traffic crept cautiously through the murk. If the fog got worse, the traffic would seize up altogether.

It was only two months since Nigel and Clare had moved to Greenwich, but these river noises, which even on a clear night seemed to come from no particular direction but to sound stereophonically all round one's house, were already familiar to them—an intermittent background music to their work and days.

"I love this place," said Clare, slipping her hand into Nigel's overcoat pocket. "I can work here."

They had rented two floors of a Queen Anne house overlooking the Park. The ground floor, for all its age, was solid enough to support the masses of stone that Clare worked on. They had turned the double drawing room into a studio, and acquired a daily to do the cleaning. This admirable woman, Em, a lighterman's wife of proportions almost as titanic as the over-life-size nude that Clare was sculpting, had reeled back when she first saw it, exclaiming, "God! What's that thing?"

"A female nude."

Em eyed it as if it were some convulsion of nature. "Fair gives you the creeps, don't it," she said. "See its bloody double, I did once, when our Stan took me to one of them horror films."

But after this shaky start, though Em would never take a duster to any of the figures in the studio, she and Clare got on famously, gossiping away like mad while the chips flew and the cups of char flowed down Em's enormous gullet.

Through Em, they were already well briefed about the Loudrons, with whom they were dining that night. Dr. Piers Loudron had been in practice here for nearly forty years; a lovely man, a real gent, don't stand no nonsense, though; saved our Stan when we all thought he was going to croak—these were some of the tributes paid by Em, whose view of the medical profession otherwise ranged from the sardonic to the blistering. Dr. Piers' eldest son, Dr. James Loudron, who was in practice with him, she dismissed as a poor substitute for his dad; he took all day to make up his mind whether you'd got sunburn or leprosy; he had newfangled notions; he failed to hand out those "bottles of the pink" that were Dr. Piers' panacea for wind; he was a stickler for etiquette and printed forms—"wouldn't cut you up without he had a dotted line to cut along." James' younger brother, Harold, was something in the City and lived in a house on the riverbank with his wife, Sharon, as to whom Em said she couldn't half tell you some dirt if you pressed her—and told you a good deal without pressure. Dr. Piers' own household was made up by an adopted son, Graham, and a daughter, Rebecca, who now housekept for him, his wife having died some twenty years before. Rebecca, according to Em, "favors her mum, poor soul." As to Graham, Em gave the impression that he was a dark horse and a bit of a lad, and that Dr. Piers had a special soft spot for him.

The amber street lighting, which turned Clare's magnolia-white skin to an implausible mauve, filtered through the fog to show the façade of an early-Georgian house, one of two pairs, at the corner of Crooms Hill and Burney Street. The woodwork outside was painted white. So, they found when they went in, was the paneling of the hall, the stairs, and the first-floor drawing room to which Rebecca Loudron led them.

"My goodness, what a lovely room!" exclaimed Clare, her eyes roving over the yellow fitted carpet, the glowing little landscapes set within the white panels, the richly patterned curtains with their design of yellow flowers and gray feathers in swags on a white background, the button-back chairs, yellow, green, dove-gray, and a single tomato-colored one echoing the red in a picture on the far wall.

"And what exquisite proportions! It's almost a perfect cube, isn't it?"

"What? Oh, is it? I'm afraid I don't know much about architecture. I'm glad you like it." Rebecca Loudron was clearly not at ease with strangers. Her sentences came blurting out, as though she had not breath enough for more than a few words at a time, and her sallow face flushed darker. She'd be quite handsome, thought Nigel, if she took herself in hand; but what possessed her, with that complexion, to wear a coffee-colored dress?

"Well, I do congratulate you on this room," he said.

"Oh, it's Father, really. He's the one with taste. He's very fastidious—you know, about colors and things, I mean."

"Unusual in a doctor, that, isn't it?" said Clare, appearing not to notice the overtones in Miss Loudron's last remarks.

"I suppose so. But it needs money, and time too." Rebecca lapsed back into the artificial hostessy manner of a small girl

3

entertaining her dolls at a tea party. "My brothers will be down soon. The fog seems to be getting worse; James must have been delayed on his rounds. How do you like living in Greenwich, Mrs. Strangeways?"

"Very much. But I'm not Mrs. Strangeways, you know. Clare Massinger," said Clare, smiling pleasantly.

"Oh. But I thought—I mean—" Rebecca flushed and floundered. Nigel came to her rescue.

"No. We live together. But Clare is tremendously old-fashioned. She believes that marriage is for the procreation of children and the raising of families. And her lifework is making her children out of stone and wood. She simply couldn't divide her attention between them and real ones. So we've never married. But it's all very respectable."

"Oh, I do admire that!" exclaimed Rebecca, unexpectedly.

"What do you admire, Becky dear?" came a voice from the door.

"Mr. Strangeways was telling me about Miss Massinger's sculpture. Miss Massinger, let me introduce my brother James."

Dr. James Loudron was a bulky, awkward man of about thirty, with a distinct resemblance to his sister. His eyes had a guarded look, which might mean discretion or secretiveness, and made the heartiness of his manner seem superficial.

"Well, you might have given them a drink," he said.

"I was waiting for you."

James Loudron dispensed drinks, with the air of pouring them from a graduated measure. While he was thus engaged, his sister murmured aside to Clare, "I wouldn't mention—what we were talking about. James is rather conventional, you know."

James came over from the piano, on which the drink tray rested. When he had given them their glasses, he stooped down, washing his hands at the fire.

"Devilish cold tonight. And the fog's going to get worse.

Hope Mrs. Hyams doesn't start."

"You doctors," remarked Clare, in her high, light voice, "do live restless lives. Always leaping up from the table to rush out and deliver another baby."

"We're used to that," said Rebecca. "Meals in this house are movable feasts."

James was looking at Clare as if he had not properly seen her before. "You know Mrs. Hyams?"

"No. I was just making a deduction."

"I see," he solemnly replied. "Quite. She is expecting to be confined any day now. Have you any children, Miss—er—Mrs.—"

"Only stone and wood ones," Rebecca put in, with a skittishness Nigel found slightly embarrassing.

"Stone and wood babies?" asked James, baffled.

A voice from behind them said, "She carves them, brother James. She's a sculptor. She sculpts. Or should it be sculptress?"

"Sculptor," said Clare. "How do you do?"

"I'm honored to meet you. I'm Graham Loudron."

The young man who came forward, after delivering these remarks with a perfectly expressionless face, was of medium height, lean and whippy—about twenty years old, Nigel judged, though it was difficult to tell with a face in which experience and immaturity were so patently blended; the cosmopolitan sort of face one might expect to see above a white sharkskin dinner jacket in some smarty night club.

Taking a drink, Graham perched himself easily on the arm of Rebecca's chair. "Hullo, ducky. How's the dinner going? My sister is a first-class cook. That's because she's so greedy."

"I'm not!" cried Rebecca, highly delighted. "Anyway, it'll spoil if Papa doesn't come soon. Where is he?"

"Waiting to make an entrance," replied Graham, his face still expressionless, which left it open whether the remark had been malicious or just teasing.

"I don't find that awfully amusing, in front of strangers —visitors," James said gruffly.

"Amusing? Of course not; it's merely true. And I like people who have a sense of occasion. Pop makes his exits and his entrances as if the spotlights were on him. What's wrong with the grand manner?"

James Loudron grunted, shaking his large head in a baffled, angry way, like a bull baited. It was another zoological simile, however, that vaguely stirred at the back of Nigel's mind as he studied Graham. Glancing at Clare, he saw that, in the telepathic way by which their thoughts occasionally communicated, she was with him. Her lips silently formed the words "fruit bat." Yes, that was what Graham reminded him of: triangular face, broad low forehead sloping down to narrow chin; ears a little pointed; small, fleshy, pouted mouth. But did fruit bats have long noses? Graham's was long, and its tip seemed likely at any moment to quiver with an animal sort of curiosity. An inquisitive nose.

What he had said about making an entrance was abundantly justified in a few minutes. The door opened, and Dr. Piers Loudron stood inside it for a moment before advancing to greet his guests. Clare was instantly reminded of B.B.— the great Bernard Berenson, with whom she had often stayed at Settignano; it was not only the pause at the door, and the ceremonious touch of being last to arrive, like an ambassador at a private party: the small, frail, spruce, upright figure; the neat white beard; the hands loosely clasped in front of the black velvet jacket; the general air of urbane autocracy and an almost *petit-maître* elegance—all these brought back to Clare her beloved though exigent B.B.

Dr. Piers came forward and took both her hands, gazing at her for a moment, his old eyes blue as lapis lazuli.

"My dear, this is a very great pleasure to me. The genius I have long recognized, but I had not known that such beauty went with it."

Nigel overheard Graham mutter to Rebecca, "Giving her the full treatment, what?" He had been aware, at Dr. Piers Loudron's entrance, of a sudden tension in the room—a tension he presumed at the time to come from the other Loudrons' unconscious screwing of themselves up to resist the strong personality of their father.

After an exchange of compliments with Clare, their host turned to Nigel. "And your name is not unfamiliar to me either. Welcome to my house. I am delighted that we are to be neighbors. You must forgive me, you and Miss Massinger, for not being here to receive you. You will understand what kept me, Strangeways, when I tell you that I was writing and quite lost my sense of time."

"Writing, Papa?" Rebecca almost squeaked. "Whatever do you mean?"

"I should have thought the expression was not unintelligible." Sheathing his claws again, the old man turned to his guests. "I have begun to keep a diary. A personal diary. I have never done so since I was a child; and now I'm in my second childhood, the wheel has come full circle." He gave Clare a wickedly enchanting smile. "I shall have a lot to write in it tomorrow. My first meeting with the great Clare Massinger. The table talk of that distinguished expert Nigel Strangeways."

"Oh? What's he an expert in, Papa?" Rebecca blurted.

Her father said, in a velvety tone, "All in good time, Becky. What is table talk without a table? You know, if I die of starvation tonight, I shall not be able to keep up my diary."

Rebecca Loudron glared at him sulkily. "It only needs dishing up. But I can take a hint." She went out, breathing hard.

The awkward silence was broken by James. "But why have you started keeping a diary, Father? I don't see the point."

"My dear boy, at my age, and when one's tenure of life is unlikely to be long protracted, one feels the need not exactly"—he gestured with a delicate white hand—"not exactly for confession but for the drawing up of a balance sheet."

"Nonsense, Father," James broke in; "you're good for another twenty years. Well, ten years at least."

"Thank you, dear boy, for your prognosis. It is meant well, I am sure. But prognosis was never your strongest point."

James Loudron's childishly disgruntled expression made him look more than ever like his sister. The old man, thought Nigel, must be Jewish: the cutting, snubbing manner, the opulent verbiage, the autocratic air of one who is beyond challenge the head of his tribe; he's an old show-off too, but excellent company—if you're not a member of his family.

"Yes," Dr. Piers was saying to Clare, "my diary is giving me quite a new interest in life. It may even prolong it. Who knows?"

"I shouldn't bank on that," remarked Graham Loudron, in an unexpectedly controversial tone.

"Oh, I'm not *banking* on it, Graham. But why do *you* say—"

A scream from belowstairs, which startled Clare, proved to be Rebecca Loudron announcing dinner.

"Why on earth can't we have a gong?" asked James.

"Gongs," his father answered, "are for butlers or suburban householders."

"Isn't S.E. 10 suburban enough for a gong?" murmured Graham.

" 'The clamorous harbinger of victuals,' " quoted Dr. Piers. "Will you come, Miss Massinger?"

The dining room would certainly not have disgraced a butler, its round rosewood table set with Georgian silver, the paneled walls painted the color of eucalyptus leaf. On the wall behind Dr. Piers hung an oil of a severe-looking rawboned lady, evidently the mother of James and Rebecca; Nigel caught James glancing at it with an expression that gave life to his heavy face, while Graham went into the adjoining

8

kitchen to help Rebecca with the dishes.

She was certainly a first-class cook. After the œuf mimosa, they ate a delicious coq au vin. Dr. Piers, in a manner which suggested that he normally left such duties to others but was doing it as a mark of special favor for her, had poured Clare a glass of wine, then resigned the decanter to James.

"Bonnes Mares, isn't it?" said Clare. "My favorite Burgundy. Aren't we in luck tonight?"

"So, Miss Massinger? You're quite right. But what expertise!"

Rebecca, coming in from the kitchen with her own plate, and having caught only the tail end of these exchanges, said, "Now you must tell us, Mr. Strangeways, what you're an expert at. I'm sure I ought to know, but—"

"He's an expert," announced their host, "in criminology."

"You mean he writes books about murders?"

"No. He catches murderers," Dr. Piers said, with a flatness of statement far removed from his normal style.

There was a second or two of absolute silence. Then Rebecca, staring at Nigel in consternation or incredulity, came out with "You catch? Are you at Scotland Yard?"

"No. But I have friends there."

"You mean you're a sort of private detective?" asked James.

"Sort of."

"But isn't this exciting!" Rebecca gasped. "Do tell us how you work."

Nigel had opened his mouth to reply, when he perceived that Clare, affected perhaps by the tension in this household of which he himself had been intermittently aware, was about to have one of her occasional fits of Going Too Far.

"It's really quite simple," she began, her tone crystal clear and twinkling like the drops on a chandelier. "One of Nigel's uncles was an Assistant Commissioner at Scotland Yard—he got Nigel to help unofficially over one or two cases. That's how it started—that, and Nigel's passion for poking his nose into other people's affairs, particularly the unsavory ones. No one can compete with the C.I.D. at collecting and sifting evidence; their machine is about as good as any could be for dealing with the ordinary gamut of crime. But now and then something turns up that needs inside knowledge—some nonprofessional crime, so to speak. Then Nigel insinuates himself into the confidence of the suspects; they've often no notion what a viper they've taken into their bosom until it's too late. He worms his way along, deeper and deeper through the secret passages of people's lives—"

"Your metaphor is quite revolting," said Nigel.

"Talking of secret passages," Rebecca put in hurriedly, "did you know there are supposed to be a lot in Greenwich, under the Park?"

James said, "Yes, when Harold and I were kids, we spent hours down in the cellars here, tapping the walls to see if we could find the entrance to one of the passages. We never did, though."

"Reverting to the Strangeways method," said Clare, "it has to be mentioned that he does rather attract crime; things tend to happen in his vicinity. I suppose it's quite natural, when —good God, what's that?"

A harsh, strangulated howl tore the air.

" 'Adiposity,' " said James.

" 'Acidity,' I think," said Rebecca, giggling.

"I beg your pardon?"

"There's a line of coastal ships that come into Deptford Creek," James explained. "They all have those peculiar sirens, and names ending in '-ity.' One is called 'Argosity,' for instance."

"And another 'Aridity.' Fancy a ship being called 'Aridity'!"

"That's because it carries sand, no doubt—to the cement works."

"James used to invent absurd names for them, to amuse me when I was little," Rebecca added.

"And they still amuse you, it seems," said Dr. Piers Loudron.

His daughter's heavy face, which had been animated for a few moments, looked quenched again. There was an uncomfortable silence. Graham Loudron switched his curiously intent gaze from Clare to Nigel.

"But *why* do you do it?" he asked.

"Criminal investigation, you mean?"

"Yes. Do you have noble ideas about justice and retribution and all that? Do you see yourself as a hound of heaven tracking down the wrongdoer?"

"No," Nigel equably replied. "It's chiefly that I'm curious about people—particularly the pathological states of mind."

"You think you can really understand them without sharing them—those states of mind?"

"Up to a point. Also, it's just as well that murderers shouldn't be allowed to indulge in their pastime. Or don't you agree?" Nigel added, seeing that Graham was determined to be controversial.

"So you are, in fact, high-minded about it," said the young man, the sneer in his tone contrasting oddly with the serious, almost deferential expression on his face. "I can't understand why you don't leave this sort of dirty work to the police. They are at least paid for it."

"Oh, so am I. I charge high fees."

"So you should." Graham was openly malicious now. "I agree with Shaw that men who clean out sewers should get the highest wages in the country."

"So do I," remarked Clare. "And what are you doing, Mr. Loudron, to implement this excellent principle?"

"My brother preaches. He leaves practice to the lower grades of humanity," said James, who had taken a second helping of each course.

"I think the fog is getting into our brains," said Dr. Piers mildly. Nigel had noticed him glancing vivaciously at the disputants during these exchanges; the old man seemed indulgent toward his adopted son—to be tacitly encouraging Graham, almost, in his provocative remarks—with a favoritism that must have been galling to James and Rebecca. "Wouldn't you say, Miss Massinger, that natural talent and acquired skills should be rewarded more highly than the sort of mechanical labor that any moron can perform?"

"Cooking, for instance," interrupted Graham Loudron. "Look at Becky's talent and skill. Oughtn't we to pay her more?"

"Oh, really!" James broke out indignantly. "This conversation is ridiculous."

"I don't agree," said Graham. "I'm being perfectly logical."

"Well, then, you have a tremendous talent for doing damn-all; how much ought you to be paid for—"

"Children, children!" their father said. "You'll be giving our guests the impression that they are dining in the nursery. Let's go upstairs now. Harold and his wife are coming in after dinner, so you'll have an opportunity of meeting the rest of my quarrelsome family, Miss Massinger. Sharon is quite a beauty; good bone; her head might interest you."

His own, thought Clare, as they sat in the drawing room, is interesting enough, but in my medium I could never do justice to the most interesting thing about it—the swift, unpredictable alternations of vivacity and melancholy; when he withdraws into himself, it is like the sun going in; the whole room seems overcast. Of course, he's an old man, frail. These withdrawals are a way he conserves his energy? Well, partly that; but also a way of impressing his personality on us, of dominating the company without expending effort? Because he's a bit of a domestic pasha, all right. Unobtrusively Clare studied Dr. Piers' face, steeped just now in melancholy, the square, thin mouth turned down at the corners in an expression of bitter, tragic acceptance. For a moment she seemed to be looking at his death mask.

The next moment, Sharon and Harold Loudron entering, Dr. Piers was all animation again. He fussed over his daughter-in-law, led her to a chair by the fire, introduced her to Clare and Nigel, teased her about a new sable scarf she was wearing.

"What did I tell you, Miss Massinger?" he said, with a kind of proprietorial gaiety. "Beautiful bone, eh?" He patted Sharon's cheek.

"You're a very susceptible, flattering old man," she coolly remarked, snatching a cigarette from a box, her hand shaking as she put a match to it. "B'rrh, it's cold outside. I've swallowed about a hundred cubic feet of fog walking here."

"You smoke too much, my dear. And eat too little," said Dr. Piers, giving her a clinical scrutiny.

"I have to keep my figure. Never know when I shan't need it again. Harold's—"

"Now, darling! Please," said her husband quickly. "That can keep."

Harold Loudron is like a shadow of his father, thought Nigel; a silhouette. The same features, but no depth to them. A smallish, spruce, upright figure. Uxorious, too—hovering over that red-headed young harpy as if she were a prize orchid. Not that, in her febrile way, she isn't highly attractive. He could still feel the hot, hard rubbery texture of her small hand when they were introduced; it felt like an animal's paw, and there was a glitter in her green eyes—the eyes which now, glancing to and fro over the others as she talked, noticeably missed out those of Graham Loudron, though his were fastened upon her.

Presently, getting into conversation with Harold, Nigel found to his surprise that this rather colorless young businessman had another ruling passion besides his wife. He was a river enthusiast. He and Sharon lived in one of several houses that his mother had bought before the war. It was right on the river wall, beyond the Greenwich power station. "At high tide, I could dive straight into eight feet of water out of our

13

dining-room window. Only I'd be certain to get typhoid, Papa says—the Thames is absolutely foul, you know, in this reach."

The house had been badly shaken by bombing, but they had reconditioned it, and Harold had even bought an old spritsail barge, which he moored at a wharf adjoining the house.

"But you can't sail her singlehanded, surely?" said Nigel.

"No. Afraid not. She's on the mud now." Harold's face, suddenly overcast with melancholy, took on a still closer resemblance to his father's. "I used to get friends down. And Sharon was keen at first. But . . . I've got a launch now. Rather a beauty—" He came out with a flood of technical detail. "But it's not the same as sail."

"Couldn't you have a sailing dinghy, or a little yawl—something like that?"

"Current's too strong. We get a six-knot tide round the Isle of Dogs, you know. Fierce. You need a strong wind to move against it."

He went on to talk interestingly about the history of the river. But Nigel felt that it was all rather mechanical; half Harold's mind seemed to be elsewhere, and his eyes kept restlessly glancing off to where his father was deep in conversation with Clare and Sharon. It was as if Harold were doing calculations in his head while he talked.

Rising, Sharon walked gracefully over. "General post," she said to her husband. "Jehovah commands. You go and exercise your charms on Miss Massinger. Not," she added, after Harold had obediently moved across, "that the poor sweet can compete with his aged parent. Piers is a real killer, you know; twenty years ago none of us would have been safe from him."

Sharon had lowered her voice to a husky murmur. Disposing herself on the sofa beside Nigel, she contrived to give a strong impression that she was getting into bed with him. Her green eyes, gazing into his, had a moony, swimming look. "I've been hearing all about you from Piers. Tell me, how many secret passages have you found tonight?"

Damn and blast Clare, thought Nigel. He said, "Give me time. I've only been here a couple of hours."

"You wait. We're honeycombed with them."

"Like a Compton-Burnett family?"

"Probably. But a book is a thing I never read. Well, then, tell me, who is the most interesting person in this room?"

"Interesting how?"

"Interesting to you as a student of crime."

Nigel had a disconcerting habit of taking such gambits more seriously than they were offered. "Well," he said briskly, allowing his pale-blue eyes to rest upon the girl's, "there's you. I'd say you would do almost anything for a kick."

"Almost?" Her green eyes swooned over him.

"What are you trying just now? Larceny? Blackmail? Drugs? Piracy? Murder?"

At one of these words, Sharon's eyes flickered as if the current had been momentarily cut off. "Well, I must say! I'm not sure you're very nice after all."

"But, of course, if you ask me which of the present company is potentially the most delinquent, I'd—"

Nigel's revelations were cut short by a loud tattoo on the front-door knocker.

"Oh, hell!" exclaimed James Loudron. "A call, I suppose."

"It may be Walter. He said he might drop in." Rebecca glanced defiantly at her father as she hurried to the door. His elegant white hand set down the coffee cup trembling.

"That mountebank!" he exclaimed. "So now he's started inviting himself to my house." But Rebecca was already out of the room.

"Another skeleton for you," whispered Sharon to Nigel. "But he won't stay in the cupboard. Becky's sweet on him. It's her maternal instinct. He's Pop's uttermost bête noire. Walt Barn. He paints."

"Mountebank" seemed an all too apt description of the

young man who now entered, with the air of one who at any moment might do a double backward somersault. He was little more than five feet high; his extremely broad and powerful-looking shoulders were surmounted by a small, quite round head, a fringe of hair low over the forehead. He had a snub nose, and blue eyes that danced with intelligence or mischief, yet looked incorruptibly innocent. Whether or no he knew there would be a dinner party on tonight, he had made no concessions to Greenwich high life; he wore a thick, scarlet fisherman's sweater and paint-stained blue corduroys.

After offering his hand to Dr. Piers, who ignored it, he drew up all his sixty inches in front of the fireplace and surveyed the company.

"Ha!" he cried. "All the beauty and some of the brains of Greenwich assembled. Sharon"—he bobbed at her—"our well-known ex-yachtswoman and ex-commodore of the flouncing flotilla of ex-models. Hiya, James, you earnest old quack! Hysterectomies coming along nicely? And Harold—big-deal Harold, the terror of Mincepudding Lane. And who do I see cowering in the corner over there? None other than our inscrutable Graham, the beatest beat on the South Bank."

"Do stop showing off, Walt," said Rebecca. "You haven't met Miss Clare Massinger."

"Only in the spirit." Walter Barn went down on his hunkers in front of Clare, hands on knees. "What d'ya love?" he inquired.

"My art, and my comforts," she composedly replied.

"You have a right to. You're good." He jerked his little round head sideways at the others. "She's very good. I, Walt Barn, am telling you, so let's have a few moments' silence to mark our appreciation of a great artist." Ignoring his own request, he sprang up like a jack-in-the-box and addressed Nigel. "Are you one of this lady's comforts?"

"Yes."

"A pity," remarked the young painter gloomily. "I could fancy a slice of her myself."

"You stick to your painting, Mr. Barn," said Clare. "You've got something."

"Do you honestly think so?" His clowning slipped like a mask. "You've seen my work?"

"Yes. But those muddy tones—you'll never get anywhere with them. It's not the way you see things. Come now, is it?"

"By God, I believe you're right!" he muttered, after a long, agonized pause. "But how the devil could you know?"

"I didn't. Till I met you."

Walter Barn plumped himself down at her feet again. "Oh, man! What a moment in Barn's life! The scales fall from his eyes. No more mud, says Massinger. Well, what do you know?" He fell silent, awed by the revelation. Even the glass of whisky that Rebecca had put on the floor beside him went unnoticed.

During these exchanges Dr. Piers had made no attempt to conceal his distaste for the young man or his displeasure at Rebecca's having brought him in. He sat stiffly upright in his wing chair, hands folded, eyes closed, dissociating himself from the conversation like a delicate ivory figurine, an idol, temporarily forgotten. But, seeing the clasped hands quivering, Nigel wondered if it were just because Dr. Piers must always be the center of attention that he was now disgruntled, was positively sulking. Or had he some graver reason for detesting Walter Barn? At least he had not made a scene and ordered this unwelcome visitor out of the house.

James and Harold were now standing together in a far corner of the room, talking in undertones. From the way their eyes glanced discreetly from their father to their sister, Nigel gathered they must be talking about Dr. Piers' attitude toward Rebecca and her impossible young man. James had a stiff, outraged expression on his heavy features; Harold ap-

17

peared to be agreeing with him, but in a distrait manner, as though he had more important things on his mind.

Graham Loudron had come to perch on the arm of the sofa beside Sharon.

"I'll be getting that record for you in a few days," he said.

"Good. I can hardly wait." She turned to Nigel, on her other side. "Graham'd be tops as a jazz pianist if he wasn't so lazy. He used to play with Lew Lindy's band."

"Which Mr. Strangeways has never heard of."

Nigel admitted ignorance.

"Which do you like best— Rock? Bop? Classical jazz? No. You're a thirties' type, aren't you? It'd be the blues."

Going over to the piano, he started playing "St. James Infirmary." But after a minute he slid into "Frankie and Johnnie," of which he gave a scintillating but unnerving performance, for he distorted each successive stanza of the ballad into a different rhythm, from the proper one to a waltz, then to a tango, then a fox trot, then a stony, stunning rock beat, and so on, but always returning to the original rhythm for the refrain. He stopped in the middle of a bar.

"Period music," he said, leaving the piano.

"I don't dig it," said Walter Barn.

"The new barbarism," Dr. Piers remarked. "It's the sign of ultimate decadence when the civilized start aping the savage." He spoke for some minutes, with elegant and mordant satire, about what he called "the cult of the tough," "the worship of the morally and intellectually muscle-bound." Before he had finished, a querulous note had crept into the old man's voice, but it was a mark of his authority, rather than a concession to his age, that no one in the room ventured to dispute his argument.

"Well, I can't help it," said Rebecca into the ensuing silence. "I like an old-fashioned waltz better than anything."

"Good for you, ducks," remarked Walter. "The old-time fragrance. You're a lavender-and-coffee-lace girl. That's what *they* think. But we know better, don't we?" He gave her a smacking kiss.

"Mother used to play waltzes—on that very piano," said James Loudron. "D'you remember, Becky, how we used to caper round? Pretend we were at a ball?"

"Yes," said his sister. "And then one day she locked the piano and never played it again."

"She played a lot of wrong notes, I expect," said Harold, "but I was too young to know."

"She didn't have Graham's—er—dexterity. But—"

"But she played, no doubt," said Graham softly, "with intense feeling."

James Loudron's large hands clenched, and he looked dangerous.

"Ah, yes," their father interposed, his old voice thin and sad as the last of many echoes. "Yes. Janet was a woman of feeling."

2.

Missing from His Home

Three days later, Clare opened the front door to let in Em, swathed by a coiling ectoplasm of fog.

"You shouldn't have bothered to come in this, Em."

"Anything to get out of me own house. My old man's been sitting about best part of three days now, wearing out his fanny. No work, see, not with the fog. Lighterman's disease he's got. Constipation. All that stuff piling up at the wharf, and he can't unload. Proper foul temper he's in. Don't know how you can stand having Him"— Em jerked her thumb up in the direction of Nigel's study—"mooning about here all day. Ain't natural."

Em divested herself of several coats and mufflers, entered the studio, and cast her usual unillusioned look at the Female Nude.

"You aren't half taking a time at That," she said.

"It's slow work."

"Well, you know best. What happens when it's finished?"

"I exhibit it. In a gallery."

Em chuckled phlegmily. "She's making an exhibition of herself, if you ask me. I wouldn't half catch it if my old man found me like that. Before 'e'd turned the light off, I mean. Well, I must do me stairs. Funny thing about Dr. Piers, ain't it?"

"Dr. Piers?"

"What? Didn't you know?" Em, in the manner of her kind, assumed that gossip arrived everywhere at the same moment. "He's scarpered."

"Run away?"

"Well, he's not there, anyway. They comes down to breakfast yesterday, and he's disappeared. Not in his room. Not in the house nowhere. That Dr. James was trying to hush it up like, but my niece Joan, who cleans for them, she heard him and Miss Rebecca arguing about it. She was for telling the cops, but he said no, maybe their dad had had a call—you know, emergency—and didn't have time to leave a message. But that was yesterday morning, and he's still not back. Joan said Dr. James said his dad might have had magnesia."

Em favored Clare with the blank expression she always put on when she was trying out her comic-Cockney-char turn. Clare had been caught out once, and she was not buying it again.

"Amnesia, presumably?"

"That's right," said Em. "Joan's an ignorant piece. Just what would 'amnesia' mean?"

"Loss of memory," said Nigel, who had just entered. The situation was explained to him.

"How do you get this amnesia?" Em asked.

"A knock on the head. Or a long period of acute strain —mental strain. Most of the people reported as missing are suffering from amnesia."

"You mean," said Em shrewdly, "they're taking a sort of rest cure from themselves?"

"That's just about it."

Em pondered a moment. "Can't see the old doc doing

that. To look at, you'd think you could blow him away like a cobweb, but he's tough as they come."

"It's often the tough who crack up, Em. No resilience. Too rigid. Can't let up on themselves."

"Well, I don't rightly know about that, sir. But I remember when that little old Hitler started his blitzes, Dr. Piers used to be out all day and night—we had it bad round here —saved hundreds of lives, I reckon. When we was bombed out—that was when my poor old dad got his—Dr. Piers turned up before the dust had settled, bandaged us up, took Mum to the hospital, bedded us kids down in his own house —I was fifteen then. Bloody marvel that man was. Night after night he'd be there, going into burning houses, crawling about under the rubble. They all said it was like he didn't care whether he lived or died. My dad was on the Heavy Rescue before he got his lot; I remember him telling us he was at an incident, and Dr. Piers was there, and another bomb fell and the blast blew the doctor right across the street up against a lamppost. Well, they picked him up and told him to go off home and have a kip. 'No, boys,' says Dr. Piers, 'I can't sleep nowadays. Let's get on with it!' White as a ghost he looked, my dad says; and sad—sort of blue look on his face as if nothing couldn't do no more to him. Well," Em turned away with a gusty sigh, "I must get out me vacuum. Time and tide wait for no man. But I tell you this—if anyone done anything to old Dr. Piers, 'e better clear out of these parts quick or 'e'd find himself hung out to dry in someone's back yard."

Nigel and Clare talked about it in a desultory way over lunch. It was difficult to reconcile Em's picture of Dr. Piers as the desperate hero with the urbane, cultivated, frail, rather tyrannical old man they had met at dinner three nights before. But crisis could bring out an alter ego, and twenty years was long enough to obliterate it again. Certainly at dinner they had not been conscious of any suppressed strain in the old man that might have caused a sudden amnesia; tension there had been, but distributed evenly—or so it seemed—over his oddly assorted family.

"The one queer thing," said Nigel, "is that he should have made such a point, at a family gathering, of bringing out my interest in crime. It was somehow not quite in character with his—his kind of fastidiousness."

"And what may we infer from that, my darling old muckraker? You're surely not suggesting that he was putting you forward as the man to be consulted if some such problem arose? He could hardly know that he was going to have an attack of amnesia and walk out on them."

"No. But—" Nigel broke off. "Ah, well, as my old tutor used to say, speculation in this field is idle. I wonder will any of them come to me."

"It won't be Dr. James, anyway. If he can't hush it up, he'd do everything through the regulation channels. But why should he try and hush it up?"

"The practice. One little puff of scandal, and patients start going elsewhere. Graham Loudron might."

"Consult you? Young fruit bat? Why?"

"He's inquisitive. He's the type, I suspect, who enjoys setting the cat among the pigeons. And he doesn't like me; he'd get a kick out of seeing me fall down on the job."

"I think he's rather pathetic."

"I think he's rather bloody-minded. How long has he been living there?"

"According to Em, Dr. Piers adopted him about ten years ago. He was an orphan. His mother was dead, and his father, who'd been Dr. Piers' closest friend, was killed in the war."

"But Dr. Piers waited till 1950 to adopt him?"

"Presumably his mother was alive till then. What about Harold? I didn't have any talk with him after dinner."

"I'm not sure about Harold. I don't much go for the City smoothie type. He's quite agreeable. But I'd say he was out

23

for Number 1 every time, which includes that expensive wife of his."

"Expensive?"

"Her clothes cost a lot. And drugs don't come cheap."

"Drugs! How do you know?"

"She told me. Unwittingly, of course. The question is, would Harold be anxious about his father? Anxious enough to come and consult me? He'd something on his mind that night. At a guess, I'd say he would come if it was thoroughly inconvenient for him for his father to be missing."

"In other words?"

"If, for example, his business, whatever it is, was badly in the red, and he needed a large loan, without interest."

"Well, I must say, that's a low view to take of a harmless young man."

"Speculation, in his field, can be a good deal worse than idle. There's the telephone."

It was neither Harold nor Graham Loudron speaking. Rebecca Loudron asked if she might bring Walter Barn that evening and have a talk with Nigel.

"So much," remarked Clare when she had given him the message, "for Mr. Nigel Know-All Strangeways."

They received their visitors in the studio, at one end of which were comfortable chairs and a cozy-stove. The fog, seeping in, slightly blurred the hard outlines of Clare's Female Nude, round which Walt Barn began to circulate, in the obsessive manner of a dog inspecting a lamppost, the moment he entered. Whether it was her well-cut tweeds, or the presence of emergency, or merely the absence of her father, Rebecca Loudron looked more mature, more integrated.

"It's very good of you to let us come, Mr. Strangeways."

"Not a bit. Have some armagnac with your coffee. Warm you up."

"Thank you, perhaps I will. How beautifully warm your studio is, though. Our house has been quite perishing since

24

this fog started. It really needs central heating. But Papa never seems to feel the cold. Walter, do stop prowling round that statue."

"First things first, Becky love." Walter Barn was lying on the floor, gazing upward at the rear elevation of the towering figure. Leaping to his feet, he smoothed the air behind it with his hand. "Nice job, Miss Massinger. Very nice. But I'm not sure about this plane here. Won't you have to modify it a bit in relation to—"

"Oh, *Walt! Do please* attend!" There was exasperation, but something like tearfulness too, in Rebecca's voice.

Walter came over at once and, taking the glass of armagnac Nigel offered him, sat down on the arm of Rebecca's chair.

"I honestly don't know if we ought to bother you with this," she said. "James wouldn't approve, I'm sure. But I can't just sit about doing nothing. And after what you told us at dinner—I mean—"

"They've mislaid their dad," said Walter.

"Yes, I know," Clare put in soothingly. "We heard about it from Em, our char."

"You see, Papa's never done this before—just going off without telling anyone. There are his patients. Of course, James can manage them for a bit. But—"

"Let's start at the beginning," said Nigel gently. By tactful questioning, he elicited Rebecca's story.

Yesterday morning she had brought her father's breakfast on a tray to his bedroom, as she normally did, at nine o'clock. He was not there. She went into his study, then called out for him on each floor of the house, but got no answer. She thought he must have gone out early on an emergency call, though she had not heard the house telephone. However, at ten o'clock Dr. Piers' secretary, Miss Anson, had come in from the annex, where he and Dr. James had their consulting rooms, to say that two of Dr. Piers' patients were waiting; he had not yet come into the consulting room that morning,

Miss Anson said. James Loudron had already gone out on his rounds, so Rebecca went to look for Graham, whom she found at breakfast in the dining room.

"I told him Papa couldn't be found. Graham said, 'Oh, nonsense. He's probably overslept for once.' I said he wasn't in his bedroom; I'd looked. Well, Graham and I hunted through every room in the house. Then I thought I'd look in the bedroom again. Papa sleeps on the mezzanine floor, above the annex. His bedroom and bathroom are the only rooms on that floor. Of course, he wasn't there. Then Graham said we'd better just try the bathroom, in case Papa had fainted in the bath or something. So he went through the bedroom into the bathroom, and then he called out, 'He's not here.' It gave me quite a shock. I suppose I'd keyed myself up to finding him there. By this time Graham was terribly worried. So we got Miss Anson to phone round and contact James and tell him to come home." Rebecca smiled wryly. "Poor Papa. He loathed that word 'contact.' "

James Loudron had at first pooh-poohed the idea that anything was wrong. But when his father was still absent eight hours later, he rang the police. The sergeant who came after dinner went straight to the point. He asked them if any hand luggage was missing. They went up to the box room with him. All Dr. Piers' bags and suitcases and their own were still there. So it did not look as if the old doctor had gone off on a journey. His car was in the garage, and a telephone inquiry at the station, where he was well known, confirmed that he had not taken a train. The sergeant next asked them to look through Dr. Piers' clothes. Here they were in some difficulty, for their father was a dressy man and had a large number of suits, and none of his children could be sure whether or no one of these was missing. The suit he had worn at dinner the previous night was folded neatly on a chair in the bedroom, with shirt, underclothes, socks, and evening slippers to hand, just as the old man had taken them off when he retired early after dinner, saying that he felt sleepy. The only garment of his that they could identify with certainty as missing was a thick Connemara-tweed overcoat of a distinctive black-and-white pattern.

"Of course he must have taken a suit," said Walter now. "He'd not have walked out into this bloody fog wearing nothing but an overcoat."

Throughout this recital, Nigel had been sitting gazing noncommittally down his nose and apparently quite relaxed, even when he asked Rebecca some pertinent question to fill out the picture. In fact, he was giving the concentrated attention, both to fact and to nuances of tone, that was one of his most formidable powers as an investigator. Clare said, smiling at Rebecca, "Strangeways is a human tape recorder, you know. Every word you've said is now printed on his mind."

Rebecca gave a nervous laugh. "Oh, I wish I could do something!" she cried.

"You can. There's one thing that seems to have been overlooked," said Nigel.

"What's that?"

"The diary. At dinner the other night, your father told us he'd started to keep a diary. It might tell us why he has disappeared."

"Oh, yes! I never thought of that." Rebecca's large brown eyes were staring intently at Nigel. "I'll start looking for it tomorrow."

"Let me get this clear in my mind. You say your father felt sleepy and retired to bed about 8:45 P.M. This was unusually early for him?"

"Yes. He generally stayed up till 10:30 at least."

"Did he seem worried at dinner? Absent-minded? Jumpy? In any way not his usual self?"

There was a slight pause. Then Rebecca said, "The sergeant asked us that. And the inspector who came yesterday. And, well—" she broke off. Nigel was aware of Walter Barn's bright blue eyes fixed almost hypnotically upon her.

"Why do you hesitate?" he prompted.

"Well, we didn't seem to agree. I mean, I thought Papa was distrait at dinner. But James said he thought he was sulking, and Graham said *his* impression was that Papa was waiting for something."

"Waiting?"

"Yes. I know it sounds odd. 'Waiting for something to happen,' Graham said. He couldn't explain it to the police better than that."

"It happened, all right," said Walter, making Rebecca visibly wince.

"And that was the last any of you saw or heard of him? When he went up to his bedroom?"

"Yes. I wouldn't have heard anything, anyway. I was in my room—it's on the top floor—playing gramophone records. And James had to go out immediately after dinner to a confinement." Rebecca related this rapidly, in her rather monotonous voice, as though reciting a lesson she had learned by heart—as she probably had, thought Nigel, after two interviews with the police.

"And Graham?" he asked.

"He didn't hear anything, either. He was pottering about in his room. It's on the first floor." A strange expression fleeted over her face. "It used to be Mother's."

Rising, Nigel gave them some more armagnac. "Well, I don't honestly think I can do much to help at this stage. The police will have put their organization to work; they notify hospitals and so on about persons missing. The main thing is to find that diary."

"There is one thing you might be able to tell us about." Walter Barn's round head, the shaggy hair falling in a fringe over his brow, looked like a lichen-covered stone ball on a gatepost. "The money. What are the arrangements over the money?"

"Household expenses, you mean? I suppose Dr. James will get power of attorney if his father's absence is at all protracted."

"Look. I'm just a blunt, proletarian painter. Pardon if my vulgar mind's showing, but if the old man never does turn up, when is the loot distributed?"

Even Rebecca looked rather shocked at this brashness, and Walter evidently felt the antipathy he had aroused. It made him the more aggressive. "It's all very well for you people, rolling in it, to turn up your delicate noses when money is mentioned. It's a dirty word—I know, I know. Just tell that to a family of six, like mine was, living in two rooms—"

"Walt! Please! This really isn't necessary."

"Shut up, woman! Don't you want to get married?"

Nigel interposed firmly. "When a person disappears, his will cannot be proved till the lawyers have established presumption of death. There's no reason whatsoever for supposing that Miss Loudron's father is—"

"Got all the answers, hasn't he, Becky?" Walter grinned at her. "Well then, Strangeways, if—just *if*—the old boy doesn't show up again, how long does it take to establish this what-d'you-call-it?"

"A period of seven years has to elapse, I believe."

"Years? Jesus Christ!"

"A great deal of investigation has to be done."

"So he could keep Becky on the bread line long *after* he's dead? That'd be like him."

The young woman's eyes were suffused with tears. She tried to speak, but her voice failed and she could only gaze at Walter imploringly. He disregarded it.

"All right. I wanted to marry Becky. He couldn't stand me at any price. Fair enough. I make barely enough to live on by myself. Her dad told her if she married me he'd stop her allowance—and a right miserable allowance it is, too. What riles me is that the old man should be able to vanish into thin air—if you can call this bloody fog thin air—and still keep her on a ball and chain like he's done all her life. I don't see what's wrong in—"

"There's nothing wrong in taking thought for the future," Clare cut in, her high, light voice like drops of ice. The sight of Rebecca, openly weeping now, had broken her own self-control. "What's wrong is bellyaching about all this and making Rebecca miserable at the very time she needs your sympathy and support most."

"Huh! The women getting together," Walter jeered.

"Don't talk like an oaf!"

"I'm talking honestly. We don't wrap things up in cellophane—not where I come from."

Clare's eyes blazed. Her long black hair swirled like smoke on a gusty day as she turned upon him. "To hell with where you come from! Do you think there's some virtue in bad manners and moronic insensitivity? Does your being working class give you a permit to behave like a bloody-minded little clown? No, you wait, young Walt Barn, I've not finished with you. People like you make me sick. You boast of your poverty and your slum origins; you behave as if they gave you a divine dispensation from showing ordinary human decency. I'm just a plain, blunt proletarian painter, so I don't have to think about anyone else's feelings. Van Gogh was uncouth, van Gogh was a genius; therefore I'll show them I'm a genius by behaving uncouthly. Lovely logic, isn't it? Exhibitionism as the short cut to success, eh?"

"Here, I never—"

Clare galloped on over him. "The trouble with you and your lot is that you don't have any values except success. That's why you'll do anything for publicity, and when you get it, you can't take it; it goes to your heads. You're just a rabble of overgrown Peter Pans posturing as roughhewn geniuses or noble martyrs to society. You yourself can at least paint. But you'll never make a good painter till you've learned that the artist must be anonymous. So for God's sake stop splashing your virility over everyone and keep it for your canvases."

Clare paused, if only to regain breath.

"How dare you talk to Walter like that?" cried Rebecca. "How dare you?"

"Take it easy, old girl. I can defend myself," said Walter. He turned to Nigel with a rueful grin. "Proper spitfire you've got there. Haven't had such a dressing down since Mum found me in the back yard with the local tart. Mind you, I wouldn't take all that from any old stone-chipper. But Clare Massinger has a right to talk. And she's talked a fair bit of sense, I reckon. I'm sorry if I upset you, Becky love, but next time I do, just throw the kitchen stove at me, like Miss Massinger here."

When they had left, a few minutes later, Nigel mopped his brow. "Good for you, Clare. But it was hot while it lasted."

"I hope I wasn't too rough on him. He's not a bad sort. He took it pretty well, I must say."

"Yes," said Nigel, a bit dubiously. He had seen what Clare had been too wound up to notice—a very ugly glint in the mercurial Walt Barn's eye at one point of her tirade.

3.

A Wind from the Northeast

Six days later—it was a Saturday—Nigel awoke early with the vague sensation that some change had occurred since he went to sleep. His attention focused drowsily upon the curtains. They were no longer, as they had been every morning for over a week, gray-black rectangles backed by the blanketing fog outside; they glowed, and a strip of dazzling gold showed between them. Getting up, he parted them and looked out. Sunlight. Trees in the park waving their branches. A clear, cold, gray-blue sky. The claustrophobic hood of fog had been lifted away during the night by a wind that was tugging straight in his direction the white ensign over the Naval College. A northeaster.

Dressing quietly so as not to waken Clare, he went out. High up the hill here, the wind drilled into his right eye and numbed the cheekbone below it. Presently he was passing the Loudrons' house. In the sunlight, the white paint of its windows and noble portico looked as if they had just been hosed down. Whatever its secret might be, the house was keeping it; no trace of its owner had been discovered since he disappeared eight days before—not even the diary, which might have explained the aberration, the despair, the stratagem—whatever it was that had taken him out to be swallowed up alive in the fog.

Alive? One had to presume so. The local D.D.I., with whom Nigel had got in touch through the medium of Chief Detective-Inspector Wright at Scotland Yard, assured him that they had given Number 6 a discreet going over, and there was no evidence whatsoever of its owner's having left the house dead. Radio and newspaper appeals had produced the usual crop of eyewitnesses who claimed to have seen Dr. Piers Loudron in a variety of places, from Deptford to Barrow-on-Furness, and the usual handful of harmless lunatics who eagerly confessed to having murdered him. These had all been sieved out, and nothing material was left in the mesh. If indeed he had suffered an attack of amnesia, he would probably be dead by now—of starvation, for his wallet was in the pocket of the suit he had taken off that night, he had drawn no money from a bank since his disappearance, and no hospitals or casual wards had taken him in.

He might just conceivably have been kidnaped. But why? And why should the kidnapers remain silently undemanding?

The local police, faced by this blind wall of negatives, were inclined to think that he must have left the house that night and fallen, either accidentally or on purpose, into the river. The Connemara-tweed overcoat was, after all, missing, and it was not altogether inconceivable that, in a state of mental derangement, the old man should put on no other clothing to walk out of the house to his death. Late at night or in the early hours of the morning, the fog being so thick, he could easily have got to the river, three minutes' walk from his house, unobserved. But the fog, clamped down on the river day after day, had prevented any effective testing of this theory.

As Nigel strode into the High Road, the clock on St. Alfege's church said twenty-five past seven. Unconsciously he quickened his pace. The river seemed to be drawing him toward it. The bodies of the drowned, made buoyant by the gases of their putrefaction, rise slowly to float on the surface again after six to ten days. It was now the eighth day since Dr. Piers Loudron had vanished, and the first of clear visibility.

All the way down the hill, Nigel had been hearing the steam whistles of ships, released from the fog's thrall, making their way upstream or downstream round the U bend of the Isle of Dogs. As he turned left out of Nelson Parade, he saw the derricks, mast, high bridge structure, and funnel of a vessel sliding past the pier. High tide, or something near it. The air thrummed with a vibration of many engines, and was impregnated with familiar river smells—diesel oil, mud, tar, rotting detritus, chemical fumes—a sour amalgam of smells blown inland by the wind, which had a taste of salt in it too. The pier turnstile gates would be padlocked still. Nigel walked past the great brown-black hull of the "Cutty Sark," under the towering tracery of its three masts and rigging, onto the railed space to the left of the pier. Early workers were pouring into the domed building that housed the lift that would take them down to the tunnel beneath the Thames; they would push their bicycles along its quarter mile of white-tiled walls, while tugs, coasters, cargo liners thrashed their way overhead.

Leaning on the rail and looking left, Nigel watched a huge, blue-funnelled Swedish cargo liner, in ballast, being maneuvered away from its moorings opposite Deptford creek by two "Sun"-class tugs, whose raked smokestacks and squat hulls, dwarfed by the Swede's tremendous hulk, gave them a prissy, self-important air. Hugging the far bank to avoid the full thrust of the ebb, three deep-waisted Dutch family ships followed one another upriver, their motors pulsing heavily. The wash of passing vessels slopped lumps of water up the stone steps between Nigel and the domed building, from which Graham Loudron at this moment emerged and walked rapidly away. What could the young man have been doing across the river at this hour of the morning, Nigel wondered.

He himself now moved off toward the Naval College. In the right angle formed by the river wall beyond the pier, an old man was leaning over the iron railing and gazing lugubriously down at the water. Nigel stopped beside him. The water was covered with a sluggishly heaving carpet of debris, driven here by the northeast wind—packing cases, bales of hay, tins of polish, halves of grapefruit, a dead cat, a gym shoe, a motor tire, and thousands of pieces of wood; timbers big enough to have been the sternposts of vanished sailing ships, planks from Scandinavian sawmills, a mass of smaller lengths like kindling wood, all jostled together in a sort of flexuous, sodden mosaic that, like oil on water, subdued the waves made by passing ships and by the wind blowing diagonally across the tide.

"All that wood," said the lugubrious man, spitting copiously into it. "Floats down the river. Then it floats up again. Backward and forward. Year after year. Makes you think, Guv, don't it?"

"What I can't understand," said Nigel, "is why the whole river isn't blocked by it, like pack ice. Where does all the rest of the wood go? Year after year, for centuries, people have been chucking wood into the river; it's been falling off ships and barges, floating out from wharves. And it doesn't sink for ages. It ought to have choked up the river long ago."

"Time," remarked his companion, "like an ever-rolling stream, bears all its sons away."

"Yes, but—"

"Funny tricks this old river plays," said the man, sucking his mustache. "Bloke I knew, years ago, got knocked in one night making fast a German ship at Grunton's Wharf. Couldn't swim. 'E just went under, like a bit of bleeding pig iron. Grunton's Wharf's on this side of the river, beyond the power station." The old man pointed east. "Now, Guv, where d'you reckon they'd find the corpse?"

Nigel gave the problem his full attention. "Depends what

the state of the tide was when he fell in."

"Top of the ebb. Like now, as it might be."

"Well, I suppose the ebb might pull him out, along the river bottom. But the current round the Isle of Dogs has a strong southerly thrust at the bend there, so he'd be bound to get pushed back to this bank, wouldn't he?"

"That's what you'd think," replied the old man with relish. "But they found him, couple of weeks later, over there." He jerked his head toward the Luralda Wharf, on the far side of the river. "Nobody couldn't account for it. Might've been an eddy; he could have got into the outflow from the power station. Some said suction."

"Suction?"

"Screws of all them vessels passing. Pull you out toward them, see? Mash you up too. Old Bert was mashed up something horrible."

"In the midst of life, we are in death."

"You bloody said it, Guv." His faded eyes gazed dreamily at Nigel. "Ah. Old Father Thames. 'E's sly, all right. You've got to watch him. Mate of mine—he was master of a tug . . ."

After hearing another mortuary reminiscence, Nigel bade the old longshoreman good morning and walked on past the Naval College, its gray stone gleaming in the sunshine, to the far end of the esplanade. Here, in the shallow inlet by the Trafalgar Tavern, another carpet of flotsam sullenly heaved. On the black wall beneath the building a high-water mark showed, only two feet below the little balcony of the central ground-floor window. It occurred to Nigel that at high water a body could be put into the river from such a window with hardly a splash. Gazing unseeingly at the wooden jetty of the Curlew rowing club, he did a sum in his head. High water to-day was at about 6 A.M. On the night Dr. Piers Loudron had disappeared, high tide must have been around 10 P.M., and by 11 P.M. the ebb would have been running strongly.

He walked round the back of the Trafalgar Tavern, along

Crane Street, and past Holy Trinity Hospital, the seventeenth-century almshouse over whose toylike façade towered the chimneys of the power station; then under the clattering conveyors of the power station, through a scrap-iron yard, to emerge again on the river front opposite the "Cutty Sark" pub. At a wharf just beyond, partly hidden by a wall, a green flag with "Wreck" lettered upon it fluttering from the mast, lay a Thames sailing barge. This must be the one that Harold Loudron had bought some years ago. Nigel peered round the wall, from which the bows of the barge projected. The bulwarks were broken off in places. A section of the deck planking amidships was gone, revealing a turgid compost of mud and water in the hold. The wheel, unlashed, made half turns as the waves thumped the great rudder, whose banging was answered by a kind of hollow, distant thunder, like the sound of the skittle game in "Rip Van Winkle," as the swell bumped together a row of empty lighters moored side by side at Lovell's Wharf.

Just beyond this barge, there showed the roof and upper story of a house, the rest concealed by the high wall. A door in the wall gave access to it; the front of the house must be right over the river. "Between the 'Cutty Sark' pub and Lovell's Wharf," Harold Loudron had told him. It was certainly a strange place for the Loudrons to live in—the dapper young City gent and his exotic, restless wife—here amongst the racket of riveting, the grime from the power station, the hissing roar of oxyacetylene burners in the scrapyard. They had the pub handy, and a glorious view down the reach past the Isle of Dogs. But otherwise the situation seemed quite out of character for both of them. No doubt, thought Nigel, it had seemed "amusing" at first: a new sensation for Sharon; and, of course, they got a rent-free house—it had belonged to Harold's mother—but the novelty must have worn off pretty soon.

Sirens blew from across the Thames. Eight o'clock. Nigel

began to retrace his steps, hungry for breakfast. From Ballast Quay he saw a police launch on patrol approaching upriver from the direction of the West India docks, a white mustache of foam bristling at its bows. He came out again on the esplanade by the Trafalgar Tavern. A white-hulled Spanish steamer, of graceful outlines, was gliding eastward. Between this vessel and the shore, a pack of sea gulls screamed and skidded in the air, circling over some debris. As Nigel took out his field glasses and began to focus them, the police launch emerged from behind a collier unloading at the power-house jetty, and its bows lifted to the acceleration of its powerful engine. The river police had seen what Nigel too was looking at now, clear in the circle of his binoculars—the thing he had not come out this early morning with the least expectation of seeing, yet which, the moment he set eyes on it, made him feel that it had been waiting for him all these days to come out and find it, directing his steps this way like a destiny—a hulk of flesh, waterlogged and dirty white, screamed over by gulls, lumbering and sliding with other flotsam on the choppy river.

The launch stopped on the leeward side of the body, obscuring Nigel's view. On its afterdeck, behind the cabin, two policemen got busy, one with a boat hook, the other with a coil of rope. Wind and tide swinging the launch round, Nigel was shortly able to observe their catch. As it was hauled aboard, the rope noosed beneath its arms, the torso stood upright for a moment on the water. Decay and long immersion had bloated the face almost out of recognition; the swollen tongue protruded from blubber lips in a grimace; the ruined eyes were smears of white. Only the silver-white of hair and beard suggested that this could be the remains of the elegant, vivacious Dr. Piers Loudron.

The policemen hauled again, their faces tight with repugnance. As the body slid over the gunwale, Nigel saw that it had no legs. The policemen laid it on deck, putting a tarpaulin over it, and the launch kicked into full speed.

Nigel took a few steps homeward; then, on an impulse, he turned round and hurried back toward Harold Loudron's house. The door in the wall was not locked. He passed through, across a small yard; hammered on the front door, rang the bell several times. At last Harold Loudron appeared, in a cardinal-red dressing gown, his black hair disheveled.

"What the devil? Oh, it's you. Has something happened?"

"Can I come in a minute?"

Harold led the way into a sitting room, which ran the length of the house, with three tall sash windows overlooking the river. Nigel sat down on a window seat cushioned with red leather. The room was paneled with birch, unpainted, and at one end of it was a dining alcove divided from the rest by a movable glass partition. Brilliant Mexican mats adorned the pearwood floor. It all looked singularly like a model for gracious, modernistic living out of an Ideal Home exhibition, except for the dust which lay thick on rubber plants, tables, and shelves—a general air of *tristesse* and seediness, which gave it the pathos of a room in an expensive dollhouse neglected by some spoiled child.

"I think your father has been found," said Nigel.

Harold Loudron stared at him a moment, in what looked very like consternation. Then his eyes lit up (artificial lighting? Nigel wondered).

"Found! Oh, but that's splendid. Thank God! We were—"

"I'm sorry. Not alive. I've just seen a body taken out of the river. I'm afraid it's very likely his."

"Oh, God! How awful!" Harold lit a cigarette shakily; then, remembering his manners, offered his gold case to Nigel and said, "Good of you to tell us. You know, in a way it's a sort of relief. We'd been worrying terribly. The suspense, you know."

A relief it certainly was, of some kind, judging by the relaxation of Harold's tense body.

"I thought you might like to ring up your brothers straightway—break it to them before the police. Sometimes the police are a bit heavy-handed about—"

"Yes, of course. I'm really most grateful to—"

He broke off. Had he been on the point of saying "most grateful to your good self"? The meaningless, vulgar businessman's jargon would come naturally to him, thought Nigel.

"It's a great shock," said Harold Loudron. "I can hardly take it in yet. My father was a fine man. Greatly beloved. And so full of life."

Harold seemed well launched upon a Rotarian-type oration, which would be more than Nigel could take on an empty stomach.

"Hadn't you better telephone?"

"Quite." But still Harold made no move. "You say—where did you see—er—the body being—"

"Just beyond the Trafalgar Tavern. It had no legs."

"What had no legs?" came a husky voice from the door. Sharon had slashed on some lipstick, but her puffy face and bedroom hair were not prepossessing.

"Darling, you shouldn't have—Strangeways has very kindly looked in to—you must prepare yourself for a shock, I'm afraid." Harold dithered round his wife in an uxorious manner that evidently tried her patience.

"They've found him, you mean?" she asked, coughing harshly.

Nigel told what he had seen. "Of course, I can't be absolutely certain. But it had white hair and a white beard. And it was the right build. We shall know soon."

Sharon threw back her tangled red mane from over her eyes.

"But what's this about no legs?" she asked.

"He must have been caught by a ship's propeller."

Sharon took three long, graceful strides to a kidney-shaped chair and sat down.

"Well, he wouldn't have felt it."

"Sharon! *Darling!*" Harold protested.

"Well, he was dead, wasn't he? Drowned, I mean, before that?"

"I presume so," said Nigel. "And drowning is a good deal more painful than—"

"My wife only meant that she was glad he didn't suffer—er—from what you say happened later." Harold spoke quite stuffily. He's still besotted with this beautiful harpy of his, thought Nigel, glancing out of the window. Waves spanked the river wall directly below it; five or six feet below. A tug, dirty-white foam piled at its blunt bows and four empty lighters in tow, approached up the reach. It hooted four times, then twice.

"Ninety-degree turn to port," said Harold absently.

"Sailor boy!" Sharon's voice was mildly satirical. She turned her diminished green eyes upon Nigel. "He'll run away to sea one day if he isn't careful."

"Well, I'd better go and telephone," said Harold doubtfully. No one gainsaying him, he went. Sharon at once slipped over to occupy the window seat beside Nigel. Her wrap fell open, and a waft of warm flesh smell came from her.

"This is going to upset poor old brother James," she said.

"Him particularly?"

"Becky will *feel* upset. But actually it'll be a merciful release for her. But James—he's been shaking in his shoes. The practice. What'll the patients say? The senior partner committing suicide. Oh dear, oh dear!"

"What makes you think Dr. Piers committed suicide?"

"Well, what else could it be?" Her eyes held his in a long, calculating look; there was a sort of excitement in them too. "You don't mean—what they call 'foul play'?"

"Or accident. Who knows? I see it'll be awkward for James, though, whatever it turns out to be. And Graham?"

Her eyes filmed over. "What about him?"

"Will *he* be very upset? I got the impression he was the favorite son."

"It would take an earthquake to upset young Graham," she murmured, frowning a little.

"Which brings us to Harold."

"I suppose it does. But what's all this in aid of? Why should you worry which of us is worried? Not that those anxious wrinkles on your forehead aren't rather fascinating."

"You and Harold will be glad of the money, I imagine."

For a moment Nigel thought she was going to claw at his face with those blood-red nails of hers. But she controlled herself, digging them into the palms of her hands instead, and replied, in a sort of husky purr, "Yes, we shall. For one thing, we can get out of this dreary dump."

"You don't like it? I think it's rather a romantic house."

"So did I, once," she said bitterly. "Of course, your generation were suckers for romance, weren't you?"

Romance? thought Nigel. The distressed areas, the hunger marchers, the new barbarism of tin-pot Tamerlanes? "And your lot is clear-eyed, disillusioned, realistic? The I'm-all-right-Jack brigade?"

"We only live once. Why the hell shouldn't we enjoy ourselves?"

"Why not? Only it seems to make you either bored or bad-tempered. But perhaps you enjoy *that*."

Sharon smiled a secret smile, her eyes glittering. She had roused this impassive man; the only antagonism she recognized was sex antagonism, to her the first sign of sexual interest.

"Not all the time," she said. "Tell me, are you a one-woman man?"

"I never consider propositions before breakfast."

Sharon gasped, as if he had punched her. "You're damned insulting, I must say."

"I thought you were against the romantic approach."

She looked at him consideringly. Then, leaning back so

that her collarbones stood out in ridges, she said, "Shall I give you breakfast here?"

"Why not?" said Harold Loudron, entering. "Do stay, won't you, Strangeways? We could ring up your house and tell them—"

"It's very kind of you, but I'd better be off."

Sharon gave him a hot, dry hand. As he went out, he felt her gaze upon his back, tenacious as brambles across a path.

4.

Unkindest Cuts

Next morning, after breakfast, Nigel walked down to the Loudrons' house. James Loudron had telephoned him the night before, asking him to come. A Sunday quiet was over the town. In the Park a few people walked, exercising their dogs; bits of paper blew about the road as Nigel came to the bottom of the hill, his mind at grips with the pathologist's report, the gist of which the D.D.I. had passed on to him the previous evening. It was a report that made the death of Dr. Piers even more mysterious and bizarre than his disappearance.

Dr. James brought him into a room on the left of the hall—a square room, its paneled walls painted with graining and knots to resemble stripped wood, a large desk in the middle, and bookshelves built into the alcoves on either side of the fireplace.

"This was my father's study."

Nigel commented on the paneling.

"Yes. My mother had it done for him. Not long before she died. As a present for his birthday." James Loudron's heavy face was bleak with some unhappy reminiscence. He paused, then jerked out, "He didn't really like it at all."

"No?"

"He could be very cutting. I suppose I oughtn't to say that, but—"

"I can imagine," ventured Nigel, "he was not altogether easy to live with."

"My mother was a saint," James blurted out; then, as if aware that along this line he might quickly go too far, he twitched his ponderous shoulders and said, "We're in rather a spot, you know."

"The pathologist's findings?"

"You've heard about that? Yes. I've not told the others yet. The fact is—I don't quite know how to approach this—"

"You'd like me to help? Professionally?"

"That's it." James seemed absurdly relieved. "Sort of friend at court. You told us at dinner you sometimes took on this sort of thing."

"Certainly. But I must make it quite clear that I don't work *against* the police."

James looked quite shocked. "Of course. I should be the last person to ask you to compound a felony, or whatever it's called. Not," he added hastily, "that there can be any question of a felony here. I mean, in the sense of—" He spluttered to a stop, like a car with a choked petrol feed. Nigel tactfully helped him out, then asked if he could talk to all the members of the family together. James went out to collect them and ring up Harold.

Pompous, earnest, socially inept, humorless, single-minded; overshadowed by his father, but likely to blossom out now the shadow is removed, and become with greater self-confidence a more than adequate practitioner; devoted to his mother, and probably resented his father's treatment of her; is appalled—as he and everyone else keep drumming into my head—by the possible effect of the tragedy upon his practice; but would this be sufficient to account for the terrible uneasi-

45

ness that he so ineffectually tries to conceal? Uneasiness? Or bewilderment?

Dragging himself out of these sterile meditations, Nigel began to prowl about the room. The books told him little he did not know about Dr. Piers' refined taste; there were two shelves of art books, an array of biography, a good selection of classics and modern novelists, little poetry. The medical textbooks were kept, presumably, in the surgery. The drawers of the leather-topped desk were not locked; they had been left open, no doubt, after the search for the missing diary.

It was this diary that most exercised Nigel's mind just now. Either Dr. Piers had started writing it or for some unimaginable reason he had told a lie when he said he was keeping a diary. If there had been a diary, four possibilities arose: either Dr. Piers had destroyed it himself or hidden it, or someone else had destroyed it or was hiding it. It seemed unlikely that Dr. Piers could have hidden it so successfully as to elude a search by his own family. Did he destroy it, then? Surely he would do so only if it contained matter he did not wish to be made public after his death, which implied that, after his announcement at the dinner party, he somehow became aware that he was shortly going to be dead, which implied suicide. And suicide, as the pathologist's report showed, was almost (but not quite) out of the question. Well, then, had some member of the household destroyed it? A murderer, because it gave him away? Possible, but the diary might also have been destroyed, after the doctor's disappearance, by one of the family, either to protect a murderer or merely to get rid of something that would prove embarrassing to himself if it were exposed. The fourth alternative—that one of the household was concealing it—implied that the diary was dangerous or embarrassing to him at present, but later might become useful. Useful for blackmail? For self-defense? For the vindication of someone or something?

Nigel turned his mind to something less ambiguous. The

physical diary itself. What would Dr. Piers be likely to write in? He was the kind of man who might well have bought a sumptuous, tooled-leather article. But also, Nigel's intuition told him, the old man might equally well have started jotting down—how had he put it?—"not exactly for confession but for the drawing up of a balance sheet"—on the first paper that came handy. And what would come handy for a doctor? A prescription pad? Too small for the purpose. A casebook? Yes, thought Nigel excitedly, and that could account for why the diary had not been found: a doctor's casebooks are top secret; even his own family would feel inhibited from prying into them—Rebecca, certainly, if it had been she who did the searching. Presumably the subsequent search by the police would have covered the surgery, but by that time the casebook, with its diary pages, might have been taken away and concealed. It should be simple enough to find out, from an inspection of Dr. Piers' records, whether one of his casebooks was missing.

A car drew up outside—a Jaguar—from which Harold Loudron emerged. Letting himself in at the front door, he called out for James, who ran downstairs and took Nigel and Harold up to the drawing room. In the morning sunshine its white-paneled walls, the brilliant pictures, and the exquisite blending of colors in carpet and hangings and upholstery, together with the figures of Rebecca, Graham, and Walter Barn, who were sitting there like people in a painter's conversation piece, all made it resemble a distinguished salon. Even Walt Barn had, somewhat surprisingly, got himself into a Sunday suit. And it was not only the sunlit room itself, so gracious and airy, that gave Nigel the impression of a lightening—an atmosphere easier to breathe, as it were, than it had been that night after dinner when the presence of the patriarchal Dr. Loudron had overcast the assembly.

James, leaning his elbow on the mantelshelf and clumsily stuffing a pipe, told them he had asked for Nigel's help; then, with a brusque gesture, handed over to him. After offering his condolences, Nigel turned to Rebecca.

"Your brother and I have heard the gist of the pathologist's report. It won't be very pleasant to listen to. If you'd rather—"

"No. Please tell us everything," she said, with a lift of her chin and a steady look at Nigel. There was a new, unconscious dignity in her bearing, though her eyes were heavy with grief or sleeplessness. "I am a doctor's daughter," she added.

"Well, then. The medical evidence is consistent with your father's having died on the night he disappeared. But it does not rule out his dying up to two days later. The cause of death is not absolutely established."

"But surely—wasn't he drowned?" Graham Loudron's expressionless eyes were fixed attentively upon Nigel's.

"No. His body was found in the river, as you know. It had been badly mutilated by the screw of a steamer. But, fortunately for this investigation, it was his legs and not his arms that were cut off."

Nigel paused as he stood by one of the tall windows, closely scrutinizing the five of them. They all looked—or managed to look—blankly puzzled.

"The Inspector—he came twice yesterday—didn't tell us that," said Rebecca.

"He told me—in confidence," said James.

"Why," asked Graham, "is this fortunate for the investigation?"

"Because the arteries of both wrists were severed," Nigel flatly replied.

"Then he did commit suicide," said Harold, almost to himself.

Walter Barn cocked up his round head. "But that's fantastic. D'you mean the old man walked down to the river, through that fog, in nothing but an overcoat, and cut his wrists and threw himself in—all in one motion, like?"

James coughed—in embarrassment or warningly.

"We don't know for certain," Rebecca put in, "that there wasn't a suit missing, and underclothes."

"He must have had a brain storm," Harold said. "That's the only thing that would account for it."

"Yes, but the clothes, the overcoat—" began Walter.

"The body was naked. But they could easily have been ripped off by the ship's propeller and shredded. Or they may yet be found." Nigel stopped, and began to prowl along the length of the three windows. "How he got into the water, we simply don't know. But he was certainly dead by then; the autopsy proves it. You agree?"

"Yes. No doubt at all," said James, with a worried frown.

Nigel paused again, to see if anyone would take up the running. At last Harold Loudron hesitantly remarked, "I don't see it's all that improbable. Couldn't he have gone to the river—assuming some kind of brain storm—and severed the arteries, and then fallen in in a faint, or—or decided to finish himself off by jumping in?"

Rebecca gave a little sob.

"The trouble with that theory," said Nigel, "is that no bloodstains have been found, and the nature of the cuts."

All but James, who was nodding sapiently, gazed at Nigel perplexed. He felt a tightening of tension in the room, but could not tell who was its source. Someone—or more than one—had keyed himself up at that "nature of the cuts."

"Yes," he went on. "You see, there are only two cuts, and they are of an equal depth."

Graham Loudron rose abruptly to his feet, looked around for a cigarette box, took a cigarette and lighted it, and sat down again. At the mantelshelf Dr. James stood, stiff as a caryatid. Walter Barn was feverishly scratching his flaxen poll.

"Could you favor us," asked Graham coldly, "with some explanation? We're not all authorities on forensic medicine here."

"Certainly. Suicides who—I'm sorry to have to go into all

these details, Miss Loudron—who cut an artery generally go for the jugular. And they almost invariably make several tentative, exploratory cuts before they give the slash that kills them. Whether this is because they haven't the nerve to do it decisively the first time, or because they are ignorant of anatomy and searching for the exact place—"

"But you can hardly argue," interrupted Graham, "that my father was ignorant of anatomy."

"Indeed not. In the case of a doctor and a resolute man, the absence of exploratory cuts would mean a good deal less."

"Well, then—"

"It's the *depth* that tells against suicide. Don't you see? Was your father ambidextrous?"

"Not particularly. Why?"

"If you are normally right-handed, you would take the razor in your right hand to slash your left wrist. This cut would, partly at least, disable your left hand, so that, when you transferred the razor to it, you could not possibly make so deep a cut in the other wrist."

"I see," said Graham woodenly. There was a considerable silence, broken finally by Walter Barn.

"Must've been a gang."

"Oh, for God's sake!" Harold wearily protested.

"No, I'm serious. Suppose he just took it into his head to go for a walk. Foggy night. Some ted bumps up against him, demands his wallet. Easy meat. But the old man resists. Puts up his hands, see, to ward off this ted. Who slashes at him, cuts both wrists, then dumps him in the river."

"I never heard such a ridiculous notion," drawled Harold. "Why on earth should Father go for a walk in the middle of a foggy night?"

"Maybe he went along after dinner to see you and your missus," Walter answered, with an irresponsible grin.

"She wasn't— What the hell d'you mean, to see *us!*" Harold exclaimed violently.

"Well, to see you, then. I heard him talking to you on the telephone before dinner that night. 'No, it can't be as urgent as that,' he said. 'We'll discuss it tomorrow.' Maybe he changed his mind and toddled along after all."

Harold was quite white with anger. "Are you suggesting—"

"Let's drop this," interposed James. "My father went to bed early that night."

"People can get out of bed," said Walter.

"But they usually don't when they've taken a sedative," said James.

"A sedative?" Rebecca's eyes were opened wide.

"He told us he was feeling sleepy. A fair amount of a barbiturate has been found in the stomach," said James. "They can't be certain how big the actual dose was. But it would have been enough, at least, to make him very drowsy for several hours."

Walt Barn bobbed up again. "Well, this beats everything! First someone tries to do him with a drug; then he's—"

"This isn't the time or the place for clowning," James heavily rebuked him.

"Anyway, what were you doing here that night?" asked Harold. "It's the first I've heard—"

Walter's bead-bright eyes switched to him. "I just looked in to see Becky. Before dinner. Next question?"

Nigel intercepted a look that Rebecca gave the young painter at this point—a look of reproach, was it? Or distrust? Or apprehension? He decided to take a grip on the situation again.

"The police will have to investigate all your movements that night. Very thoroughly. So I suggest we do not go into them now. But since Dr. James has asked me to hold a watching brief for the family, let me impress on you how important it is to tell them the exact truth. Being evasive, or telling lies with the mistaken object of protecting someone else, would cause endless trouble and confusion."

"Quite. Absolutely," commented James, in an authoritative manner.

"It looks as if you were going to earn your money pretty easily." Graham's small mouth had a cynical twist. "And why should the protection of someone else be a mistaken object?"

"Mr. Strangeways means that to suppose you can protect a person by telling lies to the police is a mistake," said Rebecca severely, looking extraordinarily like her mother in the dining-room portrait.

"I stand corrected," Graham murmured. "Perhaps our private and personal investigator can tell us what deduction he draws from the missing razor?"

"Missing razor?" Harold echoed.

"Yes," said Nigel. "Your father stopped shaving years ago, of course. But he kept his case of cutthroat razors. According to the Inspector, one is missing from the case, and cannot be found in this house."

"And the deduction?" Graham persisted, in his smooth, acid tone.

"Either Dr. Piers did leave the house, taking the razor, with the intention of using it on himself elsewhere—"

"Tactful, eh?" Walter outrageously muttered.

"—or someone used it on him in this house and disposed of it later, probably in the same way the body was disposed of."

James Loudron broke the shocked silence. "But that would mean—would seem to imply that one of us—it's inconceivable."

"If I used a razor on anyone, I'd simply wipe it off and put it back in the case," said Walter brightly.

"I can just imagine that," remarked Harold.

"Nasty, nasty!"

Rebecca spoke up. "I think we ought to try to remember that it's Father who is dead, and not be flippant about it all."

Walter's mouth sprang open, but he managed to hold back

whatever unconscionable utterance he had been on the point of making.

"Your father kept casebooks, I presume?" Nigel suddenly asked.

"Oh, yes," said James. "In the surgery. In a cupboard he kept locked."

"Miss Loudron, when you searched for the diary, you didn't think of looking in that cupboard?"

"Yes. I did. There was no diary there."

"But you didn't examine the casebooks themselves?"

"Certainly not. They are absolutely confidential."

"Then I think I'd better do so now."

"Oh, no." Rebecca was flustered but exceedingly firm. "That is quite out of the question. And in any case I can't see why—"

"Mr. Strangeways," said Graham, looking at him with something nearer respect than he had yet shown, "has it in mind that Father might have used the empty pages of a casebook for his diary."

"Exactly. And if you will not allow me to look through them, there would surely be no breach of professional etiquette in Dr. James doing so? In my presence, of course?" And it's not hard to see why the intelligent Dr. Piers had a soft spot for Graham Loudron, thought Nigel, when he is evidently so much quicker on the uptake than the others.

"I can see no objection," said James. He knocked out his pipe in the grate, and moved to go, but Graham made a slight gesture.

"Reverting to what you said just now, Strangeways, how can the police suppose that my father was killed in this house? Surely there'd be traces? And also traces of the body's being taken away?"

"They were nosing about in Father's car, and mine, yesterday afternoon," said James grimly.

"They've been all over the house," Rebecca added. "And

I suppose they'll be back again soon. I must say they're very polite and give as little trouble as possible."

"Like the bailiffs," said Walter, grinning.

"I'm afraid I'm going to ask if I may do just the same. Perhaps you would show me round"—Nigel smiled at Rebecca—"after your brother and I have visited the surgery."

James took Nigel down some back stairs and unlocked the door into the annex. This contained a surgery, a dispensary, and a waiting room. The surgery was a long, cream-washed room, with French windows at the far end opening onto the garden. While Dr. James unlocked a cupboard and took out a pile of foolscap-size manuscript books, Nigel surveyed the garden. On his left was a full-grown lime tree; in front, a bed filled with rosebushes heavily pruned; beyond that, a square of grass; and at the far end were some terraced beds in which crocuses and snowdrops were showing, backed by the side wall of a house.

"These really ought to go to his old hospital," said James. "They're quite exceptional. He was a remarkable diagnostician, you know. It's partly experience, of course, but that isn't enough in itself; one needs intuition, instinct, I don't know what to call it." His voice tailed off, and he began to read at random with an absorbed professional interest.

"Are they dated? Each book, I mean?" Nigel gently asked.

"What? Oh, yes."

"Then try the most recent one first."

Dr. James went through the pile, found the 1959 and 1960 volumes, began to glance rapidly through the pages.

"This is a bore for you," he said over his shoulder. "Wouldn't you rather go over the house while I'm doing this?"

"I'm sorry, but I must be present. Then no one could accuse you of destroying the evidence." Nigel's tone was light, but James frowned and twitched his shoulders as if there was a load on them.

"If I'd wanted to destroy evidence, I could have done it any time in the last ten days," he said. "Besides, how do you know I'm going to tell you if I do come to the diary pages?"

"Of course you are, because the police will soon be examining those books, and it'd look bad if you missed out something and they found it."

There was nothing in the recent volumes. James worked back, through the nineteen-fifties and nineteen-forties. Three quarters of an hour had passed. He came to the book for 1940, flipped his way through it. "Hello! Look. There are some pages missing at the end."

Nigel took the volume from his hands. There were indications that four pages had been roughly removed. "So perhaps somebody has destroyed the evidence."

"My father could have torn them out himself, I suppose."

"But he wasn't in the habit of taking out pages. None of the books so far have any missing?"

"No."

"Well, carry on. Work backward. It may not mean anything."

James finally put down the earliest volume. "Nothing more," he said, sighing heavily. "No diary. No other pages missing."

"Then I'll take the 1940 book and give it to the police. There may be fingerprints. Have you some newspaper I can wrap it in? I'll write you a receipt now. And please tell no one about what we've found."

Presently Nigel walked out into the garden, the wrapped volume under his arm, to get some fresh air. Forsythia was blooming on the wall to the right of the rose bed. Behind this wall, he discovered, lay a yard with tall wooden doors giving onto Burney Street and the old coach house, which had been converted into a double garage. He strolled to the far end of the garden and gazed unseeingly at the clumps of golden crocuses. "Now why," he silently asked them, "why should Dr. Piers choose the 1940 book to keep his diary in, supposing those missing pages were a diary? Wouldn't it have been more natural for him to have used the 1960 book, which has any number of blank pages?" The crocuses offered no reply. "What happened in 1940? The first blitzes. His finest hour? Twenty years ago. Does this mean anything, or is it just the alluring mouth of a blind alley?"

Nigel walked slowly back to the house. Rebecca Loudron was waiting for him in her father's study. Her eyes at once turned to the parcel under his arm. "Did you find anything?" she asked.

"We didn't find any diary pages, I'm afraid."

Rebecca waited for him to enlarge upon this, but, since he did not, bit her lip in obvious chagrin and rose abruptly. "You want to see over the house now?"

"Yes, please. May we start at the top and work down?"

The top floor consisted in a box room and two others. These two were used for spare rooms, she told him; they used to have maids in them, but servants were difficult to get nowadays and foreign help was often unreliable, so they had been managing lately with a woman to clean and another who came in occasionally to do the cooking if Rebecca was ill or away.

"But you're fond of cooking, yourself, or you wouldn't be so good at it?"

"Oh, yes. But it *is* a tie."

What a strange mixture she is, thought Nigel; so dull and conventional on the surface, and rather childlike—even now it's as if she were *playing* at being the grown-up hostess; yet underneath there is real vitality, something long suppressed, ready to flower—or to explode?

"You'll miss your father very much?" he tentatively inquired.

Her large, almost handsome face closed up. "I don't know. I was used to him. At present I feel nothing. Just sort of dazed and empty." She paused, struggling to make her thoughts articulate. "I suppose we all depended upon him too much. I don't mean just for money."

Rather brusquely, as if she had given herself away, Rebecca led him down to the next floor. "These used to be the nurseries. We turned them into bed-sitting rooms. That's a bathroom. James and I share it. And Graham uses it. This is James' room. I'm afraid it's rather untidy; the woman doesn't come today, and I haven't had time to do it yet."

It was a pleasant, low-ceilinged room, its windows looking out onto the street. A smell of stale tobacco hung in the air. The bedclothes were rumpled and wrinkled, as though James had spent a restless night. There was an electric fire, a comfortable armchair, shelves with medical works, detective novels, and travel books meticulously segregated. A cabinet in one corner held a collection of botanical specimens.

Next, they entered Rebecca's own room. Whatever Nigel might have fancied, he would never have guessed it would be like this. A large room, overlooking the garden, low-ceilinged like James', the nursery bars still on the windows, and crammed with old-fashioned furniture—a large four-poster, a frilled dressing table, a round mahogany Victorian table, an array of futile knickknacks on the mantelshelf, daguerreotypes and silhouettes and gloomy landscapes on the walls, two basket chairs and a nursing chair, a thick Turkey carpet, occasional tables littered with photographs in silver frames, bowls of potpourri, nameless objects in poker work—the eye was surfeited at one glance. Only one contemporary article could be descried amid the chaos: a magnificent phonograph.

"They're all my mother's," said Rebecca, flushing. "Papa wanted to auction them after she died, but he finally let me keep some of her things."

"How old were you then?"

"Eighteen. She died eight years ago."

"So you won that battle, anyway."

"Won—what do you mean?"

"Your father *finally* let you keep some of her things, you said."

Rebecca looked a bit uncomfortable. "Well, yes, it *was* rather a struggle. Of course, I can understand now. He didn't like them—Mother had no taste, I suppose; like me; not his sort of taste, anyway."

"And you were shocked to think he wanted to get rid of every trace of her? One can get tremendously indignant at eighteen."

"One can get tremendously indignant a good deal older than that," she answered, with a sudden dryness that Nigel could imagine as inherited from her Scottish mother.

"Yes," he said. "On one's own behalf. But the passionate, quixotic loyalty that makes one fight for someone else's memory—that's a youthful thing. An admirable thing, too."

Rebecca bowed her head, touched by the oblique praise.

"Is this your mother? May I look?"

"Yes. It was taken on their honeymoon. She looks very happy, doesn't she?"

But the face Nigel was observing in the silver-framed, faded photograph was that of the man who stood beside Mrs. Loudron. Dr. Piers had been clean-shaven in those days, so the lines of his intelligent face, tapering down from broad brow to narrow chin, and the slightly mischievous pout of the little mouth, were unobscured.

"Funny," he said, "your father reminds me of someone."

"Oh? Who?"

"Who can it be? Does it remind you of anyone?"

She studied the photograph. "I don't think so. Perhaps I know it too well," Rebecca slowly answered.

Nigel did not press her. "That's a noble bed. Though I don't know how people didn't get claustrophobia when they drew the bed curtains."

She gave him a fleeting, timid glance, then unexpectedly giggled.

"Papa said I was made on that bed, so I might as well lie on it."

"What music do you like best?" Nigel asked, pointing to the phonograph and the disc holders beside it.

"Mozart. He makes me feel young and—and bubbly. Don't you think he's marvelous?"

"I do. And does Walter like him?"

"I'm getting him to. In fact, we were playing the clarinet quintet and some piano concertos that night when—" Rebecca broke off abruptly. "Did you hear it?"

"The clarinet quintet?"

"I thought I heard the telephone." She ran out to the head of the stairs and listened. "Perhaps someone has answered it. Well, we'd better be getting on."

"I hope I'm not taking up too much of your time."

"Oh, it's all right. Graham said he'd cook the dinner today. He's quite good at it. He cooked at the Seamen's Hospital here for a bit, a year or two ago. Do you want to see his room?"

"Yes, please. It was your mother's, I think you told me."

"Yes. None of us felt much like using it after she died, and Papa had built a suite over the annex, so he put Graham into the room."

They were walking down another flight of stairs. At the bottom of it, next to the drawing room, a door was ajar. Rebecca led the way in, after knocking. The room was empty—in more senses than one, Nigel felt. Its occupant was not there; cooking, presumably. But, although it was well furnished, Graham's room gave a curious impression of anonymity, or of transient occupancy, like a college room in the vacation at the end of an academic year. No photographs, no books, no clothes thrown onto chairs, a pad of clean blotting paper on the desk.

"I say, it's all very vacant, isn't it?" remarked Nigel cheerfully.

"Graham keeps everything in his cupboards and drawers. Locked up."

"This is directly under your room, I take it. How long has Graham lived here?"

"Let me see. Seven years, it'd be."

"It must have been strange for you at first—to have an adopted brother. But you all seem to get on pretty well now."

"Graham *was* rather difficult at first—to get to know, I mean. Of course, he was only thirteen, and he'd had rather a bad time, apparently."

"So you mothered him?" said Nigel, smiling at her.

"Well, I tried." A frown came and went on Rebecca's face. "Actually, we sort of split up quite soon. James and I taking after Mother, I suppose it was inevitable we should feel closest to each other. Harold is built more on Father's lines. Of course, he was nine years older than Graham, but Graham used to tail round after him a lot in the holidays. I'm afraid I'm putting it all rather badly."

She has become so voluble, thought Nigel, because she wants to postpone going into her father's room.

"Would you rather I finished the tour by myself?" he asked.

She looked momentarily puzzled; then her chin went up. "No. It's all right, thank you."

They went down eight stairs to a half landing, and turned right and then left along a short passage, at the end of which Rebecca opened a door. Dr. Piers' bedroom had a large window in its left-hand wall, looking out onto the lime tree and the gardens of houses farther up the hill. It was luxuriously furnished; a big built-in wardrobe contained at least two dozen suits, all on hangers, and many pairs of shoes with shoe trees in them. Nigel noticed three Picasso drawings on the wall opposite the bed. On the bedside table stood a telephone, a charming converted oil lamp, and a copy of "Albertine Disparue"; the lower shelf of this table held a portable radio.

"And this is the bathroom?"

"Yes," said Rebecca, who was still standing in the bedroom door. "Do go in if you want."

The bathroom was equally luxurious in its way, but had nothing to say to Nigel. After glancing round it, he walked out again, and pointed to the bedroom window. "Was that shut when you and Graham came in, the morning of your father's disappearance?"

"Yes. It had been a foggy night."

"And the bedroom door was shut?"

"Yes."

"I'd like to try an experiment. What time did you start playing records that night?"

A flash of apprehension came and went in her eyes. "It must have been about nine o'clock."

"And for how long?"

"Well, off and on, till eleven."

"Will you go up to your room now and put on an L.P. record in three minutes' time. Play it for a couple of minutes at the volume you were playing that night, then take it off. When you've taken it off, sit still and listen. I shall come up and ask you if you heard anything from below. Oh, and shut your window; I presume it was shut against the fog that night?"

"Yes. All right. But I don't understand—"

As soon as she was gone, Nigel switched on at medium volume Dr. Piers' bedside radio. A rather sepulchral voice came out of it: "—text is, 'Am I my brother's keeper?' "

A sermon. Couldn't be better. Nigel ran upstairs into Graham Loudron's room. With the window shut he could still just hear the radio preacher's voice. Presently he caught the Mozart D-minor piano concerto from Rebecca's room above; it was faint, and he could hear in occasional intervals the preacher's voice. After a few minutes the gramophone stopped. Nigel waited for another couple of minutes, then he started to walk about, talking to himself, opening the window, moving a chair. Finally he went down and switched off the radio, and then walked up to Rebecca's room. His questions evidently puzzled her. She said she had heard nothing for a couple of minutes after she had stopped the gramophone, but then she thought she had heard someone talking and moving about on the floor below, though she wasn't sure.

"Won't you tell me what it's all about?"

"I hardly know myself," replied Nigel. "I've discovered that from Graham's room you can hear someone talking in your father's, but from your room you can't. Also that from your room you can hear movements in Graham's."

"Well, I could have told you that."

"*Did* you hear any, that night?"

Rebecca hesitated, flushing deeply. "I don't remember. I couldn't have, surely, with the gramophone on?"

Nigel did not pursue it. But he felt sure that Rebecca was not speaking the truth.

5.

$$7 + 13 = 20$$

Nigel glanced at the sheet of paper on the arm of his chair. It was his practice during an investigation to jot down anything done or said by those concerned that had struck him as out of character, self-betraying, contradictory, cryptic, or in some other way significant, not because, with his phenomenal memory, he would forget them, but because, committed to paper, these random and heterogeneous items sometimes formed chemical associations, as it were, and created the beginnings of a pattern.

Piers Loudron: "My dear boy, at my age, and when one's tenure of life is unlikely to be long protracted, one feels the need not exactly for confession but for the drawing up of a balance sheet . . . My diary is giving me quite a new interest in life. It may even prolong it!"

James Loudron: A very heavy eater—insecurity, or energy? "If I'd wanted to destroy evidence, I could have done it any time in the last ten days."

Harold Loudron: In reply to Walter's suggestion that Piers might have gone along after dinner to see Harold and Sharon

—"She wasn't—what the hell d'you mean, to see *us!*" . . . Wasn't at *home?*

Rebecca Loudron: Her account of going with Graham to look for their father—why does this stick in my mind?

Also, "we were playing the clarinet quintet and some piano concertos that night when—"

Graham Loudron: According to Rebecca, described the atmosphere at dinner the night his father disappeared as "Papa was waiting for something to happen."

And what was he doing across the river so early on Saturday morning?

Walter Barn: Not just the clown—one look enough for me.

Nigel read through the above. Then, after a pause, he took out his pen and wrote beneath them:

$7 + 13 = 20$: $1960 - 20 = 1940$: cf. Em's statement that during the 1940 blitzes P.L. acted "like he didn't care whether he lived or died."

A car stopped outside. Going to the window, Nigel saw it was a police car, and observed his old friend Chief Inspector Wright, of the Yard's C. Division, get out. Wright looked more than ever like a film director—lantern-jawed face, horn-rimmed spectacles, alert, darting eyes. Nigel brought him into the studio, where Clare kissed him warmly. In her presence, Wright loved to give an exaggerated performance of the bumbling middlebrow, the man who knows what he likes. He bent a cautious look upon the Female Nude.

"Well, you've got something there," he opined. "Massive and concrete."

"You should hear what my char says about it."

"Don't tell me! I know." Wright went outside, re-entered the studio with a heavy, bunioned gait, apprehensively circled the Female Nude. "Gruesome, ain't it? Gives yer the creeps. Do I 'ave to dust *that?*"

Clare's laughter pealed out. "I'll get some drinks."

"So they've sent for the Murder Squad," said Nigel.

"Your D.D.I.'s a first-rate man, but he's got too much on his plate just now. A wave of theft at the docks. And there's a mob of teds terrorizing the respectable residents of Shooters Hill—but can Henderson get any witnesses to come forward? 'You were at home, sir, yesterday evening when a gang of youths broke every window in the multiple stores opposite your house?' 'Yes, but I didn't see or hear nothing, didn't pay no attention.' Here lies the dear old British Public, and the epitaph on its tombstone is, 'I don't want to have nothing to do with that.' And then they've had a buzz that there's a drug-distributing racket shifted its base to just across the river; our Narcotics boys are working on that with Henderson. Thank you, Miss Massinger, just a touch of cyanide and plenty of soda."

The sound of the St. Alfege bells ringing for Sunday evensong could be distinctly heard.

"To heaven or to hell," said Wright. "I've just had a long talk with Henderson, and he's given me acres of homework tonight. So you've got your foot in the door again, Strangeways?"

"Yes. Are you and the D.D.I. convinced it's murder?"

"Hey, what's this? The family bribing you to prove it's suicide or something?" The Chief Inspector's tone was gently mocking, but his eyes on Nigel were sharp as dressed flints.

"Well, did you ever hear of someone being murdered by severing his wrist arteries? The jugular, yes. But—"

"There's got to be a first time for everything."

"And, even if the old man died quickly of shock, there'd be a hell of a lot of blood. But there are no traces of it anywhere in the house or annex or garden."

"Which makes the suicide theory even more impossible than the murder one."

"I know. So far as his own house is concerned. It looks as

if it must have happened somewhere else."

"Why?" said Clare dreamily.

"Why? But don't you see—"

"The Romans used to do it in their bath. Cut their arteries. Suppose Dr. Piers did just that. And bled to death. And someone ran the water out of the bath. There'd be no trace —not if you wiped the bath round afterward."

Wright was gazing at her keenly, his eyes sparking.

"But if that's how it happened, Clare, why should the person who found him dead go to the trouble and danger of putting him in the river?"

"And if he was *murdered* in his bath," said Nigel, "he would have been killed in that way to make it look like suicide. So, again, why throw the body in the river?"

"And why remove one of his cutthroat razors?" asked Wright. "Why not leave the weapon beside him in the bath?"

"The sleeping draught could work either way, I suppose. The murderer gives it to him at dinner to make him go upstairs early—to his bedroom adjoining a bathroom—and soften him up. Or Dr. Piers might have taken it himself, after dinner, to dull the suicide process."

Curled up on the sofa, Clare shivered delicately, like a cat. "I think it's all perfectly horrible. I doubt if one could wholly approve of Dr. Piers, but at least he was *someone*—he stood out." She sighed, then added, "Don't suicides generally leave notes?"

"The missing diary pages might have constituted a suicide note. Has the D.D.I. had any luck with them?"

"There are two sets of fingerprints," Wright answered. "Both on the left-hand page facing the first missing page. One lot are Dr. Piers'; the other will probably be Dr. James Loudron's—we're taking his tomorrow, and everyone else's in the family and household. The pages were ripped out, not cut out." He pantomimed, bending wide open an imaginary exercise book with the fingers of his left hand while tearing out pages with the other. "You see, it should leave a very strong thumbprint on the left-hand page. But there isn't one; only faint marks. What does that suggest?" The C.I.D. man had developed a habit of shooting such questions at his subordinates; it was part of their education, and kept them up to the mark.

"Gloves, of course," Nigel replied. "And you would hardly wear gloves to tear pages out of a book unless those pages incriminated you."

"Incriminated you for what?"

Nigel smiled. "You're trying to edge me over to the murder theory. But Jack the Book Ripper could have had other reasons."

"Such as what?"

"For example, he might prefer that his fingerprints should not be found on the book, supposing that he planned to use those missing pages as a lever against someone else."

"Oh, lord! Don't start bringing blackmail in now. Isn't one crime enough for you?" Wright jumped impatiently to his feet, strode over to a shelf that held a herd of the little archaic clay horses, with spoutlike muzzles, that were Clare's form of doodling. "We're doing what I'm always on at my chaps not to do—theorizing without enough facts." He took up one of the horses, gave it an imaginary lump of sugar, and put it down again. "Murder cases are solved by dozens of men in macintoshes going into thousands of houses and asking tens of thousands of people a few simple questions. Not," he continued, moving over to Nigel's chair and stubbing his finger on the sheet of paper, "by doing abstract equations. '7 + 13 = 20: 1960 − 20 = 1940'—what the devil's this in aid of?"

"Not so abstract, my dear fellow. It struck me as odd that *if* those missing pages are in fact Dr. Piers' diary, he should have used his 1940 casebook for it instead of his 1960 one, which has plenty of blank pages. Did the year 1940 have some special meaning for him? Well, he was a hero in the blitzes, by all accounts—and a desperate hero."

"I daresay. But what's this '7 + 13 = 20'?"

"Rebecca Loudron told me that Graham Loudron was adopted by Dr. Piers, at the age of thirteen, seven years ago. So he was born in 1940."

"So?"

"So I don't know what. Perhaps I'm becoming a number fetishist."

"I'd stick to shoes, if I were you."

"Has it occurred to anyone," asked Clare, after a pause, "that Graham's adoption was a bit peculiar?"

"In what way?" said Wright.

"Well, we are told his father was Dr. Piers' best friend and killed in the war. Why did Dr. Piers wait till 1953 to adopt him? Because Graham's mother was alive till then? Possibly, but we don't *know* when she died. And wasn't it rather excessive to *adopt* him? I mean, for a rather selfish *and* patriarchal man like the doctor? I'm surprised he didn't just take Graham into his house, educate him and so on, without making him one of the family and giving him his name."

"I'm not," said Nigel.

Clare opened her dark eyes wide at him.

"You see, I strongly suspect Graham is Dr. Piers' real son. Rebecca has a photograph of her father on honeymoon with his wife in the early twenties. And there's a distinct resemblance between the young Piers and Graham."

"Do you suppose his—any of the family know this?"

Nigel shrugged. "No idea. But they'd better not know that we suspect it. If it's true, it would account for Piers' rather strange action in adopting a boy soon after his wife died. He couldn't while she was alive, either because it would be bad taste or because she knew about his peccadillo. Or, of course, both."

"Well," said Chief Inspector Wright, "that's an interesting little bit of home chat. I don't see what bearing it could have on the case, but you follow it up if you like. Just your line. The mad archaeologist. Loves digging up the past. I must go and do some work. Thank you kindly for the drink, ma'am."

"Just a moment. I suggest you get the Fraud Squad to look discreetly into Harold Loudron's affairs. I—"

"It's being done. Henderson's idea. Any further instructions?" Wright grinned cockily at Nigel.

"Yes, you hard-faced servant of Loranorder. Tell your Narcotics chums that Mrs. Harold Loudron is, or recently has been, a drug addict. Also—no, perhaps not."

"Yes? Don't clam up on me. All contributions gratefully received."

"Well, I fancy that there's some kind of complicity between Mrs. Harold and Graham. I noticed it after dinner there one night—the first time we met the family. It may be just that they're bedmates, but it didn't feel like that."

"Very instructive, I'm sure."

"In his short career, Graham has been for brief periods a pianist in a jazz band and a cook at the Seamen's Hospital here."

"Ah. Now you're talking. Lascars smuggling in hemp, eh? And night-club hot-number types tend to coke themselves up. Any dirt on other characters involved?"

"I'm not prepared to release it at present."

"Hoity-toity."

"I like to pan my dirt, in case there's some gold in it. And that's the first time I've heard anyone say 'hoity-toity' since a scholarly great aunt of mine rebuked me, at the age of fourteen, for putting her right on a quotation she'd made from a chorus in the 'Trachiniae.'"

"I can just hear you doing it . . ."

For some time, after Wright had left, and they had finished their bacon-and-egg supper, Nigel and Clare talked over the mystery of Dr. Piers Loudron. Clare's fingers worked on a lump of clay they were shaping, of their own volition, into a spout-muzzled horse, while she gave all her attention to the problem Nigel worried at.

"Let's forget for the moment," he was saying, "the question of murder v. suicide. Take the hypothesis that it was in his own house he killed himself or was killed. How could the body have been conveyed to the river? He was frail and weighed little, but one can't imagine X carrying him there in a sack or trundling him in a wheelbarrow; too dangerous, even allowing for the fog; too bizarre altogether."

"So he must have been conveyed in a car."

"Exactly. But Henderson's chaps have been over Dr. Piers' Daimler and Dr. James' Morris with all the resources of science, and they found no trace of the body's having been carried, either inside the cars or in their luggage boots."

"Yes, but what trace would they be able to find? X could have bandaged the wrists, so there'd be no bloodstains left; and anyway he'd have stopped bleeding by then."

"Hair," said Nigel. "You couldn't bundle a body into a boot or a back seat without rubbing off a hair or two."

"Not if you'd wrapped that tweed overcoat of his round the head?"

"Ye-es. That might work."

Clare's eyes lit up. "No, I've got it! Something much simpler. If X used Dr. Piers' Daimler and set the body beside him on the front seat, it wouldn't matter if the police found hairs there—or any other traces of him except blood. You'd expect to find them in a car he was constantly using."

"Good. You may have hit it. The only alternative I could think of is that X borrowed for the job one of the cars that are parked every night on Burney Street. But, unless he's a professional car thief, he wouldn't have been able to break into one of them without causing damage, which the owner would have reported to the police. Well, then, let's imagine

X going off with the body in the front seat of the Daimler. Where would he take it?"

"In that fog, he'd not drive far, surely. The nearest point on the river is by the pier."

"But you can't drive right up to the river wall there. You'd have to hump the body nearly a hundred yards, past the 'Cutty Sark.'"

"Well, then, the next nearest point is Park Row, the road that runs past the east end of the Naval College. X could stop the car on the opposite side from the Trafalgar Tavern, and he'd only have to take about ten paces to the waterside."

"Yes. There's a street lamp there. But in that fog it'd be fairly safe, unless someone walked out of the Trafalgar Tavern just as X was dumping the body in the river," said Nigel slowly. "It might be safer still to drive down one of the streets that lead to the river farther east. The wharves would be absolutely deserted, I should think, at that time. There's Lassell Street, to the west of Harold Loudron's house, and Pelton Road, which runs down just east of it to Lovell's Wharf. All this presumes special knowledge on X's part."

"Of Greenwich?"

"Yes, and of the tide table. It'd have been unwise to throw the body off the river wall at any time except high water or the top of the ebb, if you wanted it to be pulled out from the shore."

"But if X merely wanted to get rid of the body? So that it wasn't found in the house?"

"Then he'd surely not have needed to take it as far as the river. There's all that waste ground along Burney Street, for instance. No, the fact that the body was thrown in the river suggests that X wanted its discovery to be put off as long as possible."

"So that it might be difficult to prove *how* Dr. Piers died?"

"Exactly. And if the ship's screw had cut off his arms instead of his legs, we should *never* have known how he died."

71

Clare Massinger stretched out her legs on the sofa and gazed at the lofty ceiling. "If it was murder, all I can say is that X was very lucky."

"Lucky?"

"To get a combination of thick fog and high tide at the right time, and the several members of the family dispersed in different rooms."

"Lucky or patient. He may have waited a long time for that combination of circumstances, including Mrs. Hyams' confinement, which kept Dr. James out of the house for several hours that night."

"I suppose you're safe to assume he died that night, or in the small hours of the morning?"

"Pretty safe, if it was in his own house he died. But there's no absolute certainty that he did. He may have had what Harold calls a 'brain storm,' and wandered out after the effects of the sedative had worn off, and somehow remained in concealment for a period until— But it's so unlikely one can dismiss it. No, the other possibility I have to consider is that he left the house that night, perfectly in his right mind—"

"But having changed his suit, shirt, and underclothes," Clare interrupted. "Why?"

"Yes, I know that sounds wildly improbable, but pass it over. It couldn't have been an emergency call, for his doctor's bag was not taken. The only thing I can imagine taking him out of the house on a foggy night like that would be an appeal from one of his family. Harold Loudron did ring him up before dinner; Dr. Piers was heard to say it could wait till tomorrow. Well, he might have changed his mind—"

"After sleeping on it for an hour or two with the aid of a barbiturate?" asked Clare skeptically.

"—might have changed his mind and gone along to Harold's house."

"But surely at his age he wouldn't? He'd have rung Harold

and discussed whatever it was on the telephone, or asked him to come over to Croom's Hill."

"Dr. Piers was not too old, I suspect, to act on an impulse —irrationally, even. Well, he walks along to Harold's house—"

"Remembering to take a cutthroat razor with him."

"Oh, blast you, Clare! Let me finish building my house of cards before you blow it down. There's no evidence that the missing razor had not been removed from its case days or weeks before."

"All right. So the old man gets to Harold's house, and then what?"

"If it turns out that Harold's business affairs are rocky, and if his father refuses him the money needed to straighten them out, Harold has a strong motive for killing him. And, what's more, he has an extremely convenient window, right above the water, from which to jettison the body."

"There's a king-size snag in that," said Clare.

"Oh, there is, is there?"

"Don't be grumpy. Suppose Harold is in such a desperate hurry for money; surely he'd not dispose of his father's body in such a way that it might not be found for weeks? He'd want to borrow on the strength of his expectations from the old man's will *immediately*. And anyway, what's the fair Sharon doing while Harold is cutting his father's arteries? Encouraging him with high-pitched cries?"

"You're impossible tonight, love. Actually, I suspect she was out on the tiles that night. Harold said something when I was talking to the family this morning which—and he got very hot under the collar when Walter Barn suggested that Dr. Piers might have gone to see him and Sharon that night. Still, I daresay it's all got some fairly innocent explanation. Perhaps we'd better stick to the Daimler . . ."

When Chief Inspector Wright turned up after breakfast

the next morning, Nigel at once said to him, "Before you start interrogating the suspects, I think it might be worth while getting one of your chaps to make inquiries in the Trafalgar Tavern and in the houses at the north end of Pelton Street and possibly Lassell Street."

"And what is he to inquire about?" asked Wright, with an exaggeratedly blank expression.

"Whether anyone saw Dr. Piers' Daimler standing at the river end of the street on the night he disappeared."

Wright's poker face registered a faint stir of emotion.

"Interesting you should say that. I had a man interviewing the residents of the Trafalgar Tavern last night. One of them —he's been away for the last week and only just returned— remembers seeing a Daimler, which he recognized as the doctor's, at about 11:15 that night. This gentleman had popped out to give his dog a bit of relief before going to bed. The car was standing, empty, on the opposite side of the street, about ten yards from the waterfront. Our witness strolled across the road and all but bumped into the car, the fog was so thick. And now," added Wright, "would you mind telling me just how you lighted upon this information?"

"By theorizing on insufficient facts," Nigel replied.

6.

Chain Reactions

As the police car drew up outside the Loudrons' house, the front door opened and a body flew out into the paved forecourt, followed by a camera that smashed itself against the iron railings. Wright and Nigel hurried through the wrought-iron gate. A dazed little man, with blood pouring from his nose and a vicious, frightened look in his eye, picked himself up.

"He's gone mad," the man panted. "I'll have the law on him! He can't treat the press like this."

Wright and his sergeant began dusting the man off. Nigel rang the front doorbell; then, hearing sounds of violence from within, moved to the window of the study. Looking in, he saw Walter Barn in the process of beating up a fattish man a good head taller than himself. Rebecca Loudron, her back to a bookcase on the far side of the room, was watching the massacre with an expression in which horror and a fascinated excitement unpleasingly blended. If Walt had ever heard of the Queensbury Rules, he had forgotten what he had heard. Slipping a wild right swing, he drove his fist into his opponent's belly, well below the belt; then, while the large

75

man caved forward, making a hideous sound as if his guts were falling out of his mouth, Walt clubbed him across the cheek with his right, and followed it up with a brutal kick at the kneecap. The man sprawled backward across the desk. Hammering at the window, Nigel at last attracted Rebecca's attention. She ran out of the room to open the front door. Nigel rushed in, followed by Wright, the sergeant, and the press photographer.

The large man was rolling on the floor now, whimpering and retching, forearms cradling his head, at which Walt was kicking. In a moment the frail-looking Wright had Walter Barn's powerful arm in a lock that made the young painter bend forward, gasping with pain. He pushed him down into a chair, sent Rebecca scurrying for iodine and dressings, helped his sergeant to lift Walter's victim onto the sofa, turned back to his assailant.

"I am a police officer. What's been going on here?"

Walter Barn's demoniac fit had passed away as suddenly as a summer hailstorm. He lay back in the chair, his speedwell-blue eyes dancing.

"These two bastards were making a nuisance of themselves. They insulted Becky."

"That's a damned lie," exclaimed the little photographer in an aggrieved, adenoidal whine. "We were only doing our duty. We asked for an interview with Miss Loudron, an exclusive, and this maniac here—"

"Asked for an interview! You lousy little gutter-press lap dog! What you mean is, you and that fat slob on the sofa there got your foot in the door, pushed your way in past my fiancée, started photographing this study, badgered my fiancée for what you call a 'story—' "

"You've no call to use violence. D'you realize you've broken a valuable camera?"

"I'm delighted to hear it. Your sort make me sick. You think that, because you're in the pay of some revolting press lord, you've a right to force your way into anyone's house and exploit people's grief to cook up a tasty story for your sickening readers—"

"The public," mouthed the large man, who had painfully gathered himself into a sitting position on the sofa, "has a right to be informed on all matters of general interest. You're going to be sorry for this, young man, whoever you are. We shall deal with you."

"God damn you and your public! Hasn't the private individual any rights?" Walter Barn, quivering now like a taut wire, spoke with such violence that the fat man shrank back and Wright interposed.

"All right. Break it up."

"What makes me vomit is the bloody, sanctimonious hypocrisy of muckrakers like that hero trembling on the sofa there, telling us about their sacred duty to provide dollops of sewage for the moronic millions, and—"

"I said break it up." Wright's voice was cold as a chisel. Rebecca came in with a first-aid box. "Will you attend to him?" said Wright.

"I wouldn't touch him with a barge pole," answered Rebecca, her nostrils wide with distaste.

"And you a doctor's daughter!" mocked Walter.

"Sergeant, attend to this man. You're a great nuisance, all of you," Wright equably continued. "Wasting my time with your squabbles like this."

"Are you in charge of the case now?" the large man asked him, while the sergeant applied iodine and a lint dressing to his split cheek. "Anything fresh broken? Can you give me a story?"

"Smut hound still on the trail," Walter remarked.

"Keep your wit to yourself," said Wright. "I'll take statements from you two representatives of the press, then you will leave. I'm busy today."

Ten minutes later, Nigel, Wright, and the sergeant were

alone in the study with Walter Barn.

"God-damned liars," said the young painter. "They *did* push their way in and they *did* molest Becky."

"How do you know? According to your statement, you did not arrive till later."

"Becky told me when I came in. And lucky I did. She was terribly upset."

"How did you get in?"

"Through the door."

"Now look, Mr. Barn. I've no time to waste on childish repartee. You know perfectly well what I mean."

"Oh, all right. I let myself in. I have a key."

"How long have you had it?"

"Becky gave me one—oh, a month or two ago."

"Right. Now we're going back to the night Dr. Piers Loudron disappeared. I understand you visited this house before dinner?"

"What the nobs call 'dinner,' yes. About 6:30. I chatted with Becky in the kitchen for half an hour or so; then I walked back to my humble abode."

"Had you any special reason for visiting Miss Loudron that night?"

"Just lerv, Inspector. Can't seem to keep away from the girl."

"You walked a mile, in a thick fog, and a mile back, simply to have a chat?"

"Beneath a rugged exterior, I'm ever so romantic."

Chief Inspector Wright, appearing satisfied, dropped this subject. Nigel had often witnessed his interrogations, but was still fascinated by Wright's technique—a technique of suspect-tapping, one might call it; as a man might move round a room, tapping the walls for the hollow sound that would betray a hiding place, so Wright probed here and there at the surface of the person he was interrogating, his senses alert for a suspect's relaxing of tension when he moved away from a dangerous area, a tightening of tension when he returned to it. Had Mr. Barn ever been in the surgery? No. Did he remember any more of the telephone conversation between Dr. Piers and Harold Loudron than he had told the D.D.I.? No. Could he drive a car? Probably, but he'd only ridden motor bikes so far. Would he make any objection to having his fingerprints taken? None at all.

"Did you ever quarrel with the deceased?"

"No. He just froze me off—or tried to."

"Because you wished to marry his daughter?"

"Yes. He treated me like something the cat brought in."

"So Miss Loudron had to do the fighting?"

Pause. Walter Barn's eyes looked wary. "I don't get you."

"She had serious quarrels with her father, over you?"

"Well, I—yes, she did."

"And a particularly violent one the evening he disappeared —not long before you turned up?"

"Who the hell told you that?"

"Information received," Wright blandly answered. Nigel sat up. This was news to him. Or was the Inspector flying a kite?

"If you knew it already, why ask me?" said Walter.

"We have to check and countercheck every bit of evidence. Is it true?"

"There was a quarrel that day. I don't know how violent. I wasn't in attendance."

"But surely you do. That's why you walked over here in the fog. Miss Loudron had telephoned you. She needed your help, your comfort, urgently?"

The painter made no reply, and Wright did not press him. Instead, he put a few dummy questions about Dr. Piers— had Mr. Barn felt him to have been apprehensive, or unusually depressed, recently? No: he wouldn't know anyway.

With the perfunctory air of one asking a merely routine question, Wright said, "So you left the house that night about seven, and walked straight home? You didn't go out again?"

Nigel, for whom Walter Barn's small round head perched on his square shoulders had always seemed like a stone ball on a manorial gate pillar, now suddenly saw it as a ball not cemented there but precariously balanced, as if a puff of wind might roll it off.

"No, I didn't go out again." There was a queer intonation, a sort of smirk, in Walter's voice.

"You were here all the time?" put in Nigel, so unobtrusively that it was barely audible.

"That's what I'm—" Walter stopped, and almost instantly went on, "what I'm telling you; I went back to my studio and had supper and looked through a Piero della Francesca book Becky had lent me, and then I went to bed."

"You live alone?" asked Wright, his eyes boring into Walter.

"Yes."

"So we have to take your word for it that you went home and stayed there all night?"

"I suppose you do. But why shouldn't you? You don't think I croaked the old man, do you?"

"Well, that'll be all for the present. We'll just take your fingerprints."

When this had been done and the sergeant sent to fetch Rebecca Loudron, Nigel said to Wright, "This alleged quarrel between Dr. Piers and his daughter—were you inventing it?"

"Inventing? Certainly not," Wright replied rather curtly. "Graham Loudron gave it in evidence to the D.D.I."

"He did, did he? And did Miss Loudron admit it?"

"She agreed there'd been a row, yes. Played it down a bit, though."

"And Walter Barn may *not* have left this house that night?"

"Yes. You caught him out very neatly there."

Nigel gazed noncommittally at the Inspector. "Do you

see her as a Lady Macbeth? A parricidal Lady Macbeth?"

Before Wright could answer, Rebecca Loudron came in. The sergeant returned to his hard chair and unobtrusively took out his shorthand notebook. Rebecca had this new look of maturity still, but there was a glaze of uneasiness over it, which did not escape Wright's notice.

"I'm sorry to be badgering you, Miss Loudron—particularly after the distressing ordeal you had this morning."

"Will they make trouble for Walt? They were horrible. Can they have him arrested for—whatever it's called—assault and battery?"

Wright smiled at her. "Technically, they could sue him, yes. But I doubt if they will. Depends whether their paper decides it'd be good publicity. It'd mean washing some dirty linen in court. And, of course, I shall have to make a report to your local police about it. Incidentally, was there no one in the house who could have helped you to deal with them?"

"Well, James was having a surgery. And Graham—I don't know where he was; I called out to him, but he didn't come."

The Inspector gently sounded Rebecca about the quarrel with her father, but he did not seem to get any further than the D.D.I. had done, judging by his reception of her answers, in which there showed clearly a conflict between loyalty to the dead and resentment at her father's attitude toward Walter and herself. Nigel studied the woman's face and manner: the strong nose, the fine, slightly protuberant brown eyes, the heavy eyebrows; the odd mixture of gaucheness and dignity. Suddenly her woman's nature broke through the web of Wright's interrogation.

"Why are you asking me all these questions? Everyone knows Papa and I quarreled a lot about Walt." Her lips quivered, then set firmly. "Do you really think I could—could *kill* Papa because he wouldn't let me marry Walt?"

Wright looked at her with surprise and respect. He said

lightly, at his most charming, "I expect you often *felt* like doing it."

Rebecca returned his gaze, shocked for a moment by Wright's unofficial comment, then timidly smiling. "Well, of course he did make me very angry sometimes. But—"

"And you have no alibi," continued Wright, smiling still as if he were a friend, a brother, gently teasing her. "Sitting up there all alone playing gramophone records."

Rebecca glanced at him suspiciously. Her instinct told her this was not just a bit of rather tasteless badinage. She remained silent, watchful.

"Or were you? What would you say if I told you that we have evidence you were not alone that night?" It was a common gambit in police interrogation, but it still made Nigel uncomfortable. He quickly said, "You told me that yourself. Yesterday morning. You said, 'We were playing the clarinet quintet and some piano concertos that night when—' and then you broke off and pretended to have heard the telephone."

"It was a slip of the tongue," she got out hurriedly.

"Oh, come, Miss Loudron. That really won't do, will it?" said Wright. "Anyway, why should you be afraid to say Mr. Barn was with you that night? It gives you both an alibi, doesn't it? At any rate, up to the time he left you? What time did he leave?"

Rebecca Loudron simply did not have the resources to cope with this sort of thing. The flustered, mutinous look that Nigel had seen on her face when her father had been exercising his sarcasm showed again now.

"About midnight," she muttered. "But there was nothing —we did nothing wrong," she defiantly added.

She's talking about sex, not about murder, thought Nigel; either she's innocent or a very remarkable actress, like Lady Macbeth. Wright continued to probe. Walter Barn, whom

Rebecca had telephoned in great distress after the last scene with her father, had talked with her in the kitchen till dinner, then gone up to her room, where she rejoined him at about quarter to nine after her father went to bed. She and Walter had been together there all the time till he left; neither had gone out of the room, even for a minute; she had smuggled him up some supper, and they talked and played records.

"It all sounds extremely innocent," Wright remarked. "Why didn't you tell us this before?"

Rebecca looked indecisive, as if trying to work out not an answer but the implications of the answer. Finally, she threw up her head, giving it to them fair and square. "Walt asked me not to."

"Isn't that rather odd, since it gives you both an alibi? For some of that night, anyway, and assuming you are telling the truth."

"Oh, I'm telling the truth." Rebecca threw it off almost negligently, as if it hardly needed saying. "You see, Walt isn't—he's working class, and they don't like being mixed up in anything to do with—well, the police."

" 'I don't want to have nothing to do with that,' " Nigel murmured, quoting the Inspector's own words of Sunday evening.

"Let's leave that. Now, Miss Loudron"—Wright spoke slowly and with the utmost seriousness—"when you were up in your room with Mr. Barn, did you hear anything? Anything out of the usual? Anything that puzzles you now?"

There was a protracted pause. Rebecca seemed to be struggling with something in her mind. At last she said uncertainly, in a low tone, "Well, we did think we heard voices, from Graham's room."

"Whose voices?"

"Graham's. And—well, it sounded like Sharon's, the other one; but it couldn't have been, because she was at home."

"A woman's voice, at any rate? Angry? Frightened? How did it sound?"

Rebecca's face flushed darkly. She jerked out, "It was—sort of laughing. And then—then it cried out." She lowered her eyes. "We—Walt thought they were love-making."

"What time was this?"

"Oh, I don't know. Perhaps an hour after I'd gone up."

Wright could get nothing more precise than this out of her. "And that was all? You didn't hear anyone leave the house later?"

"No. You see, the gramophone was on most of the time."

"Or—your room's at the back, isn't it—a car leaving your garage?"

"No. But nobody'd have taken out a car in a fog like that, surely?"

After a few more questions, Wright took Rebecca's fingerprints and let her go. The sergeant was sent to fetch Graham Loudron. One of Inspector Wright's great gifts as a detective officer was his capacity for intuitively adapting himself to the personality of each different witness. With the bouncy, like Walter Barn, he could enter into the game, become jolly and unofficial, but also, if need arose, bounce them so hard that they were deflated. Rebecca he had handled not just with sympathy but with a kind of gentle firmness and decisiveness that would feel like moral support to one lacking in self-confidence and mental clarity. When he interviewed Graham Loudron, Nigel saw Wright's method with a natural arguer of the toss.

As soon as Graham saw Nigel in the study, he asked Wright, "Is Mr. Strangeways here officially?"

"Do you object to his presence?" said Wright, no less coolly.

"No, I'm just surprised."

"Inspector Wright has allowed me to co-operate," Nigel

put in. "I'm here to see that none of you makes a fool of himself."

While Wright questioned Graham Loudron about his movements on the night of Dr. Piers' disappearance, Nigel studied the young man's personality. It was difficult to believe he was only twenty; the triangular face, the small, protrusive mouth, the eyes that fastened like limpets on whomsoever he was talking to, together with Graham's self-contained manner, deferential yet obscurely derisive—all gave the impression of an experience beyond his years; experience, but not maturity.

"You told Inspector Henderson that the deceased was 'waiting for something to happen' that night at dinner. Can you enlarge upon it?"

"I don't think so. It was a feeling I had."

"You had it at the time? You're sure it didn't come to you later, as a result of what happened?"

"Perfectly sure."

"You felt he was nervous? Apprehensive?"

"No, not exactly. His mind seemed to be elsewhere. And it was as if he was keying himself up."

"To commit suicide?"

Graham shrugged. "How can I tell? I'm not a mind reader. I thought you'd rejected the idea of suicide, anyway." There was a hint of a question in his last remark, but Wright ignored it.

"You didn't see your father take a sleeping draught, at dinner or just before?"

"No."

According to Graham, he, James Loudron, and their father had had a glass of sherry together just before dinner; Dr. Piers drank nothing with the meal, but had coffee after it in the dining room; Rebecca had made the coffee and poured it out.

"As he felt sleepy soon after dinner, it looks as if he must

85

have taken the sleeping draught either in his sherry or privately before that."

Graham Loudron agreed.

"And after dinner you went up to your room and stayed there till you went to bed?"

"Yes."

"Alone all the time?"

"I've already told Inspector Henderson all this."

"Yet your sister heard voices from your room—at about ten o'clock."

Graham's eyes, expressionless as shellfish, gave nothing away. "She's mistaken."

"A woman's voice. You say you did not have a woman in your room?"

"What woman am I supposed to have had?"

"Please answer the question, Mr. Loudron."

"If I had had a woman there, I should certainly not tell you who it was," replied Graham coolly.

"I'm not asking for her name. I'm asking, was there a woman in your room?"

"Is there any reason why I should tell you?"

"Yes. Two reasons. If you don't, you are obstructing the police in their duties, and you are depriving yourself of a possible alibi for part of the period, at least, during which your father died."

"Died? You evidently mean 'was murdered.'"

"Well?"

Graham's lips twisted sourly. "I don't want an alibi, and I don't care a damn about obstructing the police."

"Tell me, did you love your adopted father?"

Graham swallowed hard. "He was very good to me. But I wouldn't say he was a lovable man. If you mean, do I want to see his murder avenged, I'm sorry, but I can't think in melodramatic terms like that."

86

"Did you ever suspect he might be your real father?"

The young man crossed his knees and began smoothing his sleek hair. His voice remained quite smooth. "Well, of course I have wondered. I couldn't imagine why he should be so fond of me, do so much for me. But he never said anything about it."

"And your mother, when she was alive—did she not talk about your father?"

"Do you have to drag my mother into this?" For the first time, Graham showed emotion. Then, controlling himself, he said, "She didn't. All she told me was that he had died, in the war, soon after I was born."

Inspector Wright switched back to the night of Dr. Piers' death. No, Graham had heard no sounds from Dr. Piers' room. Yes, he thought he had heard a car that night, driving out of the garage yard; it was just after he had gone to bed— about eleven o'clock. Why had he not mentioned this before? Nobody had asked him. Whose car did he think it was? He hadn't given it a thought, but assumed now it must have been Dr. James going out to an emergency call.

"Why did you go over to the Isle of Dogs last Saturday morning so early?" asked Wright, switching the probe again.

"But I didn't."

"But I saw you coming out of the Greenwich tunnel, on this side, at half past seven," said Nigel.

"Ah. The household spy at work," remarked Graham. His naked antipathy for Nigel, which the latter had felt the first time they met, again made the air vibrate between them.

"So you admit you were lying?" asked Wright at his chilliest.

"I admit nothing of the sort. You asked why I went over to the Isle of Dogs on Saturday morning. I didn't. I went there on Friday night and stayed overnight."

The Inspector was on his feet, quick as a spring released, and standing over Graham. "Don't you try this schoolboy logic-chopping on me, young man—I don't wear that sort of thing. Why did you go to the Isle of Dogs?"

"I went to visit an old tart in Poplar, and we got talking, and by then it was so late I stayed the night in her house," replied Graham, his composure quite unruffled.

"Her name and address, please."

"I fail to see what my nocturnal occupations have to do with the case you're—"

"Don't start arguing the toss with me. If you persist in being childish, I shall send men round every house in Poplar, with your photograph; they'll find out soon enough, and meanwhile I shall put you in the can for obstruction."

"And what does the family friend say about that?" Graham addressed Nigel with a sneer.

"Do what the Inspector asks you, and stop making a bloody fool of yourself," Nigel equably replied.

Graham Loudron gave the name and address. While his fingerprints were being taken, he remarked offhandedly, "You'll be wasting your time on old Nellie. I go and talk to her now and then about my mother. She used to know her. But if I'm allowed to make a suggestion—"

"Go ahead."

"Ask brother James about *his* mum. Ask him what she died of. Our friend here, who's so keen on secret passages in private lives, might be interested." Graham paused, then said, with remarkable bitterness, "Funny, isn't it, the idea of a woman in a posh house like *this* dying of neglect?"

When Graham Loudron had gone, the Inspector flashed at Nigel one of his rare smiles, which were like the edge of a hatchet. "Beginning to open up, aren't they, my dear old household spy? Why has that young chap got it in for you?"

"Natural antipathy, I suppose."

"Bit of the old lag about him, I thought; I don't mean just that sea-lawyering. Wonder if he's been inside."

"Yes, I've felt that. An approved school could have done

it; or an orphanage even, if it was a bad one."

The sergeant ushered in Dr. James Loudron, who had agreed to give Wright an interview between his surgery hour and starting his rounds.

"I hope we can get this over quickly," he said. "The work's getting on top of me with my father—"

"I'm sure we can, doctor," Wright cut in briskly. He asked James first about the sleeping draught; James had nothing to contribute here; he certainly hadn't seen the old man taking any that night, nor had he noticed anything out-of-the-way in his father's behavior at dinner, except perhaps that he talked rather less than usual.

"And now, doctor, let me make sure that I'm clear about your own movements, just for the record. You went out shortly after dinner to see a patient?"

"Yes. Mrs. Hyams. Her first confinement. I walked along to her house about 8 P.M."

"And returned here?"

"At 10:15."

"The baby having been born?"

"Just so."

"No complications?"

"I wasn't entirely happy about the patient. She was very weak, and I feared a postnatal hemorrhage. Our district nurse, who was midwifing, had to go straight off on another job, so I thought I'd look in on Mrs. Hyams again."

"You have a most excellent reputation for conscientiousness, doctor. I've discovered that already." Wright was at his most bland and disarming. "I must say, if I'd been you, I'd have thought twice about walking back again to a patient in a fog like you had here."

A shocked, slightly censorious look replaced the modestly gratified one with which James had received the Inspector's compliment. "It'd be highly unprofessional not to—"

"How long did it take you to walk back there?"

A dark flush, reminding Nigel of Rebecca Loudron, came over his face, and a bead or two of sweat started on his forehead.

"Nearly ten minutes, I should think. But I didn't walk, you know. I took out a car that time."

"Your car?"

"My father's. Mine had developed a fault—the petrol feed. I put it right a day or two later."

"What made you use a car, if I may ask, when you'd walked the first time?"

"Well, I was extremely tired, and I thought the fog had lifted a bit. I was wrong," Dr. James added ruefully.

"You found your way, though, in the end?"

"Yes."

"To? Where does this Mrs. Hyams live?"

"In Crane Street."

Oh, lord! thought Nigel. That's torn it! Wright, ignorant as yet of the topography of Greenwich, could hardly be expected to know that Crane Street was a narrow passage, not negotiable by traffic, running past the back of the Trafalgar Tavern. "So you'd naturally park the car by the Trafalgar Tavern, near the opening into Crane Street?" he said.

"Yes. That's where I left it," replied James Loudron, looking a bit puzzled. Nigel dared not meet Wright's eye. The doctor began to bluster a little: "I'm sure you know your job, Inspector. But I'm a busy man, and I can't for the life of me see the point of these questions." He hunched the heavy shoulders that had often bullocked their way through the loose in hospital cup ties.

"In my job," said Wright genially, "we have to ask millions of questions, only a few of which turn out to be the crucial ones. Between your visits to Mrs. Hyams, what did you do, sir?"

He had gone up to his room, said James Loudron, wishing to read up a medical point, but Rebecca's gramophone in the adjoining room had disturbed his concentration, so he brought the book down to the study.

"And during this period—10:15 to about eleven—you heard nothing that now strikes you as suspicious or out of the ordinary?"

"No. But, mind you, I was concentrating pretty hard. I wouldn't have noticed anything short of a telephone bell ringing."

"I appreciate that. And now tell me, doctor," Wright went on, with no change of tone or emphasis, "what did your mother die of?"

"My mother die of?" James' expression of perplexity was quite ludicrous. "What on earth do you think you're getting at?"

"I know it must seem an irrelevance. But could you please tell me?"

After a long stare at the Inspector, Dr. James launched out on a medical statement, ending, "what is generally known as fatty degeneration of the heart."

"It would be incorrect to say that she died of neglect?"

"Neglect?" James exploded. "She had the best medical attention in—where the devil did you get such a preposterous idea?"

"Your brother Graham has hinted that she died of neglect."

"Graham? The bloody little twister! Neglect, indeed! It's absolutely insufferable." For a moment, in the midst of the storm, an extraordinary change came over James' angry face —a sort of breathless, anguished calm out of which, almost inaudibly, he muttered, "But how could he know?" Then he glared suspiciously at Wright, like a bull that has discovered that a nice warm extent of sand is in fact an arena dotted with infuriating colors and inimical objects, and put down his heavy head and charged. Graham was untrustworthy, sly, disloyal. He could not stick at anything; after being asked to leave the public school to which Dr. Piers had sent him, he had been found several jobs but given each of them up—or been sacked—after a short trial. The trouble was, Graham had been overindulged and totally spoiled by Dr. Piers.

James' jealousy of his brother's preferential treatment came out clearly enough, but Nigel felt there was something fictitious about his diatribe, as though he had whipped himself up into this rage against Graham in order to conceal from them, or from himself, a deeper-rooted grievance.

When James Loudron had been fingerprinted and released, Wright turned to Nigel.

"Talk about happy families!" he said, rolling up his eyes. "Well, free period now for Strangeways. I've fixed to see Mr. and Mrs. Harold Loudron at 6:30, when he's back from the City. Pick you up at 6:25."

"And what will you be doing till then?"

"Amongst other things, I must have a talk with that district nurse, and with Mrs. Hyams . . ."

That evening, as the police car moved down Croom's Hill and into the Woolwich Road, Inspector Wright told Nigel the result of these conversations. Mrs. Hyams had suffered no postnatal complications; she and her husband had not expected Dr. James to return so soon after the birth—he had certainly not told them he would do so—but they were not surprised when he did, for he was one who "took ever so much trouble." The district nurse was a little surprised. Though the birth had been far from easy, she had not thought Dr. James unduly anxious about the mother. On the other hand, he was a bit of a fuss-pot, the nurse tactfully hinted without using the expression.

"Your comments?" asked Wright.

"If Dr. James killed his father, and it was part of a premeditated plan that he should take the Daimler and dump the body in the river, using a visit to Mrs. Hyams as pretext, I should have thought he'd have told her and the nurse that he'd be returning shortly on a second visit, just to safeguard himself. If the murder was unplanned, the result of a sudden boiling up of passion, then the murder method is wildly paradoxical. You don't neatly sever people's arteries in that state of mind; you bash them or strangle them."

The police car turned left off the Woolwich Road and hummed down toward the river. Harold Loudron took them into the room overlooking the Thames, where Sharon was already sitting. Nigel introduced Inspector Wright and the sergeant. After the usual preliminary politeness about being sorry to inconvenience them—just the routine of investigation—Wright said he wished to interview Mr. and Mrs. Loudron separately. Harold, frowning, started to protest about this, but Sharon said, "Don't be silly, Harold. The Inspector won't bite you." Her green eyes delayed upon Wright, who returned her his most antiseptic smile. "Nigel can come and talk to me while you're being grilled."

"Sorry," said Nigel, "but I'm sitting in with Inspector Wright. Duty before pleasure."

The red-haired girl pouted at him, then teetered out with her model's walk. This time, Wright aimed straight for the gold.

"I understand, Mr. Loudron, you had a telephone conversation with your father the night he died?"

"Yes. But it's quite—"

"Will you please tell me the substance of that conversation?"

"I entirely fail to see how this concerns your present business," Harold smoothly replied.

"I am trying to establish your father's state of mind. If he committed suicide—"

"But I thought there was no question about that."

"That he committed suicide?"

"I—er—no—the reverse."

"It has yet to be proved. Now, if your father had had bad news, something involving one of his family—he was very much the family man, I gather—if some disgrace threatened a member of his family, would you say he was the sort of man who might take his own life?"

"But this is quite fantastic. Purely—er—problematical."

"Your own business affairs, for example—"

"They are my own affair. And I assure you they will bear the closest investigation."

"I'm glad to hear it, sir. Because they are being investigated."

Harold started up from the kidney-shaped chair he was sitting on and flipped his cigarette into the fireplace. "This is the most unwarrantable interference with the liberties of the private citizen!"

"Oh, come, come now. In an investigation of this nature, the police are bound to inquire into background and motive. Do I take it that you refuse to tell us the substance of that telephone conversation?"

"Look here, Strangeways, is this man within his rights to put questions of this sort?"

"He is."

"Very well then. I've nothing to conceal. But, frankly, I was in a slight, temporary financial embarrassment; and I did ask my father for a loan."

"How slight?"

"I beg your pardon?"

"How much did you ask for?"

Wright's abrupt question, so alien to the gilded circumlocutions of the City, clearly put Harold off his stroke. However, after a pause, he said, "Frankly, I needed a fair sum. For consolidation and—er—development, you know. I had in mind a figure of ten thousand pounds."

Wright's eyebrows went up. "And did your father agree to back you to that extent?"

"I've no doubt he would have."

"But he made no promises? On the telephone, he was heard

to say the matter could not be as urgent as you represented it to be, and must wait till tomorrow."

As Wright pursued this line, Nigel scrutinized Harold Loudron. The smooth face, the dapper figure, the uniform dark suit—one saw hundreds of this type streaming across London Bridge in the rush hour, with their bowlers and rolled umbrellas and briefcases and copies of the *Financial Times*—an anonymous army, an army of ants swarming toward their mysterious occupations. That was the word for Harold—"anonymous." What personality was concealed behind the uniform clothes, the subfusc, evasive jargon? No one who keeps prefacing his remarks with "frankly" can be trusted an inch, thought Nigel; the Martini-and-smoked-salmon brigade; the I'm-not-in-business-for-my-health battalion; the sailing-near-the-wind flotilla.

A steam whistle roared. From his window seat, Nigel saw a cargo liner approaching, port, starboard, and masthead lights jeweling the dusk.

"I believe you have a motor launch?" Wright was saying.

"Yes. She's laid up for the winter, though."

Wright asked for the name of the yard. He strolled over to the window, now almost filled by the approaching ship. "Lovely view you have." Wright gazed down a moment at the river lapping the wall from which Harold's house front rose.

"You were at home here the night your father died?"

"That is so."

"Both you and your wife? No visitors?"

"Quite. We had dinner, then we played Scrabble a while, and later watched a television play till bedtime."

"What would you say if I told you we have information that Mrs. Loudron was not here all the evening?"

Harold Loudron seemed to be groping so hard for the right facial expression with which to receive this that he could spare no energy for a reply.

"—that she visited your father's house?" Wright persisted.

A covert look of relief was instantly replaced by one of indignation.

"We have already told the police we were at home all the evening. It appears that someone is trying to make trouble for my wife and I."

Nigel shuddered inwardly at the appalling solecism.

"Who told you this?" Harold continued.

"Information received, sir."

Nigel observed that Wright, always on for a bit of gamesmanship, had been countering Harold's business English with heavy strokes of official police jargon during this interview.

"Why on earth should my wife go out in a fog like that? It's ridiculous."

"I couldn't say. We must ask her."

Wright cut short Harold's protests, got his reluctant consent to be fingerprinted, and then asked the sergeant to fetch Mrs. Loudron.

"It's all right, I'll get her," said Harold hurriedly.

"Thank you, sir. The sergeant will go with you, then . . . And that's put a spoke in his wheel," Wright added when they had gone out. "Pompous young smoothie."

"You don't look at all like my idea of a policeman," said Sharon as she disposed herself on the sofa.

"Oh, we come in all shapes and sizes at the Yard, ma'am."

"What have you been doing to poor Harold? He looked perfectly devastated."

"Giving him the third degree," replied Wright amiably. "And now it's my turn. Goody." Sharon languished at the Inspector.

"Just so, Mrs. Loudron. Now tell me first about the night your father-in-law died. How long did you stay in his house that night?"

Sharon's long red nails screeched on the marble-topped table beside her as she convulsively drew back the hand that was reaching out languorously in Wright's direction.

"Damn! Now I've broken a nail. What were you saying?"

Wright repeated the question.

"Oh, that's absurd. I never went out that night. The fog was hellish. Harold and I had a homey evening. We had dinner, just the two of us, and then we played Scrabble and watched a television play."

"Yet we have two witnesses who heard your voice in Graham Loudron's room at about 9:45 p.m."

"Two witnesses! This is insane. What in hell's name should I be doing in Graham's room?"

"Perhaps you went to fetch that record he'd promised you." Nigel's mild comment got a quite staggering reaction. Sharon's face went suddenly haggard, the color of dead ash, fury and fear chasing one another across it. Her hands trembled as she lit a cigarette and plugged it into a long holder. At last she got herself under control.

"Will someone tell me what all this is about?" she asked, in a husk of her usual hoarse drawl.

"Yes. That night we all had dinner together, Graham Loudron told you he'd be getting that record for you 'in a few days,' and you said you could hardly wait for it. What was the record, by the way?"

"How can I remember? Some record or other." Her eyes rolled sluggishly in her head.

"Had he got it for you when you went there?"

"No. Yes, I mean."

"Could we see it?" asked Wright, who had not the faintest clue to all this, but admirably concealed it.

"I haven't got it. I left it there."

"So you were there the night Dr. Piers was murdered?"

"I—no, it was another night. I remember now."

"But you did go to Graham Loudron's room on the night in question? The night Dr. Piers—"

"For Christ's sake, will you two stop pestering me, confus-

97

ing me!" The woman almost shrieked it, her hands over her ears.

"Which room do you keep your gramophone in?" asked Nigel. "I don't see one here."

"We haven't got a bloody gramophone."

"What were you going to play the record on, then?"

Silence.

"Perhaps 'record' was a code word between you and Graham for something else?" suggested Nigel.

Wright gave him a warning glance. "I don't think we'll pursue this any further at the moment. Mrs. Loudron does not seem very well. I'll come back tomorrow, Mrs. Loudron, for another chat, and we can take your fingerprints then."

7.

A House in the Isle of Dogs

Nigel walked through the white-tiled, echoing tube, lighted by a long succession of electric globes in its roof—a roof upon which, so he felt, millions of tons of water must be relentlessly pressing. The Greenwich tunnel was almost empty at this time of the morning: a few boys skylarking at the far end, their hoarse shouts bouncing along the tube toward him; a few housewives ambling behind him with their shopping bags; these might have been extras in an early German expressionist film, heavy with symbolism, in which the hero was shown walking through an endless, monotonous tube, casting grotesque shadows upon its curved, white-glaring walls—walking alone, isolated in some obsessional neurosis, through a tunnel that had no outlet, on a mission whose end he had no knowledge of.

Nigel shook himself out of these morbid imaginings. His mission had a quite definite purpose. "You like burrowing into the past," Wright had said the evening before after the interview with Harold Loudron and Sharon. "Well, you go and have a talk with Graham's old tart tomorrow. I shall be busy elsewhere." Wright had not been too pleased with Nigel's jumping the gun at that last interview. He did not wish Sharon to know what the police suspected about her relationship with Graham Loudron, and Nigel's suggestion that "records" might be a code word between them could have put her on her guard. "But, my dear chap," Nigel had protested, "I said that to force them into the open. If she tries to communicate with him now, you'll know there's something in it. You'll have them both under observation, I take it, and you've got a man on the telephone extension at Number 6."

The lift took him and the housewives up to the surface. Strolling into the Island Gardens, he looked across the water. The two wings of the Palace faced him, battleship gray in the sunshine, surmounted by their twin towers, the white ensign flying. Between and beyond them stood the Queen's House in its plain, incomparable elegance; and on the hill high above, the statue of General Wolfe, with Wren's observatory beside it, held the skyline. Wolfe, the ailing, daring soldier, killed at his hour of spectacular triumph; and in the Palace over there the body of Nelson had lain, on its journey between Trafalgar and the tomb, while his rough seamen swilled grog and damned their eyes and wept like babies.

A smart black ship, with the label of the General Steam Navigation Company on its funnel, swept past toward the Pool of London. A Finnish tramp, its tall funnel heavily smoking, its hull rusty and patched, was moving in ballast downriver, the half-submerged screw sullenly thumping the water. A collier was unloading at the Greenwich power station, the clatter of whose conveyors could be distantly heard; high up on the Heath-Robinsonesque structure a traveling crane shifted, then let down its grab to gorge out coal from the bowels of the ship. To its right, the oily water smoothed over the place where the body of Dr. Piers Loudron had been salvaged from the river. A quick-fire burst of riveting rattled across from a shipyard near the Trafalgar Tavern where lighters were being repaired. Away to the left, a piercing, blue-white eye opened—the dazzling flame of a welder's burner.

Nigel walked out of the gardens, turned left, and presently right, down Barque Street into West Ferry Road. Here he turned right again, passing the ends of Schooner Street and Brig Street, and came to Yawl Street. These romantically named streets, running south from West Ferry Road toward the water front, had been knocked to bits in the early blitzes of the war. The dingy houses still standing were interspersed with scrofulous patches of grass, tumbled brick, bald foundations. Apart from its name on a wall, Yawl Street hardly existed, but at its far end Nigel saw a house standing, like a single, decaying stump in an otherwise toothless jaw. This must be Nellie's house, unless Graham had given them a false address.

The bell jangled. A yellow face appeared momentarily at a ground-floor window, then the dirty muslin curtain was pulled back again. Presently a girl of sluttish appearance opened the door; her body slouching against the doorpost, her ankles turning over above the pin-heeled shoes, she regarded Nigel with a sort of lifeless insolence.

"Nellie in?" he asked.

"No."

"When will she be back?"

"Search me. What d'you want with her?"

"A friend of mine, Graham Loudron, gave me her address."

"Never heard of him. She expecting you?"

"I couldn't say. Are you on the telephone?"

"Telephone! Listen to him! This ain't the Ritz, mister."

So, unless Graham had written to Nellie, or walked over since the interview yesterday morning, he could not have warned her.

"Nice shoes you've got. Really smart," he said.

"They're bloody killing me, I don't mind telling you," replied the girl.

"One must suffer to be beautiful."

"Come again?"

"Old French saying. *Il faut souffrir pour être belle.*"

The girl giggled—she couldn't have been more than fifteen —and prinked at her elaborate, messy hairdo. "*Oh la, la,*" she replied; then looked vague, almost inanimate again. "You want Nellie?"

"That's the idea."

"She's out shopping. Be back in half an hour. You like to wait?" she added, in a tone of harsh, slum coquetry.

"I'll come back later."

"What name shall I say?"

"Tell her it's a friend of Graham Loudron's. The name's Percy Popocatepetl."

"Get out!" laughed the girl, hugely delighted. "That's a bleeding mountain. Had it in a poem at school."

"Tell her the mountain'll come to Auntie Mahomet at eleven."

"Hey," said the girl, who seemed disposed to make Nigel linger, "I seen you before somewhere. You a television personality?"

"Never been so insulted in my life," returned Nigel, beaming at her. " 'By."

He took a bus that ran through Poplar to the north end of the Blackwall Tunnel. From the front seat on top he scanned the sprawling vistas of the borough: "a mighty maze without a plan." There were rows of dun little houses at all angles, depressing as those of a northern industrial town thrown up in the early nineteenth century to house the new wage slaves. There were signs of the terrible East End bombing—derelict spaces, acres of prefabs. Away to his left, over a high grassy rampart, showed the masts, funnels, and white upper works of steamers in dock. Warehouses and timberyards streamed past, Victorian tenements and blocks of flats built since the war. The bus, rounding a bend, moved cautiously over a swing bridge across an inlet that ran from the

Thames, now visible again, to a ship-lined basin. Everywhere there were congregations of cranes altitudinizing against the sky line, stiff-necked as giraffes, inclining their heads to pluck heaven knew what exotic produce from out the holds of ships.

What a muddle it all looks, thought Nigel; what diversity of occupations, all higgledy-piggledy, going on under my nose here, and I don't know the first thing about them. Like this damned Loudron case. The romantic rubbing shoulders with the workaday; the beauty of ships interleaving the drabness of slums. Is there anything so exciting in the world as to see a ship steaming past the end of a street?

The bus stopped. Nigel got out. Beyond the roadway running up from the Blackwall Tunnel, a huge loading shed stood, "Coast Lines Seaway" in white letters on its sides, and above it the mast of a vessel flying a flag of blue, white, and red in horizontal stripes. Waiting for the next bus back, riding back on it, Nigel debated with himself how he should approach the unknown Nellie; what on earth could he say to her? Would she throw him out on the first suspicion that he was trying to pump her? For all that, a pleasurable excitement rose in him after he had rung the jangling bell. Nigel's insatiable interest in human beings had pulled him into many strange situations before now—situations in which he was helped, however, by his natural bent for approaching the new without preconceptions, for taking people as he found them.

Nellie was certainly something to take—a large woman, her hair dyed the color of brass, lax in movement, but with a disconcerting sharpness in her gray eyes. She wore a tight black satin dress, from whose décolletage her exuberant breasts threatened to burst out whenever she leaned forward. Pushing an enormous ginger tom off an armchair, she asked Nigel to sit down.

"Graham sent you, the girl told me." Nellie watched him carefully. "Would you be wanting a room?"

"No, it's not that."

"I thought not. You're hardly the type, are you?"

"And Graham didn't exactly send me. He gave me your name and address. I wanted to have a talk with you."

"I'm not in business now, you know, dearie."

"The loss is ours," Nigel answered, appreciatively eying her opulent surfaces.

Nellie broke into a rich laughter that rippled her bosom. "Go on with you! Well, Mr.—er—"

"Strangeways."

"Can I tempt you to a glass of port?"

"That's very kind of you." Nigel loathed port, and never more than at eleven in the morning.

Nellie tottered over to a cupboard, her almost oval figure on top of the small ankles and feet giving her the look of one of those children's Humpty-Dumpty toys weighted so that they always come back to an upright position. Nigel glanced out of the window, which overlooked the Island Gardens and the river, then round the room; it was furnished with an expensive suite of armchairs and sofa; two budgerigars chatted away in a hanging cage; the air was scented and stuffy.

"Cozy up here, isn't it?"

"Not so bad," replied Nellie, handing him a glass. Her little finger refinedly crooked, she raised her own. "Mud in your eye. Mind you, it's not a class neighborhood. But I got the house cheap just after the war—been saving for years—and it suits me all right."

"So long as the lodgers pay up."

"That's right. Mind you, one gets all sorts. But they're nice boys, most of them—don't give any trouble—particularly the spades."

"I'm glad you don't have a color bar."

"Not me." She chuckled comfortably. "Nellie the Ever-Open Door—that's me. We're all the same underneath the skin, I always say."

"Except that some have kind hearts and others blocks of stone."

"Well, there's that," said Nellie, beaming at the implied compliment. "Though, mind you, a girl doesn't get anywhere if she's too soft. I always tell my boys, this isn't Liberty Hall; if you start a brawl, out you go on your ear; same if you don't pay up regularly. Course, most of them are only here a few days at a time, while their ships are in dock, and I'm not too fussy about what they bring in at night; live and let live, I always say. But I can tell you, Mr.—er—"

"Call me Nigel."

"I can tell you, Nigel, girls nowadays—why, they're immoral as cats." She rolled up her eyes. "Go with any fellow for a pair of nylons, half these misses round here will. Now, when I first went on the bash, you knew where you were; a girl was either in the business or she was pure. The war changed all that. Why, with so many amateurs knocking around, we brasses couldn't get near our beats."

"Dilution of labor."

"That's right. And now with this Wolfenden stuff, the game's not what it was. All they need's an advert in the tobacconist's window and a telephone and Bob's your uncle."

"Saves their feet, though."

"There's that. But, say you work with a telephone, you can't pick your clients. You might be getting one of those blokes with glaring eyes who just want to come after you with a hammer. Well, drink up, dearie, and have another."

Nigel drank up. Nellie took his glass, but stopped by the side window.

"There's Abdul going out."

"Abdul?"

"One of my regulars. He's a Lascar. That's how I got to know Graham."

A few months ago, said Nellie, she had gone into Abdul's

room and found Graham Loudron with him. Graham and Abdul had come across each other in the Seamen's Hospital, where the latter was a patient. Nellie got talking with them, and they discovered that she had known Graham's mother, Millie, during the war.

"Well, it's a small world, isn't it? But I expect Graham's told you all about this."

"No. He's not very communicative," Nigel replied. "But I gather he must have had a pretty hard time before Dr. Loudron adopted him."

"Yes. He doesn't talk about it much. But after Millie died, he was sent away to some kind of—what do they call it? I don't know. He was five or six by then. Millie's family wouldn't take him; they were Holy Joes, Chapel—the sort that kicks what they call Fallen Women in the teeth. Anyway, this place Graham was sent to, talk about concentration camps! Poor little bleeder! Half starved, beaten regular. Shameful. He had five years of that. Then he ran away and started breaking into shops. They caught him, and he got the wrong sort of magistrate, so then he had a spell in a reformatory. Never think it to look at him now, would you?"

Indeed I would, thought Nigel; the cold watchfulness, the faintly mocking obsequiousness, the habit of keeping everything locked up—in his room and in his mind. He said, "Who was his father, then? Did Millie ever tell you?"

A hard, inimical look came slowly into Nellie's gray eyes. She put down her glass of port on the table beside her. "Just what are you after? What's your stake in this? Did you ever know Millie, by any chance?"

Nigel, taken aback, gazed at the woman's suddenly hostile face. Then, very seriously, he said, "It's all right, Nellie, don't worry. I'm not Graham's father, if that's what is on your mind."

Her eyes scrutinized him for a few seconds more—eyes long used to summing up men.

"I believe you," she said at last. "But I'd like to know what you've come here for then."

"To talk about Graham. I know the family, and they've asked me to help with the inquiries about their father's death."

"Are you police?" she asked, still on her guard.

"I've worked with them. And sometimes I've found myself working against them. But do stop looking at me, old dear, as if I was the man with the glaring eyes."

A convulsion, which seemed to start at the neat ankles and work its way, gathering force, up her body, shook Nellie. "Gawd! Don't make me laugh!" She slapped her bulging left breast, as if to admonish it not to leap out at Nigel, which it showed every sign of doing. She quivered and gasped with titanic laughter. "You'll be the death of me!"

When she had finally recovered herself, she began to talk freely about Graham Loudron's mother. Millie Robertson had lived a few doors away from her in East Greenwich. Just before the blitzes of September, 1940, they were both evacuated to a country town in the Midlands. Millie was then nineteen, and pregnant; Nellie a few years older. She had seen the younger girl through her trouble. Millie never spoke about the baby's father, but money orders came at regular intervals. At first the two had worked in a local factory, but when an American Air Force station was set up in the neighborhood, Nellie went back, with some relief, to her prewar profession. She took up with an Air Force sergeant, following him when he was moved to another camp. Six months later, revisiting the Midland town, she found Millie in a bad way; the girl had developed tuberculosis and could work no longer at the factory, but she refused to go into hospital for treatment because she had no one to leave the baby with. Worse, her source of money then dried up. She had had to move her lodgings, and she suspected that her previous landlady was appropriating the money orders, or perhaps their sender had packed up on it.

"But didn't she write to him? He was the child's father, I presume."

"She did, once or twice, but there was no reply."

"Well, why didn't she go and see him? Tell him what had happened?"

"She was soft, that's why. A girl can't afford to be soft—not where men are concerned. Present company excepted, dearie."

"But—damn it—"

"I remember her saying to me—it was about the only time she talked about him—she said, 'No, Nellie,' she said, 'I won't be no millstone round his neck. He's a good man. But he's not for my sort. I fell for him, and I had my romance with him, and I'm not going to ruin his life.' "

"She sounds a bit soft, certainly."

"Don't you believe it," replied Nellie, with sudden violence. "Forget what I said about soft. That girl was a bloody angel. Never groused, never turned nasty; do anything for you, she would. I'm a tough old bag, Nigel, and I've always been tough. But I know a —— angel when I see one, if you'll pardon my language. And don't talk to me about whores with hearts of gold; there's no such thing. If there was, I'd not have left her that time; I'd have done something about it; but I was mad about this Air Force chap, and so—" Nellie shrugged her monumental shoulders.

"So what happened to Millie?"

"Use your loaf, ducky. She went on the game, too. What else could she do, without she was separated from her little boy. She doted on him, see? She couldn't have given him half what she wanted to give him if she'd gone on Public Assistance." Nellie took out a heavily scented handkerchief and dabbed at her eyes. "Course, she was too ill for it. You need to be strong as a horse. So she died. I only heard about it some time afterward. She wasn't one for writing letters much, but she did write to me once or twice in that last year —all about the little boy, how he was getting on, you know— never a word about herself. Here, for Christ's sake, let's have another glass of port."

"What did Millie look like?" inquired Nigel when his glass had been refilled. "Have you a photograph?"

"No. Wish I had. She was—she was like a flower. One of them narcissuses. Pale and delicate looking. Sweet all through. You'd have liked her. How those Holy Joes managed to produce her is a fair mystery to me. God! it turns me up, calling themselves Christians and then dusting her off their fingers just because she'd tripped up."

"Does Graham take after her?"

"In looks, a bit."

"But only in looks?"

"Well, he's got nice manners. Course, that Dr. Piers gave him a good education. But he's a cold number, don't you think? Millie was warm as a stove."

"Still, he likes to come and hear you talk about her."

"That's true. But it gives me the creeps sometimes. He sits here, just as you might be sitting, and stares at me—well, like a kid when he asks you to tell a story you've told him over and over again till you're fair sick of it."

"He never talks about his father?"

"No fear. But he knows what I think about the rat, who-ever he is. Course, he may be dead by now."

"I meant his adopted father. Dr. Piers."

"Not much. He did ask once if Dr. Piers had been our doctor when we lived in East Greenwich."

"Yours and Millie's?"

"That's right. She was a patient of his, as it happens. And now, dearie"—the gray eyes were shrewd again—"it's my turn to ask a question. Did Graham do him in?"

Nigel's pale-blue eyes looked at her steadily. "We don't know. We're not even certain yet that it was murder at all. The old man had a lot of money; he left it equally among his children, so all the Loudrons had that motive."

"Ah, well," she said comfortably, "it'll all come out in the wash."

"What happened to your chap?" asked Nigel, after a pause. "The American sergeant?"

"He got his in one of those daylight raids."

"I'm sorry."

"You needn't be. I've almost forgotten him now. He was married, anyway. And he knew I was a brass," said Nellie a bit bleakly.

"I must go. Thank you for talking to me. Why don't you come over and have tea with us one day at Greenwich?"

"Me?" She chuckled sardonically but looked pleased. "What'd your wife say?"

"She'd like it. She's all right."

"I guess you're not so bad yourself."

On an impulse, Nigel put his hands on her shoulders and gave her a kiss. "Good-by for the present, Nellie. I'll drop you a line about tea. Will you do one thing for me?"

She nodded, her plump fingers smoothing the cheek beside her mouth.

"If Graham comes over, don't tell him what we've been talking about. Just say I came to ask if he'd been with you last Saturday night. He was, wasn't he?"

"Yes. I gave him a room I had empty. O.K., dearie, mum's the word. But—"

"Yes?"

"Oh, nothing. I was just thinking, maybe it's a mercy for Millie that she isn't alive. I don't go for Graham much, you know, but he is her boy."

"Don't worry, old dear. I'll do what I can for him."

Nigel walked down the seedy staircase, out into the Island

Gardens. As he waited for the lift to take him down into the tunnel, he studied the regulations. One clause took his fancy: "No person shall drive or conduct into the tunnel any cattle, or any animal forming part of a menagerie, or any wild animal."

Now, who would want to, he asked himself. Not that it wouldn't be agreeable to drive or conduct into the tunnel a tiger, a prize bull, or a herd of giraffes.

When he got home, Clare kissed him. "My goodness, you've been drinking port."

"Yes, with an old tart in the Isle of Dogs."

"Oh, yes? Was she nice?" asked Clare, interested.

"You really are a jewel among women, my darling."

"Am I? Why?"

"Any other woman would have said, 'How old is she?' or 'You know port disagrees with you.'"

8.

Labyrinth of Lies

At six o'clock that evening, Inspector Wright looked in for
a drink and a chat. He had interviewed Sharon Loudron
again that morning. She admitted now that she had been in
Graham's room from about 9:10 on the night of his father's
~~death till 10:30, when she had let herself out by the back~~
gate so as to avoid passing the study door, for her brother-in-
law James often sat there at night. She had noticed that the
garage doors were open, and was near enough to see, despite
the fog, that both cars were in there. It was clearly a clandestine proceeding, but Wright, during the interview, allowed
it to be tacitly assumed that Sharon had visited Graham for
sexual reasons; he did not want either of them to suspect yet
that the police might give a different meaning to their code
word "record."

Following Nigel's visit that morning to Nellie, an Inspector of the Narcotics Squad had made immediate inquiries
there about Abdul the Lascar, in whose room Nellie had met
Graham. "Abdul" turned out not to be his real name; he
was already on board his ship, due to sail in a few hours, and
the Inspector did not interview the man, contenting himself

with a search of his room, which proved fruitless; he wanted to catch the man with drugs in his possession, not to frighten him off; when his ship returned next, there would be a reception committee for Abdul.

"I admit it's a bit odd—Graham Loudron consorting with a Lascar," said Nigel. "But there's no evidence that either of them is in the dope trade. Even if they are, you'll have a job finding it; presumably Graham would have passed the stuff on by now."

"Well, there's no trace of it in any of those locked cupboards of his. And Jackson has had a good look in the obvious place—"

"Obvious place?" asked Clare.

"Dr. Loudron's dispensary. Hide illicit drugs amongst the lawful ones. No sign of it. Jackson's investigating the cellars at Number 6 now—tapping and measuring the walls—all that caper. Might be a secret cache."

"All of which, if Graham *is* in the dope racket, will tell him he's been rumbled," said Nigel.

"Oh, no. Jackson's given out that he's searching for the missing diary pages. By the way, only two sets of prints on that casebook—Dr. James' and his father's."

"Why should Graham go in for that sort of thing?" asked Clare slowly. "Not for money; he got a good allowance from his father."

"Excitement? Sense of power?" Nigel replied. "He had a bloody time as a boy, kicked around by everyone. You could get your own back on society by corrupting individuals."

"Maybe. But it's not strong enough as a motive, is it? For killing his father, I mean?"

"Why not?" said Wright. "Dr. Piers would have cut his daughter off with a shilling if she'd married Walter Barn. Wouldn't he have done the same to his adopted son if he'd found out that Graham was dealing in hemp?"

"I'm not so sure," Nigel frowned. "The old man had

shown Graham such a special indulgence in the past—when he was sacked from school and walked out of one job after another. Still, you may be right. If only we knew what he wrote on those diary pages! Perhaps that he'd found out about Graham, and somebody else discovered the diary and salted away those missing pages to blackmail Graham with."

At this point the telephone rang. A message for Chief Inspector Wright. He came back looking pleased with himself. "Another of our friends not where he was supposed to be."

Inquiries at the Exchange had disclosed that on the night of Dr. Piers' death a long-distance call had come for Harold Loudron's number at 9:25, but there had been no reply from his house.

"Now that really is something," said Wright. "Particularly as the Fraud Squad tell me Harold's business affairs smell very fishy indeed."

"Have you given his car a going over?"

"It's the next job. We'll make that Jaguar wish it had never been born."

Harold Loudron received them in the room overlooking the river. It seemed to Nigel even more unreal, even more like a room left over from some Ideal Home for the up-to-date exhibition, than when he had first seen it. Looking left from the window, he observed the mast and rigging of Harold's derelict barge, with the green "Wreck" flag dangling from its yard.

"You told me, Mr. Loudron, that on the night your father died you were here with your wife," said Wright, in his flintiest tones.

"Since then," Harold answered, with an absurd attempt to stand on his dignity, "my wife has informed you, I understand, that this was not entirely correct."

"She paid a visit to your father's house?"

"She was out of this house from nine o'clock till about 10:45. I have no evidence where she went."

"Come, come, Mr. Loudron. Didn't she tell you where she was going, or where she had been?"

"I didn't know that you accepted hearsay evidence, Inspector."

"I'm not a court of law, sir. Please don't prevaricate with me."

"Well, then, my wife did say she'd pop along to Number 6."

"Were you not surprised at her venturing out in such a bad fog? Had she some urgent reason for visiting your father?"

Harold's eyes flickered. He got up and, walking to the mantelshelf, lit a cigarette with an expensive table lighter that stood there. "That is an embarrassing question, Inspector."

"You mean, because it was not your father whom Mrs. Loudron went to see?"

Harold looked genuinely astonished, and for a moment his curiously anonymous personality came to life. "Not my father? I simply don't understand you."

It became evident to Nigel that Sharon had told Harold a story different from the one she had told Wright.

"Your wife had an urgent reason, then, for visiting your father? Something that couldn't be communicated by telephone or deferred till the next morning?"

"That is so, Inspector. Frankly, she thought she might be able to persuade him, if she saw him personally—he had a soft spot for her, you know—to help me out over the—er—temporary financial difficulties I have already spoken to you about."

"But she was unsuccessful?"

Harold nodded.

"She saw your father and he refused?"

"I presume she saw him," Harold cautiously replied. "When she got back, she said 'it was no go.' Those were her words."

"All her words?"

"I'm afraid I don't quite—"

"You're telling me you had no further discussion with Mrs. Loudron about the interview with her father-in-law?"

Harold looked more than a little uncomfortable. "My wife was very tired when she got back, and not—er—very communicative. I could see she did not wish to discuss the matter, so I did not press her."

"But the next day, Mr. Loudron—surely, at some time since that night, you have talked over her interview with Dr. Piers?"

"Actually, no." Harold's expression was stubborn. "His disappearance and so on; they put it out of my head."

"But has it not occurred to you," Wright patiently asked, "that your wife may have been the last person to see your father alive? That her evidence is vital to this case?"

"Frankly," replied Harold, a boyish, almost shy look appearing on his face, "that is why we—why I decided to give a somewhat—er—simplified account of our movements that night. My wife is very highly strung, and I hoped to protect her from the distressing experience of—"

"Of having to tell the truth?" Wright's voice cracked like a whip, and Harold positively winced.

"I resent the tone of that remark," he said, recovering his normal pomposity. No one, thought Nigel, can be so absurdly pompous as a pompous young man.

"Well, then," said Wright. "Going back to your 'somewhat simplified account' of your movements—while your wife was out, you were here, in this house?"

"Certainly."

"Alone?"

"Yes."

"All the time?"

"I've already said so."

"Yet a trunk call was put through to your number, and there was no reply," said Wright, who had been watching Harold, slit-eyed and tense as a cat about to pounce.

Harold swallowed. "Oh, it was a trunk call, was it?"

"So you heard the bell ringing?"

"Of course. I'm not deaf."

"But you didn't answer it?"

"No. I had a great deal on my mind. I was concentrating on business problems, and I didn't wish to be interrupted."

"Do you happen to remember what time it was that the telephone bell rang?" asked Wright casually.

"Yes, just before 9:30. No, my watch was a few minutes fast. It would have been 9:25, I'd say."

Wright's saturnine hatchet face gave no inkling that he had just seen an apparently broken alibi rendered intact again by a few words. "May I use your telephone?"

"By all means. It's in the hall."

Wright went out.

"What does he want now?" asked Harold querulously.

"I imagine he's ringing up the Exchange to find out if anyone has rung them from this house inquiring whether they had a trunk call for you that night, and, if so, at what time."

"Oh, I see. Well, he'll be disappointed. It's really most unpleasant, living in an atmosphere of suspicion like this."

"It must be. But you've rather brought it on yourselves, you two, haven't you?"

"I cannot accept that," said Harold stiffly. "It's quite natural for one to wish to protect one's wife from—"

"Are you only human when you're sailing boats or talking about them? Can't you come out from behind that façade?"

Nigel's deliberate provocation had its effect.

"Human? What the devil d'you mean? I love my wife, and—"

"And by fabricating this ridiculous tissue of fairy tales, you've let her in for a far worse grueling from the police than if you'd told the truth at the start. How d'you expect me to help you if I can't rely on a word either of you says?"

"Judging from my family's experiences so far," returned

117

Harold sulkily, "we should be unwise to anticipate any assistance from your quarter."

"Oh, for God's sake, stop talking like the chairman at an annual general meeting! I just haven't time for all this managerial jargon. It may go down all right with the pin-striped types in the City, but—"

"How dare you talk to me like that! I will not have these damned insulting remarks! Get out!" Harold's suave surface had at last begun to crack all over.

"That's more like it," said Nigel equably; and to Inspector Wright, who had just come in, "I was pinching Mr. Loudron to see if I was only dreaming him."

"Mr. Strangeways appears to have taken leave of his senses, Inspector."

"Ah, yes, sir. He does give that impression at times. May I have the keys to your car?"

Harold's bewilderment could not have been more total if he had been confronted by a whole gang of goons. However, he finally handed over the keys, informing Wright that the Jaguar had been washed and cleaned inside by the East Greenwich Garage a week before, and that he kept the car parked in Pelton Road, having no garage. Wright, in return, told him that the Exchange had received no inquiries about the trunk call, except from the police.

"So that lets me out, I take it?" said Harold, glancing apprehensively at Nigel, who was looking as if he had been struck over the head with a mallet. It was, in point of fact, an exceedingly bizarre idea that had struck Nigel.

"I'd like to have a word with Mrs. Loudron," he said.

"She's in bed, I'm afraid. A bit out of sorts."

"Be a good chap and ask her if she'll see me."

Wright went off to get his men to work on the Jaguar— a tiresome job of elimination that had to be done, even though it was almost certainly too late or unnecessary. It was only two days before that Wright had been called in, and he could hardly have been blamed for not putting Harold's car high on his list of priorities. Nevertheless, he did blame himself, and self-blame had the same effect upon Wright as a release of adrenalin—he drove his men and himself with yet greater energy through the tasks to be done. One man was sent to inquire whether the cleaners at the East Greenwich Garage had found any stains on the Jaguar's upholstery or mats, and while the experts worked on the car, Wright himself began to inquire at the houses near which it had been parked that foggy night.

Meanwhile, a rather disgruntled Harold had told Nigel that Sharon would see him, and took him up to her room. Its combination of the functional and the luxurious, of modishness and sluttishness, made him recall by contrast the cluttered, dated, spotlessly clean bedroom of Rebecca Loudron. If Sharon was out of sorts, she certainly put a good face on it, sitting propped up in the huge low divan bed, bronze hair waterfalling about her shoulders, the pallor of her cheeks without make-up revealing the beautiful bone structure that Dr. Piers had commented on. Like many lovely women, in bed she looked curiously unsexy, defenseless, and ingenuous.

"You were foul to me yesterday," she said as soon as they were alone. "Well, don't stand about looking sheepish." She pushed a heap of glossy magazines off the bed onto the floor. "Come and make it up."

"I'm sorry you're not well," said Nigel, sitting down on the bed.

"Oh, I'm all right, really. I took to my bed to avoid any more scenes with that Inspector of yours. Now I rather wish I hadn't; Harold is so damned solicitous it sends me up the wall. He thinks you're mad, by the way. Are you?"

"Well, I *have* been getting some peculiar ideas."

Sharon's eyes brushed over his face with the insolent, incurious glance of the spoiled beauty. "Oh?" she said, uninterested.

"Yes. For instance, that you never went to your father-in-law's house at all the night he died."

"My dear man, if that's a sample of your peculiar ideas, I really shall have a headache. After having had it dragged out of me that I did go there—"

"According to Harold, you went there to see if you could persuade his father to cough up a large sum of money to rescue Harold from some financial disaster. Was that true? It sounds madly unlikely to me."

"Does it? Why?" she drawled. "Don't you think I'm capable of doing something to help my husband?"

"Oh, yes; and of course you'd be helping yourself too, wouldn't you?"

"What? Oh, saving myself from the bread line?" Sharon dismissed it with a petulant gesture. "It's not as bad as that. I could always have gone back to my job—modeling. But why do you say I never went to Dr. Piers' house?"

Nigel's pale-blue eyes gazed dispassionately at her. "It was your husband who went to see him. You stayed at home. That's how Harold knows the exact time the trunk call came through that night."

"Trunk call? Now what are you talking about?" Sharon looked genuinely mystified.

Nigel explained, adding, "It's Harold's only alibi. And very nice, too, considering he had the strongest reason of you all for wanting Dr. Piers dead. I only hope you are telling the truth: the police will chivy you like fury if they think you and Harold cooked up this tale between you."

"But why the hell shouldn't I be telling the truth? It wasn't much fun having to admit I'd been with Graham."

"Women are interested in the truth only when they can make use of it."

Sharon's green eyes stared boldly at him. "So you're an authority on the sex, are you?"

"I've made a lifelong study of it."

"In theory, maybe. What you need is a few practical lessons. Lock the door and take off your clothes."

"Is that what you said to Graham?"

"Ah, you're shocked, aren't you?" the husky voice jeered. "Frightened of getting involved in something you can't tie down with a string of platitudes?"

"So you did seduce Graham that night? Another scalp for you. I congratulate you."

Stung by Nigel's scathing tone, she cried, "Seduce? He's worth ten of you. He goes for what he wants."

"Meaning that I want you and daren't? Your vanity is pathological. Yes, I shouldn't be surprised if you haven't made up all this about yourself and Graham just to gratify it."

"You ask *him*, then."

"I'd rather ask you. If you can convince me you went to Number 6 that night, and slept with Graham, you'd probably convince the police too. Come on, tell me exactly what happened. You didn't go there to wheedle money out of your father-in-law, I take it? That story was just to keep Harold quiet?"

"You really are the most extraordinary man."

"And you're a tremendously attractive woman. Let's take all that as read."

"You infuriate me, but I don't seem able to stay infuriated. Kiss and make up."

Nigel put his hands on her bare shoulders, which shivered under them, and kissed her hard, once. "Now, girl, to business. You went there to meet Graham. Secretly. And for some urgent reason, on a foggy night like that."

"Yes, sir."

"What reason?"

121

"He had something for me." Sharon was gazing into his eyes as if they hypnotized her.

"Had what? Apart from his youthful charm?"

"That's a secret. Give you three guesses."

"I'd need only one."

She winced a little, then gave him a defiant look. "Well, it's my affair, isn't it?"

"I suppose so. And it'd be my affair if I lay down on an anthill and allowed myself to be eaten alive. Which is just about what you've been doing to yourself."

"Actually, I'm going to give up my anthill."

"Good. Well, you went to the house?"

She had let herself in at the front door and gone straight up to Graham's room, unobserved and seeing nobody. About ten minutes later, Graham came into the room. "He seemed —I don't know how to say it—madly above himself; you know what a cold number he usually is. It gave me quite a turn."

"Manic?"

"Yes. I'd never thought of him as—well, a lover. Honestly. He just locked the door and grinned at me like a boy who has brought off a dare, and the next moment he'd sent me sprawling onto the bed. I couldn't do anything. I was so— so *surprised*. I told him so, afterward."

"And what did he say?"

"I don't remember. He hardly talked at all. There was no tenderness. He made me feel as if—as if I was just a sort of instrument he was playing some triumphal march on. Or as if he was taking revenge on me for something somebody else had done to him. A bit of both, perhaps. It was awfully queer. But exciting. I hate men to be respectful in bed—well, you know what I mean. Oh, yes, he did mutter something about his mother having been a tart. Yes, that never occurred to me; he was getting his own back on me, for her—treating me like one. Is that possible?"

"Quite possible. And then?"

They had made love several times. After this, Sharon crept downstairs and let herself out at the back door, so as to avoid passing the study. In the passage leading past the surgery to the garden she stopped a moment, blinded by the fog, wondering if she would be able to get home; also, because she felt dazed by what had happened, and wished to find her own mental bearings again.

"I got my stockings wet," she absently remarked.

"*Stockings wet?*"

"Yes. I was standing just where the waste pipe runs down the wall into a drain, and it splashed me."

"This was at 10:30?"

"Near enough."

The splashing water had made her move on, through the garden, into the garage yard. She could just see that both cars were in the garage. The yard doors were closed, but not bolted.

"I wonder who was having a bath," said Nigel idly.

"Graham, I expect. No, how stupid of me. It was the waste pipe from Dr. Piers' bathroom." Sharon's eyes started wide open as she realized what she had said. "God! That never occurred to me! What does it mean? He must have been alive still, at half past ten."

Nigel was eying her with an attentiveness she found disquieting.

"Well, say something, Nigel. Don't you believe me? What are you thinking?"

"I'm thinking that waste pipe provides two pretty alibis. For Graham and yourself."

"Oh, damn you! So you believe I've made all this up."

"You've made up so much—well, forget that; how do you know the water didn't come from some other bathroom?"

"Because it doesn't. When Dr. Piers had his bedroom and bathroom built above the annex, the plumbers fixed up a separate pipe to take the outflow."

"Ex-model's innocence established by waste pipe. Wonderful!"

"Why can't you be serious? You never thought I killed the old man, did you?"

"I keep an open mind."

Sharon was sitting bolt upright now in the bed. Her clenched fists beat on the coverlet. "Oh, why won't you believe me! I swear I've been telling the truth."

"But I do believe you," said Nigel mildly. "Every word. You haven't the imagination to make up all that about you and Graham—what he said and the impression he gave you. How long was it from the time you left him till you got your stockings wet?"

"A minute. Less than two, anyway."

"Have you got the stockings?"

"Yes. But I've washed them since."

"Pity. Never mind. May I borrow them?"

"I suppose so. But really, you have the nastiest, most suspicious mind—"

"Inspector Wright has. The stockings *might* help to establish an alibi for Graham."

"How can they, when they've been washed?"

"You're not really interested, are you, in what happens to Graham?"

"Why should I be? He's been avoiding me since that night—hardly spoken a word to me. Not that I wanted him to. Honestly, it was all so queer, it gives me the willies to remember it."

"Are you afraid of him now?"

"Perhaps I am. I don't know—why should I be? It's just that he's not quite human. Like you," she added, smiling provocatively at Nigel, who ignored it.

"You're not afraid he'll force you to buy more records?"

"Records? Oh, I see. Records and anthills. No, what I'm

afraid of is what they might do if they found I'd been *talking* about that little racket of his."

" 'They'? He and his associates, you mean?"

"Yes. Whoever they are."

"Well, I won't tell them. And now may I have the stockings?"

She got gracefully out of bed, her long legs exposed to the thigh by the short nightie she wore, and rummaged in a drawer. "I think this is the pair." She moved close to him, holding out the sheer stockings. "Now," she said, looking up at him through her long eyelashes, "strangle me with a stocking. Wouldn't you like to?"

"I've felt like it sometimes."

"Why must you play hard to get?"

"Because I *am* hard to get."

"Don't boast. You and I would be dynamite, and you know it. Shall I light the fuse?"

"And blow up Harold?"

Sharon gazed at him meditatively for a few moments. "Well, then, tell me why you want the stockings?"

"I don't really want them any more. I wanted to see if you'd give me them."

9.

Whiffs from the Past

"But you don't even know if she gave you the right pair," said Clare later that evening.

"No. But I had a word with Wright as I came away. He's examining all her other stockings."

"What for? If she took part in the murder and got blood on them, she'd destroy them. If she told you the truth and just got them wetted by the outflow pipe, then I don't see—"

"There's another way she could have got blood on her stockings," said Nigel inscrutably.

"This sphinx act is tiresome."

"You yourself made a suggestion a few days ago about how Dr. Piers might have died. . . . Now do you see?"

Clare's eyes had lit up. "*Oh!* Yes. But surely it'd be too diluted to leave stains."

"It almost certainly would. But we can't afford to take that for granted."

"Then Graham wouldn't have an alibi for that period?"

"No. Nor Sharon, of course. But his alibi would only be partial, anyway—if she told me the truth, and I think she did for once."

"So either Dr. Piers was alive at 10:30, and had just had a bath, or—"

"Exactly."

Clare looked puzzled. "I still can't see those two as accomplices. What motive would they have—as a couple, I mean—for killing Dr. Piers?"

"If he'd found out about the drug racket?"

"Would that be really strong enough? For Graham, perhaps. But surely not for her?"

"I think I agree. No, I don't see them as accomplices. There's something Sharon said, though, while she was talking to me this evening. . . ."

Nigel told her what it was. Clare stared at him, chewing her lip. "Well, that's a nasty thought, isn't it, one way and another."

"Yes," Nigel slowly replied.

"But then, why move the body? Or, rather, who moved it?"

"The why reveals the who."

"Oh, come off it, darling."

"I think I know who put the body in the river."

"Well, come on, tell me."

He told her, and why, at some length. "But this doesn't help us much toward the identity of the murderer. We've still got Graham, and Rebecca and Walt Barn; and Harold, just possibly, though it'd be hard to get round his knowing the time of that trunk call; and of course, just possibly, James Loudron."

"And just possibly Dr. Piers himself?"

"Yes indeed. That's the trouble. But for the medical evidence, I'd go for suicide every time. I don't mind there being no exploratory cuts. But the equal depth of the two cuts—how does one get round that? He'd have had the resolution, but how could he have had the strength to make the second one?"

"How could he have had the strength to make the second cut?" Nigel inquired of Graham Loudron's impassive face.

It was the following day. Wright had telephoned to say that the search of Harold's Jaguar had proved negative, the firm that cleaned it the previous week had noticed no suspicious stains on the upholstery or mats, and the occupants of the Pelton Road houses near which the car was parked had not heard any sound of its being driven away on the night of Dr. Piers' death.

Now, in Graham's tidy and impersonal room at Number 6, Nigel faced what promised to be one of the most difficult interviews he had ever undertaken.

"So the police are baffled," murmured Graham, in his subacid way.

"For the time being. As I say, but for that one bit of medical evidence, they would probably accept suicide."

"And the dead body walked to the river and threw itself in?"

"What makes you think Dr. Piers killed himself in this house?"

Graham looked a trifle confused. "But I thought that was all settled. Harold's idea about his having had a brain storm and walked out to the river—do the police still believe that possible?"

"Does it seem to you any more improbable than that someone here should have found your father dead and gone to the trouble of dumping his body in the river?"

Graham considered it. "Well, I don't know," he said slowly. "It might be rather an embarrassment, professionally, for a body to be found in the house."

"If Dr. Piers' suicide would damage the practice, I don't see it could matter where the body was found."

"I expect you're right," said Graham indifferently.

Nigel got up, paced about the room, absently trying the locked doors of the cupboards, then walked over to the window, aware all the time of Graham's eyes following him.

"This tree must be lovely in summer," he said, looking out into the branches of the towering lime, where a troupe of sparrows were bickering.

Graham's mouth moved in a faint, disagreeable smile. He said nothing.

"Why do you keep everything locked?" asked Nigel, trying a cupboard handle again.

"It's my room. I suppose I can do what I like."

"You had no privacy in that hideous orphanage, or whatever it was they sent you to after your mother died. And all the kids stole anything they could lay hands on. No doubt those are the main reasons."

"You are a student of psychology?" the young man inquired, with polite sarcasm.

"Didn't it ever occur to you that Dr. Piers was your real father?"

"Why should it?"

"But you're not surprised at the suggestion?"

"All I knew about my father—I don't remember my mother ever talking about him—was that he let her down; when I say 'knew' I mean 'guessed.' I never believed that stuff about his having been killed in the war. Anyway, it was obvious some man had let her down. I was a bastard; she had to go on the streets."

Graham's voice held no emotion; his eyes were still expressionless.

"Do you really believe Dr. Piers was that sort of man?"

"No. I suppose that's why it never occurred to me he could be my father." The small fleshy mouth in the triangular face pushed out meditatively. "Of course, that would explain one thing."

"Yes?"

"Soon after I came here, I overheard James and Rebecca talking about their mother. I can't remember how it arose,

129

but they mentioned a quarrel their mother had had with their father. It was about some letters Janet had intercepted and kept from him. Dr. Piers found out somehow that his wife had done this. He made a flaming row, and never spoke to Janet again except asking her to pass the salt. She died about a year afterward."

"So that's why you said to the Inspector the other day that James' mother had died of neglect?"

"Yes."

"And you think those letters might have been from your mother, appealing to Dr. Piers for money, telling him she was very ill?"

"Well, it could be. Though, as I say, it hadn't occurred to me before."

"Really not?"

"I've just said so. Twice."

"Although Nellie talked to you about your mother, and told you Millie had written one or two letters to the father of her child, imploring him for money? You never linked up the two things in your mind?"

"So you've been worming information out of that old bag?"

"Do you despise everyone except yourself?" said Nigel, nettled.

"Don't preach at me," Graham coldly replied. "I take people as I find them, and—"

"You took Sharon as you found her, all right."

Graham's eyes narrowed. "Meaning?"

"You just walked into this room and raped her."

The young man grinned sourly at him. "The lady was only too willing."

"But otherwise my statement is correct?"

"I suppose so."

"Yet you told the police that you were already in this room when she arrived."

"I don't see the point."

"Now you agree that you walked in and found her here. Walked in from where?"

Graham laughed, stretching his arms up behind his head. "Oh, I see. I thought your phrase about walking in was metaphorical."

"Not a bit. Sharon tells me she waited for you here about ten minutes before you came in."

"She's congenitally incapable of telling the truth. Anyway, all this is immaterial, isn't it? Oh, I see! During those ten minutes she alleges she waited here, I'm supposed to have been killing my adopted father?" Graham said it lightly, but his eyes were sticking to Nigel's with that limpetlike fixity again.

"You might have been. At any rate, there's ten minutes lopped off your alibi, if Sharon is telling the truth."

"She isn't."

"Why should she lie about that and be truthful about the rest of the episode?"

"Search me." Graham smiled, with a sudden and unusual charm, as if to take the offense out of his words. "Perhaps she was wielding the razor during those ten minutes."

"You don't really believe that, do you?"

"Of course not. My sister-in-law is much too ladylike for that sort of thing."

"What, in fact, did she come here for that night?"

"Not for what she got," replied Graham, his mouth reminiscently twitching.

"Well, what then? A nice chat?"

"You know damn well what she came for," said Graham, after a pause.

"The 'record' you'd promised her? A neat little parcel of—"

"You're saying it, not me."

"Did Dr. Piers ever tax her with taking drugs?"

"I've no idea. Why not ask her?"

"He was a first-rate diagnostician. He must have noticed

131

the signs. And then he'd start wondering who supplied her."

"This conversation is privileged, as the needle-noses say. I should of course deny that it ever took place," said Graham smoothly.

"And of course they'd take your word rather than mine? Not that the police could do much about it, unless they found drugs in your possession, or Sharon blew the gaffe to them. You've had plenty of time to cover your traces. And Dr. Piers is dead."

"All this is rather tedious. Supposing that I had supplied Sharon with drugs, which I do not admit, and supposing that Dr. Piers had found this out, d'you really think he'd have gone to the police about it? He was far too keen on the Honor of the Family."

"I daresay you're right. What really interests me is why you tried to make Sharon contract the drug habit."

Graham, watching Nigel, offered no comment, except the faint look of derision on his face.

"It could be," Nigel went on, as if to himself, "that after your unfortunate boyhood you feel a need to exercise power over other people, and Sharon was an obvious victim with her craving for new kicks. On the other hand, it may be that you have a vindictive nature, and a strong motive for causing what havoc you can in the Loudron family; your grudge against Dr. Piers could easily extend over his children. Well, we shall find out in due course."

During this chill analysis, the fruit-bat face betrayed a certain covert animation. Graham evidently felt more gratified to be the subject of discussion than offended by the terms in which Nigel had spoken.

"When you went with Rebecca to look for your father the morning after he'd disappeared, was she very upset?"

"Well, in a bit of a flap, yes."

"You looked in the bedroom. Then you both went into the bathroom?"

132

"No. I went by myself."

"Did you get the impression that Rebecca was nervous—apprehensive about going into the bathroom? Did she hang back?"

Graham gave him a calculating look before replying, "I can't honestly be sure about that."

"Well, then, when you told her Dr. Piers was not in the bathroom, how did Rebecca react?"

"I don't remember that she said anything particular. She did look a bit stunned, I thought."

"But you wouldn't say she was afraid to enter the bathroom?"

"I—honestly, I can't tell you. At that time we weren't *badly* worried about my father's disappearance. It was still possible he'd gone out on an emergency call. We were just doing what the cops call a routine search."

"I see. And the night before, when—according to your story—you were sitting in this room and Sharon came in, what was her state of mind?"

"Good God, I'm not a mind reader. If you mean, did she look as if she'd just come from slitting my father's wrists, the answer is no." Graham's voice turned oddly peevish. "I simply can't understand why she should have told you I wasn't here when she came in. It's such a pointless lie. What do the police make of it?"

"She's not told them that bit yet, as far as I know. And just after she'd left you that night"—Nigel, moving to the window, looked out at the waste pipe running down the outside of the wall from Dr. Piers' bathroom on his right—"did you hear water splashing into the drain from that pipe?"

"Not that I remember," said the young man, after a pause. "I doubt if I could have, with my window shut. Why?"

"You realize that's the waste pipe from your father's bathroom?"

133

"Of course. But Sharon left about half past ten. He was dead by then."

"*How do you know?*"

Graham seemed unperturbed by this shattering question. "I don't *know*. I assumed it. After all, the old boy would hardly have got up again at 10:15 or so and run a bath, when he'd taken a sleeping draught and gone to bed immediately dinner was over. Anyway, he always had his bath in the morning."

"Did he? That's interesting. You know, you're the one who has inherited Dr. Piers' brains. Why on earth don't you do something with them, instead of these dead-end jobs you take up and drop?"

"I'm only twenty. Why should I, anyway? I don't owe society anything—not after the way it treated me for the first thirteen years of my life."

"But it must be so boring. Don't you have any ambitions?"

"Not now," replied Graham.

"But you used to?"

"Oh, yes. One ambition," said Graham, with a secret smile.

"What was that?"

"To be a first-rate jazz pianist and have my own band."

"I thought you were one. I'll never forget that night you played for us after dinner here. 'He was her man, and he done her wrong.' You were thinking about your mother when you plugged that refrain, weren't you?"

Graham, who had come out in the warmth of Nigel's praise and interest, now closed up again. "'Frankie and Johnny' is a song about homosexuals," he coldly replied.

Five minutes later, Nigel was sitting with Rebecca Loudron, who had just come in from shopping. In the elegant drawing room, where she had taken him, Rebecca looked out of place with her heavy limbs and country tweeds; she also looked, for no reason that Nigel could think of, on her guard. After a few polite formalities, made the more absurd both by her new *grande-dame* manner and by the cloud under which the Loudrons were living, she came out with, "I do hope the police will clear up this matter soon, Mr. Strangeways. People are beginning to talk in Greenwich."

"Unpleasant talk, you mean? About your family?"

"Yes. And they look at me in such a horrid way, some of them, in the shops."

"It must be wretched for you. But there's probably no malice behind it; only a sort of gloating curiosity. You must outface them. It'll die down soon."

"My father was very popular in the district," said Rebecca, with constraint. "They think one of us killed him, for his money."

"Which of you?"

"Harold. Or Graham. But some are saying it was me; it's got round about my father's opposition to Walter."

"But, my dear girl, how do you *know* what they're saying? They don't say it to your face."

"They wouldn't dare." Her hands gripped the arms of the high-backed chair in which she sat bolt upright. "No, one of Walt's friends heard talk, in a public house." Her formal manner suddenly cracked. "Oh, it's so beastly," she wailed. "How much longer will it go on? James is so dreadfully worried; I don't know what to do about him."

"Well, you've got Walter."

Rebecca's lip began to quiver. "I haven't seen him for nearly two days. How can he be so unkind!"

"He's busy, I expect," said Nigel soothingly.

"He told me, last time I saw him, that he didn't think my having so much money would be good for him—for his painting," she said, in a frozen little voice.

"Well, that's a new line for him. But he hasn't broken it off, has he?"

"No. I don't know. Oh, I'm so miserable! All this suspicion, poisoning everything! He even—" Rebecca paused, twisting her handkerchief.

"He even suspects you? But you and he were together till midnight."

Rebecca's eyes swerved away from his. "Father could—it could have been done before I went back to my room after dinner," she muttered. "Or after Walter left. Couldn't it?"

"It might, I suppose. And, if so, Walter could have done it; that's what's really worrying you most, isn't it? Before you went up to your room, or on his way out of the house at midnight?"

Rebecca hid her face ashamedly in her hands.

"And he's saying that marriage to a rich woman would be bad for his painting, although he'd never been troubled about that before; you're afraid it might be because he killed your father, and then lost his nerve and is trying to cut away his obvious motive for doing so?"

She nodded, her face still buried in her hands. Yes, it could be that, thought Nigel; or it could be that Walter suspects her of having murdered Dr. Piers and is pulling out so as not to get further embroiled. Walter is one who likes not to be involved, particularly where the police are concerned. On the other hand, it was he who originally asked Rebecca to say she had been alone in her room that night. If Rebecca told the truth about that. If.

Nigel decided he had come to an impasse on this line. "Tell me," he asked, "about this quarrel your father and mother had, a year before she died."

Rebecca's head went up as if sharply jerked by a bridle.

"Quarrel? How do you— I don't know what you mean."

"I'm all for loyalty. But blind loyalty can do appalling damage."

"I'd rather not talk about it. You'd better ask James. It's a private, family thing. He must decide whether you should be told about it."

"Can you give me an assurance that it is germane to this —to your investigations?" Dr. James Loudron asked, a couple of hours later.

"Certainly."

"Very well. But it's a painful matter to revive, even after all these years."

Dr. James sat at the head of the dining-room table, where he had just finished a scrambled lunch under the formidable eye of his dead mother, whose portrait hung on the wall behind him. Rebecca had not exaggerated her brother's state; he looked positively hagridden, and his burly form seemed to have shrunk within his clothes.

He poured himself another glass of water, holding up the glass to the light as if measuring a dose. "Are you quite sure you won't have a bite of lunch? Becky could easily—"

"No, thanks. I go without lunch as often as not, and I never take more than a light one."

James gave him the automatic, professional eye. "Yes? Well, you look all right on it. I daresay we make too much fuss about a regular diet, though . . ." His voice trailed away.

"You're going to tell me about the quarrel."

"Yes. Ah, here's Becky with the coffee. You'll have a cup?"

"Thanks."

They sat in silence till his sister withdrew again. Then James, with a lunging movement of his body, which suggested the breaking from some shackles of inhibition, plunged into the story.

"It was about eight years ago. One evening. I was in my third year of training. We were sitting in the drawing room after dinner—my mother, Becky, and I. Father came in with some letters in his hand. He was—I'd never seen anyone look like that before: white-hot with anger, but sort of frantic too, as if he'd just waked up and found himself buried alive. He walked over to my mother and shook the letters in her face. He said—look here, I can't see why you want to know all this."

137

"Never mind. Carry on."

"He said, 'Janet, I hope you realize you're a murderess, as well as a thief.' Mother said, 'I did it for your own good.' He said, 'You did it out of poisonous, despicable jealousy.' I'll never forget their words, or their faces. It was terrible. We'd never seen them quarrel before—not in a deadly way like that. They forgot we were in the room even, till Becky became hysterical. I had to take her out and calm her down; actually she was quite ill for several days afterward."

"So that's all you heard of the quarrel?"

"No. I came down again. Father was still at it. I didn't go in. I—I listened at the door. I was afraid he might do her some physical violence and I thought I'd better be on hand."

"So you were able to piece the story together?"

"Yes. Of course, neither of them said a word to any of us about it afterward. But from then on my father treated Mother—well, as if she simply wasn't there. It was bitterly cruel; whatever she'd done, she didn't deserve that. We had a miserable year. Then she died. Of course, she had a bad heart condition before, but she couldn't go on living, with my father behaving as he did."

Nigel watched James Loudron intently. The emotion released through that hagridden face was painful to see. The doctor was beyond embarrassment, gripped by a feeling that shook to bits his usual stolid, professional decorum.

"I take it," said Nigel, "that those letters were from a young woman who had had a child by your father and was appealing to him for help?"

"They were blackmailing letters," James grimly rejoined.

"How do you know? You didn't read them."

"That's what Mother called them."

The two Millies, thought Nigel: Janet Loudron's black-mailing bitch; Nellie's sweet-as-Narcissus friend. He said, "Your mother had intercepted the letters, then?"

Janet Loudron, according to James' account, must have

opened the first of them quite by mistake. Two or three more came, which she was then on the lookout for. Dr. Piers, a few days before this hideous scene, had somehow got to hear of Millie's death in 1945. He must have wondered why she had never written to tell him that she was very ill and no longer receiving money from him: but suppose she had written, what could have become of the letters? There was only one answer to anyone familiar with Janet's possessive, moralistic, and ambitious nature. She would see Millie as not only an episode in her husband's past that must be hushed up but as a potential menace to his career as well as their marriage; it was not in her to feel the sweetness and unselfishness (if Nellie was right about Millie's character) that breathed through the letters. But why had she hidden, not destroyed them? Because, thought Nigel, their existence would represent for her a latent source of power over her brilliant and authoritarian husband; or perhaps simply because she was the kind of woman who keeps everything. Anyway, what did it matter now?

"You and Rebecca used to talk about this sometimes, after your mother died?"

"Yes. It was partly therapeutic. I mean, Becky had taken it very hard, as I told you. And I judged it was better for her to talk about it than to keep it bottled up."

"Very wise, I daresay. And one day Graham overheard you both discussing it."

"So *that's* how you knew—it would be Graham, the little bastard."

" 'Bastard'—do you realize what you're saying?"

James Loudron gave him a puzzled look. "Well, he *is* an absolute"—his slowish wits were visibly working—"good God, you're not suggesting—"

"Surely it must have occurred to you that Graham might be this girl Millie's child by your father?"

"What? Occur to me that my father would bring his bastard into our house and give him my mother's room to live in? I must say, you credit me with a pretty lurid imagination."

Nigel was unimpressed by this disclaimer, but did not say so.

"Well, your mother was dead. Your father may have felt he must make some reparation to the other woman and her child."

"Yes, but damn it, Mother's own room! Talk about adding insult to injury!"

Nigel gazed steadily at him. "You took sides, didn't you?"

"Took sides?"

"You and Becky were against your father, on your mother's side, after the quarrel. And you still are, though they're both dead."

"What if I am?" James glared back at him with a kind of fuddled menace, almost as if his unwonted display of emotion had intoxicated him. Nigel let the silence protract itself.

"Well, what if I am?" James repeated. Then slowly, with the air of one who makes an almost incredible discovery, he went on, "You're not suggesting that I—that I've been saving up my bitterness against my father for the way he treated my mother—saving it up for eight years?"

"Savings accumulate," murmured Nigel.

"You must be mad. If I was going to kill him, I wouldn't have waited all this time. Damn it, we got on quite reasonably well together—"

"Well, then, who did kill him? Whom have you tried to protect?"

James Loudron rose abruptly and lunged out of the room.

10.

The Naked and the Dead

For the third time Nigel rang the bell of the house overlooking the green expanses of Blackheath. He was about to turn away when the door at last opened.

"Oh, it's you," said Walter Barn. "I was working. What d'you want?"

"To talk to you. I can come back later."

"Oh, that's all right. The best of the light has gone, anyway."

He led Nigel through a nondescript hall into a large room at the back of the house. The hard, cold north light came through French windows, mercilessly exposing an unmade camp bed, a gas ring with a dirty saucepan on it, muddy canvases on the walls, a kitchen table littered with paints, rags, jam jars full of brushes. There was a smell of turpentine and poverty.

"Welcome to my humble abode," said Walt. "This is Louisa, known to her wide circle of undesirable friends as Lousy."

"How do you do?" said Nigel to the girl, who sat in an

ungainly attitude upon a kitchen chair, stark naked. She glowered at him through a tangle of hair.

"Bloody cold, as you ask me," she vouchsafed.

Whether it was the north light, or the east wind outside that seeped into the room with a bone-piercing chill for which the ancient gas fire was no match, the girl's skin had a bluish tone.

"Who's this?" she growled.

"His name is Nigel Strangeways," said Walt. "He lives with Clare Massinger."

A trace of animation appeared upon the girl's doughy face.

"Clare Massinger? She's old hat now."

"You shut your silly mouth, Lousy. Massinger is first-class. What the hell do you know about it, anyway?"

"Peter says—"

"Peter knows as much about plastic values as this bit of linoleum." Bending down, Walt tore a strip off the rotting linoleum and slapped the girl smartly on the thigh with it. "If you'd use your own eyes instead of bleating out a lot of second-hand judgments—"

"When you've finished," she complained.

"I have finished. Put on your clothes and remove the body. This gentleman wants to talk to me."

"One of your Establishment friends, huh?" The girl stood up, revealing the stocky, broad-hipped figure, the thick legs, and low-slung buttocks beloved by painters. "I warned you what'd happen to your work if you got in with that lot. Peter says—"

"Peter!"

The girl put her hands on her hips, tossing back her hair and revealing a dirty neck. "All right. Marry your bloody heiress—and Annigoni won't see you for dust."

"I do believe this moronic cow is trying to be rude," remarked Walt. He seized the solid girl and held her up high,

142

her legs kicking like a frog's, then deposited her among her clothes on the bed.

"She needs her bottom smacked. You take first go?" Walt grinned at Nigel, wandering off to the easel. "Color," he muttered abstractedly. "That's all very well. But you've got to *feel* it! Here!" He thumped his barrel chest. "Young Lousy —does she make you *feel* any color?"

"She looks blue to me," said Nigel.

"Nah. That's just her bad circulation. Her father's a chartered accountant, believe it or not. . . . Figure studies . . . She's in revolt against bourgeois respectability, or some such crap, so she sits for me and goes daubing in some God-damned art school. Pathetic, isn't it?" He scraped away at the canvas with his palette knife. "Louisa, the queen of the layabouts . . . But, you mark my words, she'll end up in a semidetached in the suburbs, like the rest of them. Nappies in the bathroom and a loverly three-piece suite in the lounge."

"—— to that," mumbled the subject of his remarks, drawing a thick sweater over her head.

"Yeah, she's burning with a hard, gemlike flame, like a lodginghouse gas jet. Just look at her! All rump and no radiance. Daresay Massinger could make something of her. But *I* need someone who'll squeeze the colors out of me—get it?—a model who's *asking* for vermilion and cobalt and chrome yellow. Poor Lousy gives off about as much passionate color as a loin of refrigerated mutton."

"If you could paint like you talk," retorted the girl, "you'd be in the Academy."

"Hah! Double-barreled insult. You kill me. Run along now, Cleopatra. See you tomorrow."

"So long," said Louisa amiably, and, with a final glare at Nigel, departed.

"Well, there it is," muttered Walt. "Lar Vee Bohame. She can have it. Cup of tea?"

He unearthed a plate of buns from under a paint rag, filled

a kettle, lighted the gas ring. Nigel studied the young painter's cannon-ball head, compact body, and neat movements.

"Well," said Walt as he poured out the tea, "how's things in the great world of crime and punishment? Found any more bodies?"

"Rebecca's very upset."

A wary look came into Walter's bright blue eyes. "She sent you up here?"

"No."

"Well, then? You on the Marriage Guidance lark? Have a bun."

"I can't make out whether you've broken it off with her or not. Have you?"

"What does she say?"

"That she hasn't seen you for two days. And what do you say?"

"That I haven't seen her for two days. So what? I don't have to live in her pocket."

"You'll beat up two newspapermen who molest her, but you won't stand by her when she's in real trouble?"

"I beat them up because journalists disgust me; it wasn't my chivalry." Walt's round head rolled on his shoulders. "Hey, what's this you said? Real trouble? How d'you mean?"

Nigel gazed at him noncommittally, saying nothing.

"You mean, they suspect her of doing the old man?" Walt persisted.

"Don't you?"

"Me? It's nothing to do with me." The piercing blue eyes stared defiantly at Nigel, then swiveled away.

"You know, somebody ought to sign you on for the freaks' show in a fair."

"I don't get it."

"Young man who says it's nothing to do with him when he suspects his fiancée is a murderess."

"Look here, I—"

"Is that why you're pulling out? Afraid of her?"

"This is just bloody crazy!"

"Or am I really expected to believe you had a change of heart and decided that a rich wife would be bad for your"— Nigel glanced at a grayish still life on the wall—"your Art."

"I shall probably knock your block off before you go. But I'd like to know first why you find that idea so incredible."

"I don't. It's perfectly possible a rich wife might be the ruin of you. What I do find odd is that this should only have occurred to you a couple of days ago. The day after Rebecca's father disappeared, you came chasing round to ask me how soon you and Rebecca could get your hands onto his money. What happened in the interval?"

"Nothing." Walt Barn said it much too quickly.

"Well, I'll tell you. You started thinking about Dr. Piers' death. You realized that Rebecca might easily have caused it, either before she joined you in her room that evening, or after you left the house. You remembered the row she'd had with her father that day—how she sent for you, and you came along and found her in a murderous state of mind."

"No! Steady on! She was hysterical, I grant you. But not—"

"And then it occurred to you that she'd sent for you so as to provide her with an alibi of sorts for that evening. Had she ever asked you up to her room at night before?"

"No, as it happens. But—"

"You are aware that she has a passionate temperament, and a slightly unbalanced mind, and that she had two reasons for hating her father."

"Two reasons?"

"You didn't know that when her father and mother had a cataclysmic quarrel eight years ago, Rebecca got hysterics and was ill for some days after? That she has always believed he was responsible for her mother's death?"

"I don't know anything about that." Walt's eyes were glittering and inexpressive now, like mineralogical specimens.

145

Reaching out for his palette knife, he made stabbing motions at the wooden table. Nigel got up and walked over to the French windows; the garden outside, in the dour February light, was a mass of rank grass, bricks, balks of wood, rusting household utensils.

"I think Becky may have taken up with me," Walter was saying slowly, "because I was different from anything she'd come across—from her dad and the way they live there. It was a sort of gesture of revolt. Like Lousy's from her chartered-accountant father. If Becky really hated her dad, as you say, it'd be a way of rolling him in the mud, wouldn't it?"

Nigel made no comment on this singular interpretation of Rebecca's conduct. He asked point-blank, "Are you breaking it off with her because you've got cold feet?"

"I've not broken it off."

"Because," Nigel persisted, "you're afraid that your coming in for her share of the old man's money would make the police suspect you?"

"Well, you have got a nasty mind," said Walter, with a flickering, evasive grin.

"Maybe. But it's the only explanation I can think of. You don't like getting mixed up with trouble, do you?"

"Who does?"

"Lots of people. Do you get the impression that Rebecca is a bit doubtful about you too?"

"Doubtful?"

"You had motive and opportunity for killing her father. And you persuaded her to tell the police she'd been alone in her room all that night. Wouldn't that make her suspicious about you?"

"Not on your life. She's in love with me," Walter replied, with a disagreeable complacence.

"So you're just going to sit tight on your little raft of non-commitment and let Rebecca drown."

Walter shrugged. "I've got to concentrate on my work.

It's been going well since this happened. All I want is a bit of peace just now."

"Which is what you won't get—not till the case is cleared up. If you want to let Rebecca carry the can for you, that's your business. But you can't paint out the fact that you and she are two of the chief suspects; the police will chivy you from here to judgment day till they find out the truth."

"—— the police."

"Particularly," added Nigel, at a venture, "when Sharon comes out with the full story."

"That bitch. She'd say anything." His eyes glittered at Nigel like blue glass. "So it was her in Graham's room?"

"Yes. And I'm convinced she saw or heard something that will lead the police to the murderer."

"Well, why doesn't she tell them?"

"She's like you. All for Number 1 and a policy of non-involvement."

"Except with young Graham. I should watch that bird, if I were you. He's the killer type. A psychopath, I shouldn't be surprised."

"You think he killed Dr. Piers?"

Walter Barn gave Nigel a look both calculating and impish. "Well, I saw him come upstairs about ten past nine that night."

"Which proves that he had just murdered his father?"

"I'd nipped out of Becky's room to go to the john. Its door faces the head of the stairs. When I came out, I saw him walking up from his father's room and going into his own."

"Very sinister, I'm sure."

"Yes. He had a ghastly grin on his face, and blood dripping from his hands."

Nigel gazed contemptuously at the young painter. "Why don't you grow up? You're not even amusing as a clown."

"Just taking the micky out of you, mate. I don't like blood-hounds and I don't like intellectuals. A combination of the two makes me sick to the stomach. Now run along and be inquisitive somewhere else, sod you."

Nigel realized that Walt was about to explode with demoniac violence; the round face had gone white, the broad shoulders were hunched in menace. As he finished speaking, the young man made a sudden pass with the palette knife, his wrist turning upward, at Nigel's face. Sidestepping, Nigel brought the edge of his hand down on the inside of Walt's wrist, with such force that the knife flew to the floor and its owner doubled up in agony, thrusting his wrist between his thighs to alleviate the pain.

"Christ! You've broken it, you bastard!"

"Nonsense. You'll have a bruise, that's all."

Walt soon straightened up. One arm dangling, he came at Nigel, who straight-armed him, the heel of his hand cracking against the bridge of Walt's nose, and stopped him as if he'd been nailed to the floor.

"All right," said Nigel. "Calm down. You're tough. But I'm not a yellow-bellied newspaperman."

Walt shook his head to clear it. He looked dazed, but not a bit tamed yet. His hands went up to his bowed head, as if to cradle the injured nose, which was bleeding profusely, but Nigel sensed that Walt was looking through his fingers, measuring the distance. So, when the hands came down and Walt kicked viciously at his groin, Nigel was already moving back and to his left. Seizing Walt's boot, he gave the foot a sharp upward twist, upending his opponent, the side of whose head struck the linoleum with a stunning thud. Nigel picked up the palette knife and sat down on a kitchen chair against the wall —the chair recently occupied by the undraped Louisa.

"This could go on forever," he observed amiably, as Walt Barn sat upright on the floor, his eyes not perfectly focused yet, and wiped the blood off his face with the back of his hand. "The irrepressible in pursuit of the impossible."

Walt looked comically puzzled. "Well, who'd have thought

it?" he said. "But if you expect me to shake hands and say the better man won and all that Public School crap, you can—"

"Oh, come off it. There's only one thing I'd expect from you."

"Yes?" Walt dragged himself to his feet.

"A kick in the liver as soon as I turn my back. Or would you rather use this?" Nigel handed him the palette knife.

Walt stared at it for a moment, then threw it down on the table.

"I guess I'll keep that for my painting." He grinned at Nigel suddenly. "Proper dirty fighter, aren't you?"

"When encouraged."

"I'll have another go at you one day. Have to brush up my timing a bit first."

"Pugnacious bastard. In the meantime, why not go and have a talk with Rebecca?"

"Wedding ring and all?"

"That's your affair. Of course, if you don't love her—"

"Who the hell says I don't love her?" Walt belligerently inquired.

Inspector Wright gave the appearance of a man utterly exhausted. His eyes seemed to be looking out from the far end of deep caverns. He sat slumped in Clare's studio, the hands —usually so restless, miming his words—dangling flaccidly now from the chair arms. Even Nigel's account of the set-to with Walter Barn that afternoon produced hardly a flicker of animation.

"Well, it doesn't sound as if young Walt was the murderer," offered Clare.

"No," said Nigel. "He's a demon when he loses his temper; he boils over suddenly and silently, like milk in a pan— Welsh blood, perhaps. He'd never think up a deliberate thing like that: neat incisions with a razor."

"He was going to incise you with a palette knife, though," said Wright.

"He'd lost his temper. I provoked him."

"But he could have been provoked into losing his temper with Dr. Piers. He finds Miss Loudron in a hysterical state after the scene with her father; it makes him see red—"

"No. That won't do. He hasn't got that kind of chivalry. He'd just slap her on the bottom and say 'Cheer up, ducks, it'll all come out in the wash.'"

"You say that, when you saw him beating up the newspapermen?"

"Yes."

Wright sighed, reached out for his whisky, took a deep draught, and closed his eyes. "We're getting nowhere. Nowhere at all. A lovely set of motives. Lots of lovely opportunity. Some cockeyed alibis. But hardly one solid fact to build on. Even their lies—and they've told enough, between them —seem to cancel one another out."

Clare refilled his tumbler. "I must say it does seem odd no one heard a splash. It was a dead quiet night; no traffic on the river, only one car—"

"One car?"

"The car in which the body was brought to the river. There are only three roads, at all near, which run right down to within a few yards of the water. And there are houses at the end of each of them," said Clare. "It's a hundred to one that the murderer would use a car and would choose one of those three roads. In that fog, you can't imagine him going further afield."

"But the Loudron cars have been checked and double-checked. We took samples of dust. We went over the mats and upholstery with—"

"Dr. Piers' car included?"

"Of course. A hair or two of his on the floor by the front passenger's seat—"

"The passenger's seat?"

"Yes. It seems Graham Loudron often acted as his chauffeur."

Nigel, pacing up and down the studio, paused. He gave the Inspector a veiled look. "I think Clare's right. Somebody must have heard a splash. Somebody in the Trafalgar Tavern."

"But we inquired of every resident there. Those likeliest to hear anything—in the apartment nearest the river wall—had the radio on."

"Too bad," remarked Nigel dreamily. "Nevertheless I think I shall work on the assumption—the far from tacit assumption—that they did hear a splash. About eleven. We've got to get this log jam shifted."

Wright, looking a little revived, winked at Clare. "What's the old man cooking up?"

"Something nasty, I'll be bound. 'Eels boiled in broo, Mither.'"

"'Mak' my bed soon,'" Nigel capped the quotation. "But that's not it . . . An association . . . What did he call that dirty girl? 'Lousy.' No. Ah! 'Cleopatra.' A barge." He swung round on Wright. "The barge! Harold's old wreck. What fools we are! That'd be the place to hide the diary. Why didn't we—"

"Speak for yourself, chum. I had two men taking that barge to pieces all yesterday afternoon."

"Oh, you did, did you?" Nigel looked only momentarily disconcerted. "Nobody ever tells me anything."

"It's full of mud and rats and rotting timber. Nothing else. And I wish you'd get your mind off that diary. If it was the least danger to him, the murderer would have set a match to it long ago."

"We mustn't assume that it was the murderer who tore out those pages."

The three sat in silence for some moments—a silence broken at last by Clare's high, light voice, whose childlike

151

timbre often deceived the ignorant into imagining it went with a childish mind. "A phrase keeps running in my head: 'He's got it taped, he's got it taped.' Now what do you suppose that can mean?"

Nigel seldom made the error of not taking seriously Clare's random contributions to a subject. " 'Taped'? Let's see. Measurements. Boxer's knuckles. Ticker tape. Tape recording. Name tapes in schoolboy's underwear." His mouth fell open. "No! *Tape recording!* That's how Harold could have got his alibi. Don't you see? He sets a tape recorder going near his telephone in the hall, just in case someone should ring up or ring the doorbell while he is out. Dashes off to Croom's Hill. Kills his father. On his return, plays the tape over to himself. Hears the telephone bell ringing on it. It'd be easy to fix exactly the time at which the bell had rung—so many minutes after he'd switched the machine on and left the house. Wait a minute, though. How long does a spool of that stuff play for?"

"Half an hour," answered Wright, poker-faced.

"Are you sure?"

"I ought to be. I had a chap spending the best part of a day playing Harold Loudron's spools over."

Nigel bowed his head. Clare smiled at Wright.

"Dearest Inspector, you know I love you fondly. But sometimes you are the most provoking creature in the world."

"Of course, he could have destroyed that particular spool," said Nigel. "Or just scrubbed it."

"Oh, yes, indeed he could. But we're back where we started. By the way, I've been onto the chap who put that trunk call through to Harold's house—just in case Harold might have *asked* him to put it through at that time, so as to provide an alibi. He says Harold did not ask him. Respectable chap. No reason to suspect him of lying about it."

Nigel took up one of Clare's chisels and sighted along it.

"If our bird sits tight, you're going to have an unsolved case. I think it's time I put a cat among the pigeons."

But a very different sort of cat was already on the prowl. While Clare, Nigel, and Inspector Wright were talking, the telephone bell rang in Harold Loudron's house. Harold was out, dining with a business associate. Sharon took up the receiver. "Who? Oh," she said. "I didn't expect—"

"Listen. I've got to see you—"

"But—"

"The police have been at me again. And I've got to have another session after dinner. Don't know how long it'll go on. It should be safe about 11:30. Slip out then. I'll be waiting at the end of Lassell Street."

"But why not here? Why out?"

"I'll explain when I see you."

"Well, can't you give me some—"

"It's not advisable on the telephone. I can only tell you we've got to have a talk. Terribly urgent."

"Oh, very well."

"And keep this to yourself, my dear. Tell nobody. Repeat, nobody. 'By."

At 11:30, Sharon came out of her house. She was fully dressed, and wore a thick frieze coat and a headscarf. The east wind had died down, but the air was biting; Sharon shivered, feeling the cold at once, and a certain chill of apprehension, too, but it was partly excitement that made her shiver; Nigel had been right when he told her she would do anything for a kick.

Quietly she opened the door in the wall. She looked left, and then right. The street lamp outside the "Cutty Sark" tavern threw an amber glow over Ballast Quay. She could hear water slapping the river wall; no other sound.

The windows of the "Cutty Sark" and the houses on either side of it showed no glimmer of light. It was a dark night, but Sharon could just pick out against the sky the pyramid of scrap iron overtopping the corrugated-iron wall of the yard beyond the curving quay.

"Why did we ever come to live in this Godforsaken hole?" she muttered peevishly as she hurried in her heelless shoes over the cobbles past the public house, startling a cat, which streaked away from her like a ripple of shadow.

At the corner, she descried a figure standing in the shadow of the scrapyard wall. Was it the person she expected? The figure raised a finger to its lips. The finger looked unnaturally thick, which Sharon put down as a trick of light and shadow, being unable to see till she got close that the hand was wearing a heavy gauntlet glove.

"Why all this mystery?" she murmured, looking up into a familiar face that seemed the face of a stranger.

"Shh! I may have been followed. Come this way a little. Daren't go into the house."

Sharon could barely hear the whisper. She shivered again, but allowed herself to be drawn by the arm, which was firmly tucked into her own, toward the entrance of the narrow alley between the scrapyard and the quay where the scrap was loaded onto ships. To her right, a crane stood up against the darkness like a premonition. From downriver came one melancholy hoot of a steam whistle.

Excitement welled up in Sharon. There was something about this assignation and the tense figure of her companion that stirred her jaded senses. She clutched the arm closer to her body, groping for the gauntleted hand.

Halfway down the narrow passage, with its corrugated-iron walls rising high above their heads on either side, her companion stopped, moved behind her. She heard quickened breathing; arms came round her, and hands over her breasts. Leaning back, she shivered deliciously. There was a silence

154

of listening. Then the hands rapidly shifted, flurried; Sharon was flung down on her face and felt a dreadful constriction at her throat.

The woman's body jerked and thrashed, but she could not throw off the weight upon her back, the knees which ground into it. The silk stocking, tightening and tightening round her throat, took her voice away, so that her screams were only whimpers and gasping croaks. Nevertheless, it took her some time to be killed, and she was not quite dead when the killer heard footsteps, their noise drowned till now by the struggle, approaching the far end of the alley.

It was a Dutch seaman, returning blind drunk from a round of the pubs and subsequent potations in a private house, to his ship moored at Lovell's Quay.

The murderer dragged the body of his victim to its feet, set its back against the corrugated wall, and held it there, its knees sagging, screened by his own back from the approaching seaman. If the latter was capable of perception and inference, he would take them for a pair of lovers in a close clinch.

The seaman, who had now started to sing, wove his way along the dark, narrow alley, bouncing from wall to wall like a ball on a pin table. He struck the wall, a few yards short of the two silent figures, cannoned off it, lurched past them with a guttural curse, then resumed his singing. Arriving on Ballast Quay, the man's drunken progress took him on a swerving arc to the left, where he tripped over a low-slung chain that separated roadway from pavement and fell flat on his face. The shock must have fuddled his wits still further, for, on getting to his feet again, he walked straight to the low parapet of the river wall, tripped over that, and fell in.

Fortunately for him, it was not high tide. Sobered by the cold water, he floundered his way to the steps. His shouts and oaths, after the splash of his fall, brought heads out of windows, and presently one or two men ran out of houses and helped the seaman up the steps.

While this farce was being enacted, the murderer slid open a door in the corrugated-iron wall, deposited the victim—now at last dead—amongst the scrap, and walked decorously away in the direction from which the seaman had come.

11.

A Silk Stocking

Standing just inside the breaker's yard, Nigel Strangeways cast his eye over the dismal scene. A thin, bitter rain was falling —raindrops black with smut from the power-station chimneys. Mounds and pyramids of scrap iron towered above him, the rusting detritus of a civilization: boilers, bicycles, oxygen cylinders, coils of barbed wire, oil drums, perambulators, automobile engines, cisterns, cogwheels, pipes, pots and kettles, machinery, all tossed and jumbled together as if by a whirlwind. The oxyacetylene burners, with which the larger objects in this tangle were broken up, stayed silent today; the first arrivals at the yard had found a body there, and soon the police were in occupation, photographing, measuring, poking about for clues in the jungle of metal upon which Nigel's eyes now dully rested. At last he forced them to look down at the last piece of scrap to have been deposited here. It was covered with tarpaulin. Chief Inspector Wright, his sergeant, and the yard foreman stood beside it. Wright, Nigel noticed, was gesturing forcibly; he seemed to have a new lease on life. Last night he had complained of the dearth of material facts; well, now he'd got one—and good luck to him.

Nigel walked over and pulled back the tarpaulin. His eye traveled up from the slender feet, one of them shoeless, along the sodden frieze coat, to the neck. A silk stocking was round it, knotted presumably at the back. He had expected Sharon's face to be an atrocious sight, and it was. Her eyes stared back into his with the merciless indifference of the dead. Sharon had not been any great credit to society; smart clothes, smarty talk, selfishness, an appetite for the basic thrills; but this was no comfort to Nigel, who feared he had been indirectly responsible for her death. He pulled back the tarpaulin over the staring eyes and the pretty, snarling teeth. It was 8:45. Half an hour ago, Wright's telephone call had dragged him out of bed.

Wright gave Nigel a look both sympathetic and bracing; "Yes, I understand," it said, "but this is no time for brooding." He drew his friend aside and leaned against a rusting water tank, from which he surveyed his men at work while he talked rapidly to Nigel.

"They found her at eight o'clock. Been dead seven to ten hours, the quack says. Autopsy'll tell us nearer. Strangled—you saw that; probably in the alleyway outside; signs of a scuffle and of her being dragged in here; one shoe found just inside the yard. Face dirty and bruised; must have been thrown face downward and strangled from behind. Not nice at all. No signs of sexual assault or robbery; left her handbag and purse at home. Sergeant Reed has broken it to her husband. Harold's in a bad way; Dr. James is with him just now and will take him to Croom's Hill. Harold says he dined out with a business associate, returning home about midnight; didn't want to disturb his wife—they sleep in separate rooms —so went straight to bed. Reed and Dr. James say they found no scratches or bruises on him. Yes, Simpson?"

A plain-clothes man had hurried up to report. Several people living in the houses on Ballast Quay had just told him about the episode of the drunken sailor; it was the only disturbance during the night so far reported. Simpson pointed in the direction where the Dutch ship lay.

"Well, stop her, man," exclaimed Wright. "What are you wasting time here for?"

"It's all under control, sir. Lewis has gone aboard. He'll hold the ship."

Wright nodded at the man, smiling faintly. "Some of these chaps can actually think for themselves," he said to Nigel. "Would you believe it? All right, I'll interview him straight away."

After giving the sergeant some instructions, Wright untied the silk stocking from Sharon's neck and handed it to him. As they walked along to Lovell's Quay, he remarked, "Reed may find that one stocking of a pair is missing—amongst the dead woman's or Miss Loudron's. But if the murderer has any sense, he'll have destroyed the other one."

In a couple of minutes they were aboard the Dutch motor vessel. It was one of the ships largely manned by members of single families, who are enabled to purchase them by government grants, paid back in instalments, and who use them as floating homes. The master received them in his cabin. It was spruce and shining, meticulously tidy, a genuine Dutch interior, with potted plants on a table and bright curtains over the window; it smelt of coffee, cigars, and furniture polish. The master's buxom wife was placidly knitting, while two stolid children finished their enormous breakfast. The master himself could speak only a few words of English, but a younger brother, the mate, was reasonably fluent. After the usual introductions and civilities, the master's wife removed her children, and Jan, the drunken seaman of last night—a nephew of hers—was summoned. He turned out to be a strapping, gawky young man, suffering from a hang-over but not, as far as Wright could judge, a bad conscience as well.

The mate interpreting, Jan gave what account he could of the previous night. He remembered the last house he had visited, and this could be checked, but he had only vague recollections of his movements thereafter. Wright had to phrase his questions tactfully, for there was a strong atmosphere of family solidarity in the cabin. Jan had certainly met no women on his way back to the ship; never, he soberly averred, did he mix women and drink; one or the other, yes, but not both at the same time. He remembered falling flat on his face over a chain, which accounted for the bruise on his forehead, and then falling into the Thames. There were abrasions on the palms of his hands, caused by the first fall, but no scratches on the backs of them or on his wrists, such as a woman would have made in fighting to tear loose the hands tightening a knot at the back of her neck.

And as he came along the narrow alley through the scrapyard, just before he fell over the chain, had he seen or heard anything unusual?

No.

"Anything at all?" put in Nigel, knowing the literal-mindedness of the Dutch.

"There was a couple. In the alley. Lovers. It was very dark. I nearly ran into them," said Jan through the interpreter.

Asked if he could describe them, Jan blushed and stammered out a few phrases.

"He says he did not like to look close. He is not a—what is your phrase?"

"Not a Peeping Tom?" Nigel offered.

"Yes. Just so."

"Tell him it may be most important to remember anything—any impression he got about this couple," said Wright urgently.

The reply came. "My nephew says the man's back was toward him. He was about middle height. He seemed to be holding the woman up. My nephew thought she was perhaps drunk."

"Tell him we're most grateful for—"

"Just a minute," Nigel interjected. "Is he certain that the person holding up this woman against the wall was a man?"

The question evidently shocked Jan. He blushed up to the roots of his blond hair.

"He says, but it must have been a man. They were in the embrace of lovers."

"But it was dark. He couldn't swear on his oath that it was not a woman dressed as a man."

Jan replied that he could not absolutely swear to it, but he was certain in his own mind.

With the master's permission, Wright now got Jan to remove his trousers. A woman being strangled from behind would kick backward. There was an abrasion on one knee and a bruise beside the other. But when Wright got Jan to fetch the trousers he had been wearing the previous night, a tear and some dirt on them corresponded exactly with the marks on his legs; Sharon's heelless shoes could not have made the tear.

"Elimination," remarked Wright as they went ashore, "is the thief of time."

"You're satisfied about Jan?"

"Oh, yes. But I've left Reed to go through the women's stockings on board. Never know what the A.C. won't ask you if you've left undone."

"And now what?"

"Question the Loudrons. Find out where they all were last night."

"You think this must be linked up with Dr. Piers' death?"

"I'll take a bet on it. No robbery. No sexual interference."

They walked on in silence for half a minute.

"But *why?*" asked Nigel. "To stop her mouth? I was sure she'd finally told me all she knew about the night he died. And the Loudrons knew—or at least must have assumed—that she'd done so. Why silence her *after* she'd told all?"

"Two possible reasons," Wright briskly replied. "She didn't

tell you all; she may have had some piece of knowledge whose significance she didn't realize. Or—"

"Don't say it. That's what's on my mind. Or she may have been killed because she'd told me too much. Killed out of sheer spite."

"Ye-es. But that doesn't quite fit in with the murderer's actions up to date—the cold-blooded, planned murder of Dr. Piers, and then the sitting tight and letting us make the running."

They were at the entrance of the corrugated-iron passage. A police car waited in Lassell Street, on their left. When they had got in, Nigel said, "Why was it so dark in the alley last night? Doesn't it have a street lamp? Or was it the effect of liquor on Jan's eyes?"

"There's one of those concrete lamp standards at either end of the alley. Both the globes are smashed. Presumably by X. The lights were on all right when the 'Cutty Sark' closed."

"That proves it was a premeditated crime. I wonder how X got her out of the house into the alley?"

"Assignation by telephone? Anyway, it must have been somebody she knew well—and trusted."

When the car got to 6 Croom's Hill, Nigel surprised his friend by saying he would go home; he wanted his breakfast, and he needed to think—a process he refused to initiate on an empty stomach.

"You can tell me later all about the Loudrons' alibis and which of them you have arrested," said Nigel. "I leave the interviewing to you with perfect confidence."

"Very kind of you to say so, I'm sure," replied Wright, equally sardonic.

Half an hour later, Nigel pushed aside his empty plate and took a fourth cup of coffee. Clare, who had been reading the paper while he ate in gloomy silence, looked up at him.

"You feel bad about this."

"Yes."

"But you couldn't have prevented it. Or could you?" Clare added.

"I wish I knew."

"You liked Sharon?"

"In a way. She made several attempts to get me into bed with her, and it's difficult to dislike an attractive woman, I find, who does that."

"Did she succeed?" Clare equably inquired.

"As it happens, no."

"You didn't like her enough for that?"

"I suppose not. Anyway, she would keep asking me at such inconvenient times."

Clare went off into one of her rare gales of laughter. When it had subsided, Nigel said, "I'm obsessed with the silk-stocking motif. Poor Sharon got hers wetted that night by the waste pipe of Dr. Piers' bathroom; then she was strangled with one. Is it just a coincidence?"

"Justice sometimes works through coincidences, they say. Poetic justice."

Nigel gazed dimly at her. Then gradually his face lighted up. "Poetic justice? I wonder. I think you've hit something," he muttered. "Yes, it could make sense. Now I must go upstairs and think."

He thought all that morning, and by lunchtime a pattern had formed in his mind—an almost complete pattern, but there was one piece missing; a keypiece, it might well be, without which the pattern must remain no more than a plausible construction of the mind. Someone had said something that would give him this piece and lock the whole business together; he had a dim idea that the secret he sought lay in the intonation rather than the actual words.

Putting on his macintosh, Nigel went out into the rain. A lorry ground up the hill; written on its side was the legend "PROCESSORS OF BUTCHERS' WASTE." He crossed into the Park and began walking rapidly, past Wolfe's house, across the

163

football ground, through the flower garden, with its brooding cedars, and down the path running parallel with Mays Hill. He walked twice round the periphery of the Park, uphill and downhill, reviewing in his mind the conversations he had had with each person concerned in the case, while the cold rain beat down on him.

On his third circuit he varied the route, walking to the pond and pausing between the water and the magnolia and camellia trees to gaze at the ducks. "No, it's not here," he heard himself glumly muttering to a mallard, as if it had failed him. He moved on, but ten paces further stopped dead. A slow burn. He had got it after all, though the formula had not been quite word-perfect.

Nigel strode home, took off his clothes, and went to sleep, body and mind exhausted.

At nine o'clock Wright turned up. He tossed a bulky sheaf of typescript at Nigel, who ran his eye rapidly over the pages while Clare cooked a ham omelet with chipped potatoes and the Inspector ate it. Nigel had something of the late T. E. Lawrence's capacity for getting the meat out of a book at phenomenal speed. The verbatim interviews with the suspects, which Wright had given him, ran to a large number of type-script sheets, but he had mastered the gist of them by the time the Inspector finished his second cup of strong coffee.

"Well, how does it strike you?" the latter asked.

"Peculiar about these alibis. Four out of five very much the same as for the night of Dr. Piers' death."

"Yes."

"So Walter Barn did take my advice."

According to the evidence they had given Wright, Walt had cycled down to 6 Croom's Hill after supper, and been with Rebecca in her room till shortly after eleven. This time, they did not play gramophone records all the evening; they had a heart-to-heart talk, which apparently brought them to a satisfactory conclusion about their future. James Loudron had met Walt in the hall when he arrived, and had heard Rebecca saying good-by to him at the front door when he left, but there was no corroborating evidence that Walt and Rebecca had remained in her room over this period of two and a half hours.

"However," said Wright as they discussed it, "the crucial time is after 10:30, when the 'Cutty Sark' closed; probably a bit later. We've got a witness along there who heard a smashing of glass—thought it was local hooligans—around 11:15."

"X putting out the street lamps at either end of the alleyway? Incidentally, how did he do this? Swarm up the concrete standards with a hammer?"

"No. The padlock of the door into the breaker's yard was forced during the night. I take it X did this first, then pinched a long metal scaffolding pole—there are dozens lying about in the yard—to reach up with and smash the globes."

"Walt Barn would have had about ten minutes to get there and do this, after leaving Croom's Hill. Not enough, surely?"

"Not on foot, perhaps. But he had a bicycle, remember."

"So has Rebecca."

"Oh, Nigel, surely you can't suspect her?" said Clare. "Not this time."

"Why not?"

"If she or Walt killed Sharon, and did it after 11:15, surely they'd have given each other an alibi for a longer period than they have."

"That's a good point, of course," said Wright. "But the trouble is, we've no outside evidence yet that Miss Loudron went straight to bed, as she claims, after Barn left, or that Barn cycled straight home; no one at his own house heard him come in."

"What about Graham Loudron?" Clare asked.

Graham's story was that, after dining with James and Rebecca, he had gone up to his room, read a book, listened to the radio, and turned in at eleven.

"Short and simple," Nigel commented. "Like last time. Except that Sharon was not keeping him company."

Clare shivered and looked distressed. She had never quite got used to Nigel's occasional brutality of statement, even though she knew it to be a sign of anger, not of insensibility.

"You questioned him about the book and the radio program?" asked Nigel.

"Of course. He had no difficulty with that. Why should he? The murderer didn't have to start work till after eleven. If Graham is our man, we'll turn up sooner or later somebody who saw him leave the house, front door or back, or going along toward the scene of the crime. But the telephone call seems to clear him."

"Will someone please enlighten me?" said Clare.

"Not a confinement this time. Dr. James says he received an emergency call at 11:10, just as he was about to go up to bed. Caller—muffled voice and all, James did not recognize it—said his mother had had a fit and their own doctor was out. Gave an address in East Greenwich. Said the street was between the Woolwich Road and the river. Rang off. James got out his car and in five minutes had reached the district indicated. Swanned around looking for this street. Found it. But there was no house of the number given him by the caller. Walked up and down the length of the street to make sure. Assumed it was a hoax. Turned round and drove home. Got back at 11:40. So, if what our Dutch friend saw just after 11:30 was the murderer and his victim, Dr. James was at least near the scene of the crime at the crucial period. He could have smashed the lamps at 11:15 on his way to a mythical call, shown himself walking up and down the street in question, returned to the alleyway—"

"But I don't see how this clears Graham," Clare put in.

166

"He heard the doctor going out in his car. That was a little after 11:10. Therefore he could not have smashed the lamps at 11:15."

"But he could have heard this morning that his brother had gone out," Clare protested.

"No. Dr. James told me he'd not mentioned the call to anyone at home before we started interviewing them."

"It clears Graham, all right," said Nigel slowly, "unless it was he who made the call."

"Exactly. Let's forget the remote possibility that it was a hoax by an outsider. Either Dr. James pretended he had received the call—no one in the house heard the telephone go, but it's in the study, and they wouldn't hear it upstairs—as a pretext for taking his car out and driving to East Greenwich, or it was X, ringing from a public call box."

"X being Graham or Walter?"

"Or Harold Loudron; we'll come to him in a moment. X would make a bogus call to implicate James. If, in fact, there was no call, James is lying and he must be the murderer."

"It'd be a pretty stupid alibi to fake—saying he'd had a call that took him so near the scene of his crime," said Nigel.

"Yes. But there's the matter of his gauntlet gloves. Since these depositions were taken, we found them stuffed away in a locked cupboard in the surgery. They have scratches on their backs—the sort of marks that could have been made by a woman's nails clawing at the wearer's hands. Fresh scratches."

"What does James say about this?"

"He says they were not on the hall table, where he usually keeps them, when he went out last night. Professed himself baffled as to how they could have got into the surgery cupboard. Wasn't sure when he'd used or noticed them last; a couple of days ago, he thought."

"So either he's lying again or it was another move in a plan to frame him for the murder."

"If he killed Sharon, surely he'd have thrown the gloves

into the river?" said Clare. "It'd be asking for trouble to hide them in his own surgery."

"Yes. But murderers do the most God-damn silly things."

"So that leaves us with Harold."

Harold Loudron's evidence was somewhat incoherent. Wright had found him prostrate with shock and grief (or was it remorse?) for the death of his wife, and had not pressed him hard. Harold had met his business associate at the Savoy for dinner, leaving the restaurant at 10:45 P.M. So much the friend had confirmed.

"But I thought he'd previously told Sergeant Reed he didn't get home till midnight?" said Nigel sharply. "It'd only take twenty to thirty minutes to cover the distance at night."

"Just so. I taxed him with this. He said he'd drunk too much at dinner, and realizing soon after he started home that he wasn't in a fit condition to drive, he parked the car in a side street and waited till he'd sobered up a bit."

"What street?"

"He doesn't know. Thinks it was a turning off Tooley Street. It's an ingeniously simple fabrication, if it isn't true."

"He could easily have pinched his brother's gauntlet gloves. But how the devil would he contrive to get his wife out of the house at that time of night?" said Nigel, after a short silence. "I can't see her agreeing to take a romantic stroll with him through the scrapyard. But you're looking very sphinxlike; was it one of her own stockings that Sharon was strangled with?"

"No. It was one of Rebecca's," Wright replied.

"Rebecca's?" Clare gaped at him.

"To be precise, one of her mother's. She's got drawers stuffed with her mother's things. I thought this was rather an old-fashioned stocking—heavy silk, not nylon. We found the other one of the pair in a drawer, together with several rolled-up pairs."

"And how did Rebecca react to this discovery of yours?"

"Well, she panicked a bit. First said she didn't know a

stocking was missing; then changed her tune and said oh, yes, she remembered now, she'd torn it accidentally some years ago, while wearing it, and had thrown it away."

"Not what one would expect her to do with a sacred relic," said Nigel.

"No. But I'm not convinced she was lying when she said she didn't know one of the pair was missing."

"But she knew, before you interviewed her, that Sharon had been strangled with a silk stocking?"

"Yes. Dr. James blurted that out in the family circle as soon as I telephoned him, though I'd particularly requested him not to."

"Your X, whoever he is, seems to be flinging suspicion around rather indiscriminately," said Clare. "Isn't it odd that he should try to incriminate James and Rebecca?"

"Yes. Which inclines me to think he is one or the other of them."

"How did those two react during the interviews?" asked Nigel.

"Pity you weren't there," said Wright crisply. "Miss Loudron, as I told you, seemed panicky. Her brother looked as if he'd been hit with a mallet. I'd say they were both less upset by Sharon's death than by its effect on Harold. It's only my guess, but I had a feeling they were concealing another kind of anxiety about him."

"That Harold might have killed Sharon?"

"Yes. And I suppose he had a strongish motive. He's an uxorious type, and she'd been unfaithful to him with Graham. If James or Rebecca is not the murderer, no doubt it was their fears for Harold that made them sell me the Dutch seaman so vigorously."

Clare started up in her chair. "But how did they know about the seaman?"

"Graham told them; no, you mustn't draw the wrong inference. He accompanied James when his brother went to fetch Harold this morning; that was early, just after I'd telephoned James to break the news to him. It seems that, while James was giving Harold a sedative and so on, Graham thought he'd do a little private detection. He got into conversation with a group of women on Ballast Quay; they were all standing at their doors by then, drinking in the delicious sensation of having a murdered woman's body so near their homes. They told him about Jan's escapade."

"But he didn't pass the information on to you, I notice," said Nigel, tapping the sheaf of transcripts.

"No. Claimed he'd been too busy over Harold, and so forth. He's an unco-operative type, though."

Nigel gazed ruminatively down his nose. "You've said it. Yet he suddenly becomes madly co-operative, volunteers to accompany James to Harold's house. That's not at all in character, is it?"

"Morbid curiosity, maybe—going to the scene of the crime."

"Or returning to it," said Nigel.

There was a silence. Then Nigel said, "Sharon told me she was afraid what 'they' might do if they discovered she'd talked about Graham's drug racket. We've got to bear that in mind as a possible reason for the crime. Who are They, anyway, apart from Abdul, who's presumably on the high seas?"

"The Narcotics chums haven't been able to unearth any widespread racket here. They're inclined to think now that it's only been a matter of a small parcel conveyed to Graham Loudron and distributed by him to a few favored acquaintances."

"Perhaps that's why Graham didn't try very hard to conceal from me that he'd done a bit of drug-passing. Still, if he did have other associates—"

"They'd not go to those lengths," said Wright dogmatically. "Carve her up a bit, maybe. But not kill her. Take it from me; I know that sort of criminal."

"I believe you. But it's a tempting idea—one of Graham's

associates killing the poor girl while Graham himself sits tight at home diverting suspicion onto Rebecca and James."

Clare's beautiful eyes looked troubled. "It's confusing to have two morally irresponsible people concerned in the case."

"The other being Walter Barn?" said Wright.

"Yes. I feel that both he and Graham are capable of telling elaborate lies, of doing things like hiding James' gauntlets—of making away with Dr. Piers' diary, even—out of sheer impish cussedness. They've not started to grow up, morally. They'd enjoy confusing the issues; Graham particularly would relish leading Nigel up the garden path; he had it in for Nigel from the start."

"You may be right," commented the Inspector, but without much conviction.

"Aren't you too readily inclined, in criminal cases, to assume there are only two motives for witnesses lying: either to conceal their own connection with the crime or to protect someone else? What about the person who can't resist a piece of mischief? The grown-up child who throws a spanner in the works just to see what will happen?"

12.

The High Old Roman Way

Clare's theorizing was to be tested sooner than any of them would have predicted. Wright had been gone only half an hour, and Nigel and Clare were reading books, their chairs drawn close to the cozy-stove, when the doorbell rang. Graham Loudron was standing outside.

"Well, this is a surprise," said Clare, in markedly neutral tones, when Nigel brought him in.

"I do hope I'm not disturbing you, Miss Massinger? I imagined you wouldn't be working as late as this."

Graham's suave address and *jeune-premier* appearance made it sound, to Nigel, like the opening lines of a third-rate West End comedy. I am the elderly husband, solid but dull, whom the dashing and specious young man intends to supplant in his wife's affections. By the end of Act I, he seems likely to succeed. The wife is flattered; her maternal feeling for the young man is being diverted into a more questionable channel. But in Act II, our deb daughter appears. And so forth, and so forth.

"I really came to see your—to have a talk with Strangeways," Graham was saying.

"Talk away," said Clare crisply.

Oh, dear, thought Nigel, the dialogue's going wrong already.

"Get him a drink, darling," Clare added.

Aha, she's pretending indifference—dislike, even—to throw dust in the husband's eyes; we must be in Scene 2 of Act I. "What would you like? Whisky? Armagnac?" Or is it a thriller, not a comedy? A hand comes out from a secret panel while the husband's back is turned, shakes a powder into the young man's glass. He dies, downstage right. The husband is suspected. But the poisoner turns out to be their faithful old housekeeper, whose daughter has been seduced by the young man.

"This is ghastly about Sharon," said the young man, cradling his glass of armagnac in both palms.

"You were fond of her?" asked Clare.

Graham's eyes were fastened upon hers. With an air of rueful candor, he said, "I don't know about fond. We'd been lovers. Once. But you know about that, don't you? . . . She had such vitality. I can't believe—somehow I feel responsible for it."

"For her death? Why?" Nigel tried to make his tone sympathetic. If Graham was going to un-clam, he must not be discouraged.

The small, prehensile mouth moved, as if to get a grip on some tenable form of words. "I don't know. It's just a feeling. If I hadn't started it—"

"You mean a general feeling of guilt?" Clare put in.

Graham mumbled something incoherent.

"Or are you worried that Harold punished her for her infidelity?" Clare went on, regardless of a warning glance from Nigel, who thought she was making the pace too hot.

"Oh, not Harold, surely," said Graham, a shade overstrenuously. "After all, it wasn't the first time she'd— But anyway, isn't that Dutch seaman the likeliest person?"

"Sharon was neither robbed nor raped. We don't even know that she was killed at the time when he came along; it may have been later. Or, again, he may have seen the murder."

"Seen it?" Graham looked horrified.

Nigel told him about the couple, apparently lovers, whom Jan had passed in the alleyway. "Jan may be useful to the police. He might be able to identify the person he saw."

"Oh." Graham seemed temporarily silenced by this thought. "But it was very dark, wasn't it?" he resumed. "And the chap was blind drunk. He walked straight into the river. Or so some people living there told me."

"That's true. But a man can sometimes recall something, in a vivid flash, out of his drunk period. Something he didn't consciously take in at the time."

"That's assuming the couple he saw were Sharon and—"

"Yes. We have no evidence for it. Yet. Would you like some more armagnac?"

"Thank you." Graham held out his glass with a steady hand. "I need this. To give me courage for a confession."

Nigel and Clare withheld comment.

"Tell me"—Graham gave them his rare smile, which had considerable charm—"tell me first, are you pretty sure that Sharon's death is linked up with my father's?"

"Absolutely certain."

"Very well. Then you'd better read this."

Graham stood up and, leaning against the mantelshelf, took a folded piece of paper from his wallet and handed it to Nigel. Nigel opened it. There were seven lines of manuscript writing, the beginning of the top line charred away; the script was either Dr. Piers' or an excellent forgery.

. . . stall him. If I died before he could kill me—why didn't that occur to me?—it would solve the whole problem. Justice would be done without making him a murderer. The high old Roman way out of trouble. Fall on one's sword; only I haven't got a sword, and if I had I'm so light I should prob-

ably bounce off the point. Petronius, then. The hedonist's
method. Euthanasia. Yes, that's the answer.

"Where did you find this?" asked Nigel, passing the charred
paper to Clare.

"In the surgery. There were several pages of an old casebook; my father had started writing his diary in it."

"When did you find it?"

"The morning he disappeared."

"You found the book, or just this fragment?"

"Oh, the book."

"You were looking for it, then?"

"Of course I was looking for it," Graham answered, a little
feverishly. "He'd talked about a diary the night you came to
dinner. And when he disappeared, I thought the diary might
tell us why. So I worked out in my mind where the diary
could be. Pinched the key of the cupboard, and found the
casebook."

"You looked through them all till you came to this one?"

"Oh, no," replied Graham, with a veiled look, "I had a
pretty good idea which year to turn up."

"Then you tore out the pages and burned them, all but
this piece?"

"Not immediately. I kept them hidden for a while. Then
my father's body was found, and I knew the police would be
turning on the heat. So I burned the rest."

"Why only the rest?"

Graham looked rueful again. "I meant first to burn them
all. I put a match to the last sheet. But I suddenly realized
how important these lines at the bottom were, so I beat out
the flame just as it reached them."

There was a long stretch of silence. Graham sat down and
took a gulp at his armagnac. He was trembling a little now,
as if from a release of tension.

"I see," said Nigel at last, unable to postpone any longer

the crucial question. If Graham answered it wrong, the answer would all but convict him of murder. "And who do you suppose is the 'he' your father is writing about? Dr. James?"

"James? Good Lord, no. It's me."

Graham had not answered wrong.

". . . 'stall him'—I suppose that word was 'forestall.' You seriously mean to tell us that what your father is saying here is that he's going to commit suicide in order to prevent you killing him first? It takes a bit of swallowing."

"I know. I wouldn't believe it myself, if it wasn't written down there in black and white."

"So you had intended to kill him, and he knew it?"

"I'd better tell you the whole story."

It was not until he had met Nellie, two months before, said Graham, that he had connected Dr. Piers with his mother. When Nellie told him about the letters which Millie had sent, *in extremis*, to the father of her child, Graham had suddenly wondered if these might not be the letters that he had overheard James and Rebecca discussing—the cause of the dreadful estrangement between their parents. He had, of course, wondered about his own parentage often enough before this; but now everything fitted into place—Dr. Piers' seeking him out seven years ago, taking him into his home, adopting him, and treating his subsequent misdemeanors with such leniency—all this would carry sense as the old doctor's attempt to make restitution for what he had done to Millie.

This, Graham explained, was why he had gone straight to the casebook for 1940—the year in which, if he himself was indeed the fruit of their love, the love affair between Millie and Dr. Piers had taken place. His father had a vein of sentiment beneath his sophisticated surface, and would be likely to choose the book of that year for his confession.

After Nellie first gave him the clue, Graham had made inquiries among those who had been hers and Millie's neighbors in East Greenwich during the 1939–1940 period. He had finally found a woman who, plied with drink in a local pub, refreshed her memory to the extent of recalling that Millie had been a patient of Dr. Piers and that she (the narrator) had suspected there was something between them when, one day, she saw Dr. Piers calling the girl into his consulting room. The pair must have been remarkably discreet, for the woman admitted she had heard no gossip about them at the time or later.

With this knowledge, said Graham, he confronted his father. It had happened a day or two before Nigel and Clare went to dinner there. Dr. Piers had not attempted to deny Graham's charges, nor did Graham now attempt to deny that he had threatened his father's life. The rest of the diary pages —the material he had destroyed—gave an account of this interview and of Dr. Piers' love affair with Millie.

Nigel questioned the young man closely about the interview, getting the impression that he was holding nothing back and not minimizing the hostile attitude he had taken up.

"I must ask you this," he said. "Did you really intend to kill your father, or were they empty threats—just to frighten and punish him."

Graham considered it seriously. "No, I meant to. I'd hated my father for years, long before I knew who he was."

"But when you found out it was Dr. Piers, who'd been good to you, who'd done everything he could to make up to you for what you'd gone through—"

"It's not what I'd gone through," Graham interrupted, with a chill, restrained violence. "Not that I could forget that, mind you. But I couldn't forgive him for letting my mother down."

"Yet you knew it wasn't his fault. He never saw those letters your mother sent him till it was too late; his wife had intercepted them."

"Now you're preaching at me again," said Graham, his old Adam returning. "I can't stick sermonizing. I had enough of that from the swine I was sent to when mother died; preaching and beating—I got the whole works, day after day, and on an empty stomach." His voice had gone shrill, a self-pitying whine in it. "You people who've had it soft all your lives can't begin to understand—"

"Now you're preaching," said Clare gently.

Graham gave her his deferential smile—a smile she felt he must have cultivated during the years of inhuman treatment, so artificially ingratiating did it look, a mere baring of the teeth.

"You were going to speak about your mother," Nigel prompted.

"You think I should have forgotten about her after all this time? No use crying over spilled milk?"

"I think nothing of the sort."

A strange expression came over the fruit-bat face. "I was only a kid when she died. But I'll never forget her misery during those last weeks, and how she tried to hide it from me. I'd seen her turning away to cough into a handkerchief. She spat blood. She was so weak she could hardly get out of bed in the morning or stand up at the stove. It got so she couldn't have men any longer. And that meant we'd no money except the little she'd saved for a rainy day. Rainy day! It was a bloody deluge. She used to give me nearly all the food she bought—said she didn't feel hungry. I don't know how she could cough up so much blood and stay alive. I loved her, you see. I've never been able to love anyone since. How the hell could anyone expect me not to hate my father, who'd let all this happen?" The words came oozing out of him, like matter from a septic wound. "We had a music box. About all we did have left. We used to play it to each other when she'd put me to bed—before she went out onto the streets and brought a man back home. She loved that music box; maybe *he* had given it to her. But she had to pop it in the end. She cried a lot. I *hated* her crying."

Graham Loudron stopped abruptly, staring into the past,

178

his eyes dry, his face hard as concrete.

"I see you had very strong reasons for hating your father," said Nigel, after a pause. "You threatened to kill him. Why didn't you?"

Graham looked up, startled. "He did it for me. I don't think I'd have gone through with it, anyway."

"Why did you destroy the rest of the diary, then?"

"That's obvious, isn't it? When his body was found and everyone said he'd been murdered, I had to destroy the pages that gave away the motive I had for killing him, and the fact that I'd threatened to."

"But you kept this bit, as a sort of insurance policy? You knew what Petronius did?"

"I looked it up. Severed his arteries in a hot bath. You said it'd be impossible; the cuts could not have been equally deep. Well, if Petronius could do it, my father could."

"Petronius had a slave to do it for him, I think. Anyway, you believed this extract from his diary was proof of suicide. Why did you conceal it from us all till now?"

A sort of old lag's smirk appeared on Graham's face, and at once vanished; "Don't know nothing about that," he might have been on the point of saying. He said, "I wasn't brought up to go rushing off and Assisting the Authorities. Far otherwise. I just wanted to keep out of trouble; the police would ask what I'd been up to, pinching the diary. And so on."

"And you liked the idea of stringing them along?" said Clare.

"Something of that, I'll admit."

"In that case, why produce it now?" asked Nigel, in a neutral voice. "Because you thought you're likely to be charged with the murder?"

"I never touched Sharon. I was here all last night."

"I'm talking about Dr. Piers' death. That's the only one the diary is relevant to. Why produce this fragment *now*?"

Graham's eyes were fastened, limpetlike, upon Nigel's.

"You told me Sharon's death is linked up with my father's," he said. "That means one of us, one of the family, killed her. Right?"

"Right."

"Which means either that my father's death was not suicide—someone killed him, and then killed Sharon because she knew too much—or else this person wanted her dead for some other reason and used my father's death as a cover."

"Cover for what?"

"For his motive for killing Sharon. Let's say he believes my father was murdered, though in fact it was suicide. So he arranges to kill Sharon in such a way that suspicion falls upon the imagined murderer of my father."

"That's a bit farfetched."

"And, this being so," Graham continued, disregarding Nigel, "we have a killer in the family circle who may decide he'd like to get rid of a few more of us, perhaps so that all my father's money may come to him, not just his own share."

"Why should he start off with Sharon, then? She only inherited indirectly, through Harold," said Clare.

"That could be a blind," Graham replied, with a significant look at her.

"Meaning that Harold himself killed her, just to throw dust in our eyes—"

"He had another motive too."

"—and is now going to pick off the rest of you one by one. Do you seriously believe that?"

Nigel broke in. "You seem still convinced that your father killed himself. How on earth do you explain the disappearance of his body?"

"Obviously, someone moved it."

"But why?"

"Search me. Wait a minute, though." Graham's long nose twitched inquisitively. "Suppose someone discovered the diary before I did—while my father was still alive. The bit about

180

Petronius would give this person the idea for murdering him in such a way that it looked like suicide, but then he finds the diary pages gone, which were to be the final proof that it was suicide. No, that won't do; I didn't take them till after the body had disappeared. No. It must have been suicide. I've got it!" Graham excitedly snapped his fingers. "My father killed himself. One of us found the body, assumed it was murder, and threw the body into the Thames in the hope that, by the time it was recovered, the signs of murder would be obliterated. And I can tell you straightway which of us would be most likely to do that. Brother James. He's a terror for the conventions. Never do for a murdered body to be found in a doctor's house. Jolly bad show. How about that?"

Nigel had felt much of this eager ingenuity to be rather preposterous and disagreeably adolescent, but he made a noncommittal reply. Then, taking up the charred and crumpled piece of paper, he said, "All this theorizing of yours started with 'Suppose someone else had discovered the diary before I did.' Well, if we're going to suppose that, the one really important thing that follows is that this person would read about your threats to murder your father, and would have you as the perfect scapegoat if he decided to do the murder himself."

"Yes. That had occurred to me. But I'd have thought he'd have waited longer, to see if I wasn't going to get rid of my father for him. It must have thrown him pretty heavily when he found the diary pages had disappeared."

"Which of you seemed most exercised about hunting for the diary after Dr. Piers' death?"

"I don't know," Graham hesitantly answered. "Becky did most of the chasing round for it. But I remember James kept asking her if she'd come across it yet, and so did Harold." The young man got himself to his feet. "Well, it was good of you both to let me stay so long. It's taken a weight off my mind." He held out his hand toward Nigel. "Can I have it back?" he ingenuously asked.

"This bit from the diary? Good lord, no."

"But you've read it now."

"It'll have to go to the handwriting experts. We must make certain it's not a forgery."

13.

How the Body Vanished

"I see you're sleeping here now," remarked Nigel, glancing at the camp bed covered with a tartan rug that was ranged against one wall of the study.

"Yes," Dr. James Loudron replied. "I have to be by the telephone at night, and there isn't one in my own room. There's an extension in my father's, of course, but I don't like the idea of—"

"Sleeping there? Naturally. You sleep well?"

"Luckily. But the traffic on this side of the house wakes me up rather early. Why do you ask?"

"You look as if you needed sleep."

And indeed the doctor did. His eyes were heavy, as if it took a painful effort to move them in their sockets; the skin beneath them looked stained and pouchy. His solid shoulders drooped dejectedly. He seemed a man at the end of his tether. A haunted man. Or a bewildered ox.

"Well, I've got a half day at last. The first since . . ." His voice petered out again.

"And it's good of you to let me take up a bit of it. How did you manage?"

"One of my colleagues at the hospital agreed to do locum for a while. He's taken over some of my father's patients."

There was another silence. Dr. James seemed too exhausted even to ask Nigel why he was here. Nigel glanced round the study, at the bed, the bookshelves, the telephone, the paneling that Janet had had painted to resemble stripped wood, in a pathetically misguided attempt to please her husband. It was in here that Walt Barn had beaten up the newspaperman, while Rebecca looked on, half appalled, half fascinated. And in here, maybe, Dr. Piers Loudron had written the diary, a fragment of which was now being examined by the handwriting experts.

"That voice you heard on the telephone—"

"Voice? When?" said James dully.

"The bogus call that took you out the night Sharon—"

James visibly flinched. "Oh, for God's sake! Must I go into all that again? I told the Inspector I could not identify it."

"Not even if it was a man or a woman speaking?"

"No . . . But, look here, how could it have been a woman?"

"Why not?"

"But, damn it, wasn't it the—the person who killed Sharon? Ringing up to get me near the place where—"

"And couldn't Sharon's murderer, or an accomplice of the murderer, be a woman?"

Dr. James lowered his head, in the old, dangerous, bull-like way.

"Are you insinuating that Becky—"

"Why Becky?"

"She's the only woman left in our family, isn't she? And that stocking!" The doctor shook his head as if to clear it, then burst out, in the gravelly voice of exhaustion, "Who is it? Who is it that hates us so?"

"Hates you?"

"Using that stocking of Mother's out of Becky's drawer.

Hiding my driving gloves. It's absolutely fiendish. You know, if this goes on, I shall become paranoiac."

Nigel eyed him in silence for several moments. The time had come. He had put this off too long, and he knew why. The lie would be no more morally respectable because it was necessary in order to clear the way to the truth.

"And now," he said, "I'm afraid you're going to number me amongst the persecutors."

James Loudron gazed at him in a lackluster way.

"Will you not tell me the truth about the night when your father's body vanished?" said Nigel, without inflection.

"What on earth do you mean?" Dr. James sounded angry, but as if his will was lashing a tired mind into anger. "I resent that very much. I *have* told the truth—all I know about it—over and over again. I'm sick and tired of the whole business."

"When you came in that night, after delivering the baby, you went to your father's room—perhaps to say good night, perhaps to consult him. You found him dead. In the bath. You wrapped the body in his tweed overcoat, carried it out through the back door, put it on the front passenger's seat of his car, drove to the river, and tipped it in beside the Trafalgar Tavern."

James was staring at him stupidly, as if hypnotized. "You're mad. You must be mad. I went back in the car to my patient's house, because—"

"The woman had no complications," Nigel went on tonelessly. "There was no reason whatsoever to return there so soon after the birth. And there's no other reasonable explanation why you should have taken the car when the fog was so bad that on your first visit you had to walk there."

"But I *have* explained that. I thought the fog had lifted a bit. And who the devil are you to instruct me about my medical duties?" the doctor added, with another feeble spurt of anger.

"You were seen putting the body in the river. The police have found an eyewitness at last. I shouldn't be telling you this, but—"

James Loudron's whole face and body sagged. In his rumpled suit he looked like a Fifth of November guy. "Is that true?" he muttered, glaring sightlessly. "They're going to arrest me, you mean? For the murder?"

"They will certainly bring a charge. What that charge will be depends upon your telling the truth. If you could give me the facts now—"

"I—would you mind if my sister was here?"

After a pause, Nigel said, "Very well."

"She's in the garden, I think. I'll fetch her."

When James had gone out, with a stiff, old man's gait, Nigel had leisure to ruminate on the unpleasing ruse by which he had brought things to a head, and on James' next movements; the garden, after all, led to the garage, and at this very moment James might be making a bolt for it.

In a couple of minutes, however, James returned with Rebecca. Brother and sister sat side by side on the sofa, looking like chastened children, holding hands. James looked up at Nigel.

"You do realize this means the finish of my career?"

Nigel nodded, feeling sickened by himself. His eyes rested on James Loudron's face; its expression had changed, putting into Nigel's mind the lines "If calm at all, if any calm, a calm despair."

"James didn't do it!" exclaimed Rebecca, with a flash of her brown eyes.

"I didn't do it. But I did quite enough to, well, make the police believe I did. Sorry, that's not very coherent." He lifted his heavy gaze toward Nigel. "I've just told Becky, outside, that it was I who put my father's body in the river."

"But he didn't murder him," said Rebecca fiercely. "James would never kill anyone in a cowardly way like that."

186

"Tell that to the police, Becky!" said her brother. "Strangeways says they've found an eyewitness—someone who saw me by the Trafalgar Tavern."

Nigel would not meet Rebecca's eyes; but he felt they were scrutinizing him keenly. "You'd better tell us exactly what happened," he said.

Rising, James moved to the window and turned round with his back to it, as if he could not bear the light upon his face. Past his bulky shoulder, Nigel could see the February sunshine palely gilding the stucco of the derelict cinema, once a Victorian music hall, on the opposite side of the road; a pigeon flew out of one of its shattered windows.

"When I got back from the confinement, I went to Father's room. I was a bit worried about another patient, and wanted to consult him. You know," James added, with a rueful half smile, "he had more medicine in his little finger than I and a dozen other—"

"And he let you know it," Rebecca put in.

"Well, he wasn't there. Something made me go through into the bathroom. His body was there. In the bath. Naked. The arteries had been cut. One of his razors lay in the bath beside him. The water was pink, but I could see it. I made sure he was dead. Then I examined the cuts."

"And you realized at once it was not suicide?"

"Almost at once. I'm a bit rusty on the medicolegal stuff, but there were no preliminary cuts—I knew about the significance of that, of course—and then I examined closer and saw the two incised wounds were of equal depth."

"So you knew it was murder? And the murderer must be one of this household, or somebody who had a key to the house?" Nigel was aware of the tenseness with which Rebecca sat there, her eyes fastened on her brother. "That was why you took the terrible risk of moving the body? You were afraid of the effect it would have on the practice if Dr. Piers was found murdered in his own house?"

187

"Yes."

"No!" Rebecca cried out forcefully. "I won't let you make yourself out so mean, so—so mercenary. James was afraid that—"

"Please, Becky!"

"James was protecting me. He thought I'd done it. He'd overheard me telling Father I wished he was dead." The woman spoke in a white heat of exaltation, and went on talking, even more rapidly and incoherently, until James shook her by the shoulders, commanding, "Stop that, Becky! You're getting hysterical. Stop it at once!"

"Well, anyway," said Nigel, when she had calmed down, "whatever your reason was, you moved the body. Tell me exactly what you did. It may be important."

James Loudron had let the bloodstained water run out of the bath. He then wiped all traces of blood from the body, and cleaned the bath so that there should be no telltale rim. He pocketed the razor, fetched his father's Connemara-tweed overcoat from the bedroom, wrapped the body in it, and carried it out to the garage.

"Were the bedroom or bathroom doors locked while you did all this?"

"I'd locked the bathroom door, not the other one."

"You were so sure it was murder, you didn't look for a suicide note?"

"No. I'd no doubt. It's occurred to me since, of course, that the murderer meant it to look like suicide."

"Why the tweed coat? You'd wiped the blood off the body, and there'd be no more bleeding."

"You'll think it rather queer—I'm a doctor, after all, and used to handling cadavers—but I felt there was something indecent about carting him around naked. He was my father."

"You thought that, if you threw him into the Thames, the body would not be found till decomposition had removed the signs pointing to murder?"

188

"Well, I suppose so. Confused them, anyway. But I don't know that I really thought it out so far ahead. I—well, I was in a bit of a panic. I just wanted to get rid of the body. And I had what seemed a good excuse for going out again, to a spot just beside the river."

"Supposing it had been low tide?"

"Oh, when you've lived here as long as we have, you know the state of the tides almost by instinct."

"So you got the body to the garage; unobserved, as far as you know."

"It would have been commented on," James sourly rejoined, "if anyone had noticed me walking about with a corpse."

"And then?"

"I took him to the river and dumped him in. I've told you so. Do you want a running commentary on every stage of the process?" For a moment James was stirred out of his flat dejection.

"Yes, I do. It's not idle curiosity. You've been bottling it all up too long—what must have been the most horrible experience of your life. It'll do you good to let it out."

"You think I'm heading for a nervous breakdown otherwise? But that'd get me into the prison hospital instead of a cell."

"Oh, James!" Rebecca burst into sobs. This time her brother disregarded her, and she soon stifled them.

"Accessory after the fact," he said. "That'll be the charge, won't it?"

Nigel was silent.

"You don't think I'm making all this up to cover the fact that I killed him myself?" James persisted.

"Oh, lord no, you didn't kill him."

Rebecca's head came up sharply, as if someone had jerked it by the heavy coils of hair.

"That overcoat," Nigel went on. "Feeling it was indecent to carry him about naked. A person who killed him in that

189

way wouldn't have that sort of feeling; and I don't think you've got the sort of imagination to make it up afterward."

Yet the doctor, as he recounted the details of that grisly ride to the river, showed more imagination—or sensibility, at least—than many would have credited him with. While he talked, Nigel glanced from him to Rebecca, sitting dry-eyed now, and from her to the yellowish, derelict cinema on the far side of the street, with its medallions and broken windows and the boards fastened to the façade—"FREEHOLD FOR SALE."

"I managed to get him propped up beside me on the front seat. It was like old times, sort of. When I was qualifying, I used to drive him on his rounds during the vacations. The fog was as bad as ever. I had to open the side window to see anything at all. I remember thinking he'd get cold with nothing on but that overcoat. Bloody silly. But he—the body kept lolling up against me, as if for warmth. I got out of Burney Street and into the High Road past St. Alfege's. It was driving blind—never knew which side of the road I was on till I hit the curb. Then I damn nearly ran into the traffic island at the end of Nelson Parade. That gave me the cold shudders; suppose I had an accident and was found with a corpse on the front seat. I nearly jumped out and ran away at that point. It must have taken me five minutes to reach the Naval College. And then I nearly hit the traffic island beyond the bus stop. I had to wrench the wheel to the left, and the body—well, he gave me a sharp nudge in the ribs. I could almost hear him say, 'Keep your mind on your driving'—he was always the back-seat driver, wasn't he, Becky? Well, when we'd missed that island and got round into the Woolwich Road, I picked up a rear light in front of me—bloke crawling even slower than myself—and closed up on him as near as I dared and trailed along behind him. I had to keep one eye on him in case I bumped him, and the other on the lookout for the left turn into Park Row. Luckily there's a pedestrian crossing just before the turn, and I was able to pick out the zebra just in time to swing left. When I got down to the river, I had a violent fit of coughing—result of driving with my head out of the window all the way—so I had to shut the window in case anyone heard me. I parked as near the river wall as I could get, and dragged Father out. The overcoat nearly came off him. I did up all the buttons and put the razor in the pocket. It was dead quiet. The fog. I felt as if I was deaf as well as blind. Then I heard the water lapping, and carried him in that direction. I lifted him over the railing and dropped him in. It seemed to make a hell of a noise, after the silence. That's all there is to it. How anyone could have spotted me in that fog, I can't imagine. I remember saying—sort of in my head—just after the splash, 'Father, forgive us our trespasses.' And that's bloody queer too, since I don't believe any of that stuff; and if I was saying it to my earthly father, then we had a damn sight more trespasses to forgive him than, vice versa, Mother had, anyway."

The monotonous, compulsive voice stopped, making way for a silence as absolute as that which must have closed in after the body of Dr. Piers Loudron had fallen through the fog into the water and the ripples had died away.

"Tell me one thing," said Nigel at last. "Who did you think had killed your father?"

James Loudron gazed back at him in stubborn silence.

"I said all along you were trying to protect someone. There's only one of your family you'd go to such lengths to protect."

"Can't you leave me alone now?" said James, in a small voice that sounded as if it came from the bottom of some fathomless pit.

"Yes, why don't you leave him alone?" exclaimed Rebecca, taking her brother's hand.

"Two murders have been done."

"And James thought it was I who killed our father. No, James, of course you did. I hated him for what he'd done to Mother, and the way he treated me—always making me feel inferior—his everlasting snubs. And then when I had a chance of happiness, with Walter, Father had no use for me except as a housekeeper, but he wouldn't let me go. He—"

"Quiet, Becky! You're getting hysterical again."

"Yes. Go on, say it! I'm unbalanced, not responsible for my actions."

"Don't be absurd, Becky. You're as sane as I am."

"Still protecting your poor wretched sister?"

"Oh, for God's sake—"

"Well, *did* you kill him?" asked Nigel, in an equable tone.

Rebecca Loudron turned her blazing eyes upon him. "No. I just wished him dead. Time after time. And at last he *was* dead. Shall we take the will for the deed?"

The old James Loudron, so easily embarrassed by displays of emotion, looked out from the heavy, exhausted face of the man on the sofa. "I think we'd better call it a day. Do you want me to give myself up to the police now? I'd like to make some arrangements with Lightfoot, my locum."

Nigel could not meet his eyes. "Just a minute. I've something to tell you."

Before he could say it, Rebecca had pounced upon it with a leap of intuition. "You were lying! The police have no eyewitness."

"Becky, please! Strangeways would never—"

"If someone had really seen you throw Father's body into the river, would he wait all this time before telling the police?"

She stared implacably at Nigel, who said, "No. There was no eyewitness."

"And now you've wormed it out of James by a foul trick, you'll trot off to the police and—"

"The police suspect it was your brother who moved the body. They have no evidence. I do not propose to give them any," Nigel flatly replied.

"So you were just playing a cat-and-mouse game for your

own private amusement. That makes it more despicable still."
Rebecca Loudron was almost beautiful in the flush of her
indignation. "What sort of a creature are you?"

"One of your family has murdered twice. He must be
stopped, before it becomes a habit. He won't be stopped if
the rest of you conceal the truth. Sharon was strangled with a
silk stocking out of your drawer. Perhaps she'd concealed
something which would have saved her life if she'd come out
with it. Perhaps you know something which would have
saved her."

"How could I?" said Rebecca uncertainly. "What do you
mean?"

"Something, for instance, about Walt Barn?"

Her eyes opened wide in consternation. "Walt? But that's
absurd! He wasn't there," she cried, her voice going up on
the last word.

Nigel stared hard at her. "Say that again," he demanded.

"I said he wasn't there. He left this house soon after
eleven. I saw him off, saw him pushing his bicycle up the hill.
I stood in the door for a minute or two. He didn't come back
down the hill. He could never have got to—to where Sharon
was killed if he'd gone all the way up the hill and along the
south of the Park and down Maze Hill; there wouldn't have
been time."

Nigel cut in on her babbling. "Never mind that, Miss
Loudron. The morning your father disappeared and you and
Graham went to look for him—you told me that Graham tried
the bathroom."

"Yes," said Rebecca, mystified.

"You didn't go in yourself. Right?"

"Yes."

"When he went into the bathroom, Graham called out,
'He's not here.' You remember that?"

"Yes."

"How did he say it?"

"I don't understand you."

"Say the words as he said them. Try to remember the exact intonation," Nigel urgently asked.

Rebecca hesitated, an anxious look on her face—the same look that had so often appeared when her father cracked his intellectual whip at her. "Honestly, I don't think I can; I'm not good as a mimic."

"Well, for instance, did he say it like this"—Nigel spoke the phrase with a fairly level intonation, stressing the last word—"or was it more like this"—his voice went down in pitch on the second word and hit a high note on the last one.

"Yes, that was it," Rebecca exclaimed. "The way you said it the second time."

"Good. You see what that means, particularly when you take it in conjunction with what you told me about Graham's not having seemed at all worried about your father till that moment?"

"Well, he did seem pretty upset when he came out of the bathroom. But—"

"You mean," James put in, "he'd only say 'He's not here' in that surprised sort of way if he'd expected him to be there?"

"Precisely."

"And what deduction do we draw from that, my dear brother and sister?" came a voice from the doorway.

Graham Loudron had been listening for an unknown period of time. He now walked in and put himself on the window seat.

"So it was you, James, who disposed of the—er—remains? I always suspected it," he coolly remarked.

"Eavesdropping again, you filthy little tick!" James shouted. He made to get up from the sofa, but Rebecca restrained him.

"How could you have been so surprised that Father was not in the bathroom," she said, in an almost gloating voice, "if you hadn't seen him there the night before—if you hadn't killed him in the bath yourself?"

194

"You were always jealous of me, weren't you? Both of you?"

"Keep to the point," said James. "Answer her question. You can't wriggle out of that one, can you?"

Their enmity pulsated in the room like scorching breath from a furnace. The three Loudrons seemed to have forgotten Nigel's presence.

"My poor James, there are several answers. Becky couldn't possibly remember how I said it; she's tone-deaf."

"That's ridiculous."

"Well, what's much more likely is that she's pretending I said it in that surprised way so that she can put the blame on me for the murder. You'd like me out of the way, wouldn't you?"

"The police will be interested in that theory," said James.

"Police? I can just see you going to the police with it!" Graham uttered an uncheerful laugh. "If you do, I shall tell them about your disposal of the body. No, it'd better be Strangeways here who plays the role of talebearer. After all, he enjoys it."

"Do you know," Nigel affably remarked, gazing at Graham's head outlined against the window, "do you know that your face is the shape of an isosceles triangle the wrong way up?"

Graham's silhouetted form became rigid.

"So that if I turned you upside down, you'd be resting on your base, so to speak. Bear that in mind. I'd do it, but for the disgusting things that might fall out of your pockets."

The other two stared at Nigel, bemused. Graham, profoundly uneasy, shifted off the window seat and took a chair at the round table. "I suppose all this means something," he said.

"On the contrary, it means nothing at all. That's the beauty of it. Are you acquainted with the fruit bat, or flying fox? *Pteropidae*, they're called, if you prefer Latin."

"I simply don't know what you're talking about."

"Come, come. I asked a simple question. Either you are acquainted with the *Pteropidae* or you aren't."

"Well, I'm not, as it happens," Graham sulkily replied.

"That's better. Now, let's try another simple question. Was your father dying or dead when you found him in the bath?"

"But I didn't find him in the bath," replied Graham, in the elaborately patient manner of one humoring a lunatic. "He wasn't there."

"You see? Even now your voice goes up in that protesting way at the end of the phrase. You're still genuinely indignant that the body wasn't there. Surprised and indignant. It simply wasn't playing the game for the body to have disappeared. But I was talking about the previous night. While Sharon was waiting for you in your room. You'd gone to Dr. Piers' bathroom. Did you find him dying or dead? Surely you can remember? Or were you in such a panic that you didn't try to find out?"

"But I never went to—"

"Be careful. Think of the consequences of denying it. If you'd found him happily singing in the bath, you'd never have been in such a state—'terribly worried,' as Rebecca put it— next morning when you discovered he wasn't there. So, the night before, you found him either dead or dying."

"But I tell you—"

"Or, if you didn't, there's only one alternative—that you killed him yourself."

Nigel threw a forensic glance at James and Rebecca, as if they were members of the jury. Graham merely shrugged; Nigel's attempt to rattle him out of his composure had not quite succeeded.

"Either alternative," Nigel continued, "would account for the strange state of excitement Sharon noticed in you when you returned to your room."

"You seem to forget, I have never admitted to being out

of my room that night. It was Sharon's story that she waited ten minutes for me there."

"And now Sharon is dead, so she cannot talk about that night any more."

Graham shrugged again.

"You had threatened to kill your father," Nigel began.

"What's that?" exclaimed Dr. James. "How do you know this? Is it true?"

"Graham told me himself."

"But why should you want to kill him?" The words came out involuntarily from Rebecca. She flushed. "I mean, you were always his favorite."

"He seduced my mother, and then let her bl- bleeding well starve to death," the young man stuttered.

"I simply don't believe you," said James. "Melodramatic bosh."

"Of course, your mother was equally responsible."

"How dare you say that!" James shouted. "You take that back, or I'll—"

"Your mother intercepted the letters my mother sent him when she was dying. Have you forgotten that quarrel? Becky hasn't."

"Leave my sister out of it, you wretched little twerp!"

"I can't. She's in it. Up to the neck. She hated her father as much as I did, and you know it. Laugh that one off. She didn't dare go into the bathroom next morning. She pretends it was I who got the shock when the body wasn't there. And she put the sleeping draught in his coffee; oh, yes, she did, I saw her. You did, didn't you, Becky?"

Rebecca Loudron's eyes glared rigidly at him. Her mouth worked as if she were suffocating, then opened in a long, wailing sound, and she stumbled out of the room.

14.

The Sorrows of Walter

A few hours later, Nigel and Chief Inspector Wright were discussing the latest developments of the case. Graham Loudron's evidence about the sleeping draught had been unshaken in a tough interview with Wright. He had noticed Rebecca putting a white powder into her father's coffee cup after dinner. If he was telling the truth, it must have been a stronger dose than the post-mortem had suggested—or perhaps the old man was already sleepy—for it to have taken effect so soon. Asked why he had concealed this knowledge from the police, Graham replied that he'd been unwilling to do anything to incriminate his sister, until she and her brother set upon him during the interview just now with Nigel.

"That's all my eye, of course," Wright briskly commented. "If you ask me, he was just saving it up to blackmail her with later."

"You've a very low opinion of the young man."

"Haven't you? He's a criminal type, potentially, if not actually. We'll nail him yet."

"For the murders? He's your suspect Number 1?"

"He is."

Nigel offered Wright a cigarette and lit it for him. The smoke curling across Wright's sallow face gave him a Mephistophelean look.

"Well, what does Rebecca Loudron say?"

"She doesn't. Incommunicado. You seem to have driven her into fits. Dr. James put her to bed, gave her a sedative; says she's not in a state to be interviewed yet. I have a man at her bedside."

"But, my dear chap, if Graham's the murderer, how do you account for her doping the coffee? You're not suggesting he and Rebecca were in it together?"

"We've only Graham's word for it that she did dope the coffee. Do you believe him?"

"If his accusation was untrue, she'd have flown into a rage of indignation. Her reaction was very, very different."

"Well, damn it, if she did dope the coffee, that meant she and/or Walter Barn murdered the old man. Is that your idea?"

"It doesn't follow. I can think of a perfectly innocent reason for her administering the sleeping draught. She'd probably tell us now, if only—no, we needn't wait, we can ask Walter."

"I'm afraid we can't."

"What?"

"He's disappeared."

"Oh, lord, not another disappearance!"

"He and his bicycle are missing. I went up there this morning. Another occupant of the house saw him go off early on his bike, with a knapsack, and he's not back yet. Nothing sinister about it, probably."

"Talking of him and his bike," Nigel began, and proceeded to tell Wright what Rebecca had said about Walt's departure on the night Sharon was killed.

"So, if she was killed at the time we think she was, Barn could not have got there in time to do it," said Wright slowly. "If Miss Loudron is telling the truth. Why the devil didn't she mention this before?"

"Possibly because the point seemed of no importance till I suggested that Sharon may have been killed because she knew something about Rebecca and Walt. Possibly those two really are guilty and Rebecca made this story up to strengthen his alibi."

"Dr. James' gauntlet gloves," said the Inspector, after a pause. "You know there are scratches on the back of them. Our laboratory chaps have found traces of nail varnish in the scratches, and particles of leather beneath the dead woman's nails. They correspond."

"The blessings of science. All we need to know is who wore them. Any more enthralling pieces of evidence?"

"Negative only. The D.D.I. of the manor Tooley Street's in tells me none of his constables on the beat noticed Harold Loudron and his Jaguar the night Mrs. Loudron was killed. Mind you, that doesn't break his alibi. He doesn't remember which side street he parked in to let the alcoholic fumes dissipate. A Jag would stick out like a sore thumb in any of those streets, but there's a hell of a lot of 'em, and the police patrols wouldn't cover them all during the period in question."

"You've eliminated Harold? In your own mind?"

"I've eliminated nobody. That's the hell of this case; it's getting me dizzy. Too many motives, too many clues, and all pointing in every which direction. Even Harold—he could have pinched that silk stocking, he could have taken the gauntlet gloves and hidden them afterward—he was in and out of Number 6 often enough. Dr. James has had the luck of the devil."

"Dr. James?" said Nigel, startled.

"Oh, I don't mean he's the murderer. Though he might be. No, getting the body out of the house and into the river without a soul seeing him."

"Yes, I agree."

"It couldn't have been anyone else who moved the body."

"No."

Nigel was uncomfortably aware of his friend's piercing eyes upon him.

"What were you talking about to Dr. James and his sister this afternoon?" asked the Inspector.

"That very thing."

"He denied it?"

Nigel hesitated. The lie with which he had elicited Dr. James' confession lay heavily on his conscience. To lie to his old friend Wright was unthinkable.

"I'm sorry," he said. "Dr. James is my client. I can't tell you about our conversation."

"You have told me." The steel in Chief Inspector Wright came out, as he said coldly, "Well, I hope you know what you are doing," and abruptly took his departure.

Next morning was sunny. At eleven o'clock, when Clare was out shopping, Walt Barn turned up on Nigel's doorstep. It was the first time Nigel had seen the young painter looking thoroughly worried. Walt told him he'd been down at Number 6, but they'd told him Rebecca was ill and not allowed to have any visitors.

"Why wasn't I told before? Is she bad, do you know?"

"You couldn't be found yesterday."

"Oh, lord, she did send for me then?"

"No, the police were looking for you."

"Christ! She's not—nothing's happened to her?"

"Nothing too serious, I hope. I'd better ring the police and reassure them you haven't fled the country."

Walt stood by Nigel in the hall while he rang up and left a message for Inspector Wright.

"Let's go into the Park," said Nigel. "I need some fresh air. Where were you all yesterday?"

"I needed fresh air too. Bicycled out through Bromley.

Wandered about in those woods—you know, on the right after you've turned off onto the Westerham road. Didn't get back till late. What the hell do the coppers want with me now?"

"I've no idea. Checking up again about the night Sharon was killed, maybe."

"I wish they'd get out of my hair. My mum always told me, Walt, she said, don't you have nothing to do with that lot, she said. And she was right!"

They were climbing up the steep grassy slope, Croom's Hill on their right, the Park road to their left. At the top, Nigel led his companion, who was breathing heavily, toward a wooden bench on the knoll. They sat down.

In the clear air, all London seemed to be unrolled like a map below them. At their feet lay the consummate elegance of the Queen's House, flanked by its colonnades, with the twin domes of the Palace towering up beyond it. The river sparkled like a crystal snake, winding its way round the Isle of Dogs, sinuously curving out of sight where it turned eastward again beyond the West India Docks, Millwall, and Poplar. Colored funnels of steamers sticking up amongst the thousands of drab chimney pots. The attitudinizing cranes. The huge flour mill dominating the middle distance. And then, away to the left, through the leafless trees, they could see Greenwich reach, a few ships on it tiny as Minitoys, on its way toward the Pool of London; and beyond it the dome of St. Paul's glittered in the morning light, and Westminster Abbey was visible away to the northwest.

"You know," Walt remarked, "I never seen all this before. One hell of a panorama, isn't it?" He gave his companion an odd look. " 'And he took him up onto a high mountain, and showed him all the kingdoms of the world'—somehow like that it goes, doesn't it?"

"More or less. But I'm not the Devil, and I'm not going to tempt you. I didn't know you were religious."

"My mum was. Regular old Bible-basher, when she wasn't on the booze."

Nigel studied his companion for a moment. The cannon-ball head, the fringe of hair along his brow, the speedwell-blue eyes which flitted so restlessly from object to object, hard to pin down as butterflies; the cheeky, challenging expression of a slum child. Naïve though Rebecca Loudron was in ways, she seemed fully adult compared with Walt—this tough, brash young man who could be mischievous as a child, not from any inherent viciousness, maybe, but because he had never lost the child's irresponsibility and his need to make an impression.

"Graham says he saw Rebecca put a sleeping powder in her father's coffee," Nigel quietly remarked.

The blue eyes turned to him and flickered away.

"So what?"

"Did she?"

"How should I know? You mean the night he was murdered? I wasn't there—not at dinner, I mean."

"I know that. You were upstairs, in her room. Why do you have to be so evasive about it? Or aren't you interested?"

"The old catechism again."

"Rebecca didn't deny it."

"Well, that's her affair, isn't it?"

"You really are an extraordinary freak. The woman you're supposed to be going to marry is accused of something that, if it's true, could pretty well convict her of murder, and you say you're not interested."

A badgered look came on Walt's face. "Look, there's no 'supposed to be' about it. After you and I had that dust-up, I had a think—it sort of cleared my mind—I went to see Becky and told her I'd go through with it."

"'Go through with it'?" Nigel chuckled. "That must have made her feel on top of the world."

"Don't be so bloody daft! I didn't put it like that."

"But it was what you meant?"

Again Walter shied away. "Look," he said presently, "there's quite a simple explanation of that powder Becky gave the old man."

"I shouldn't be surprised. It was to put him to sleep, wasn't it?" said Nigel, without irony.

"That's right. She'd just had a hell of a barney with him. About us. He'd forbidden her to see me again, or else. Well, Becky sent for me and smuggled me upstairs. We'd come to a crisis—got to decide one way or the other. Defy the old —— or break it up between us. Last thing Becky wanted was for him to come trotting upstairs and find me there and turf me out before she and I had had a regular old heart-to-heart and thrashed it all out."

"Which you did to the strains of Mozart?"

"Some of the time. Why not?"

"Why not indeed? You really are a bloody silly ape."

"Now what have I said?"

"Not telling the police about this at the start."

"Oh, come off it. It'd be a cinch for them; if we'd told them it was Becky who doped the old man, they'd have jumped at the chance of arresting her, and me too, for murdering him."

"I suppose there's no use telling you that people like Inspector Wright don't jump at the chance of arresting anyone and everyone?"

"No use at all. The poor bleeders want promotion, don't they? D'you really suppose they'd have swallowed a story that Becky put her dad to sleep just so that she and I could have a nice long talk? Phooey!"

"Well, I'm prepared to swallow it."

"You're different. You're human. More or less. Your mind doesn't wear a uniform."

Nigel gave Walt a cigarette and lit it. "So now everyone is happy again."

"Don't kid yourself."

"You're still wondering if Rebecca might have killed her father before she came up to you?"

"Oh, it's not that." Walt dismissed it with a wave of his cigarette. "Maybe she did, maybe she didn't. The old man had it coming to him anyway. Phony old domestic tyrant."

"You've got more serious matters on your mind?"

"Sure I have," replied Walt, disregarding Nigel's mild irony, or not noticing it. He gazed in silence at the great distances of London unrolled beneath them. "Funny, us coming up here," he said at last. "Look at all that. The Smoke. Millions of houses and factories and shops and warehouses. Own just two or three of those millions and you're sitting pretty. Or are you?"

"Are you, you mean?"

"It's a temptation. When you're poor, anyway."

"Yes."

"You say yes, but what do you know about the problems of the artist?"

"Quite a lot. I live with one."

"That's true. But Massinger's made it. She's a success, and she's good. She doesn't have to think about the right way for her, as an artist, to live; not any more."

"I wouldn't be so sure of that."

"Now you probably think I'm a self-centered young bastard who tries to inflate a little scrap of talent with a lot of flash talk. Well, I daresay I throw my weight around a bit. But, believe me, I've no use for the layabouts, the pub-crawlers, all those bearded wonders who think a paintbrush is for signing your name with. Me, I'd cut my grandmother's throat if I knew I could paint better by doing it. But I don't know. Oh, I can paint as well as the next man. But that's not the point. It's not good enough. What I worry about is whether I have it in me to paint better than the next man, and if I have, what kind of life I should live to give myself the best chance of doing so."

"Clare felt exactly the same when she was your age."

Walt's eye brightened. "Did she now? I'd never have believed it." He relapsed again into his gloomy expression, hands loosely dangling between his knees.

"Which brings us to Becky again," Nigel prompted.

"Yeah. Poor old Becky. And poor old Barn." The words came out differently now, in jerks and rushes. "It's not just a matter of her money—will it corrupt me, make me lazy, take the edge off things. Though that's enough of a problem. No. It's more complicated. I've a responsibility toward her, and a responsibility toward my work. If I let her down now, God knows what she mightn't do. She takes things hard, you know. Abnormally, I'd say. I wouldn't want to have her on my conscience. But suppose I go through with it and then find that my work peters out; I'd be blaming it on her, on our marriage, you see? And that would wreck the marriage. Well, suppose I pluck up courage and break it off now, and then find that my work still comes to nothing, that I'd hurt her mortally to no purpose; what sort of a heel d'you suppose I'd feel?"

Nigel looked at him consideringly, then away to a tug towing its string of lighters on the Thames far below. "I think you're putting up a comparatively unreal problem to conceal the real one, which you daren't face."

"O.K., teacher, chalk it up on the blackboard."

"In the first place, you could quite easily dispose of the problem of Rebecca's wealth, if you think that might be bad for your work."

"You mean—"

"Just take enough of the money for you and her to live on very simply. Give the rest away—"

"To my fellow artists? Ha!" Walter laughed. "Corrupt *them*? Eliminate the competitors?"

"—or keep it in the bank for your children, not touch it yourselves. Would Rebecca agree to that?"

"Yes, she probably would. But—"

"But that's not the real problem either."

"Say on, professor."

"The real problem, which you're smoke-screening with these other ones, is simply this: Do you or don't you love her enough to risk everything for her—to gamble your most precious thing, your talent, on your love?"

The young man was silent, pressing his hands together, his round face tightened in a sorrowful perplexity.

"We must look like one of those Victorian problem pictures," he said at last. "The Rustic Bench, or Shall He Emigrate?" He fell silent again, then burst out, "Love her? I don't even know if I believe in love!"

"Oh, bosh! You might as well say you don't know if you believe in Greenwich Park. You're *in* Greenwich Park—you'd bloody well better believe in it."

"She'd make a good wife," said Walter presently. "She can cook and run a house and all that."

"Is she interested in your work?"

"Well, because it's *my* work. I can imagine her getting a damned sight too ambitious, on my behalf. I don't like being pushed ahead." His eyes flickered at Nigel. "D'you think she's, well, quite normal? I mean, the way she blows her top sometimes, it scares me."

"If she had a safety valve, she wouldn't blow her top."

"Meaning marriage? I wonder. What about Sharon and poor old Harold?"

"What about them?"

"She was married. Devoted husband—worshiped the ground she trod on and all that lark. Didn't stop her bursting into flames whenever a pair of trousers came in sight. If I'd been

Harold, I'd have wrung her neck long ago."

"Well, Rebecca isn't Sharon, and Harold isn't exactly like you either. Why drag them in?"

"Your talking about safety valves. The way poor old Harold looked at her with those spaniel eyes—throw me that bone, please, when all the other dogs have had the meat off it—putting up with all her discontentedness and her lousy lovers—I ask you! Either he's not a man at all or he'd screwed down the safety valve so hard that—"

"That he finally blew up and killed her? Well, it's a theory. But why should he kill his father?"

"Does he have to have killed them both?"

"Someone did."

"Well, poor old Harold needed the dough, from all I hear."

"So did you and Rebecca."

Walt Barn's eyes danced audaciously at Nigel. "I'm tired of talking. That hold you got on me the other day—can you teach me it?"

"What, here?"

"Yes."

Nigel shook his head, grinned, demonstrated the hold and then the blow to disarm a man with a knife. Walt was a quick learner.

"Let's have a fight," he said presently. "No dirty stuff. See if I can throw you."

During the wrestling match that ensued, Nigel was made aware of Walt's extraordinary competitiveness; the young man clearly took any form of contest with absurd seriousness. Nigel reflected, as they heaved and panted, how a few sons of the working class overcompensate for the utter noncompetitiveness of the rest.

A parkkeeper came pounding toward them, appalled by the spectacle of a young tough and a middle-aged gentleman locked in mortal combat. As he neared them, they hurled each other to the ground and started rolling down the hill. Blowing his whistle, the parkkeeper followed, to come to a halt open-mouthed when the furious pair rose from the grass, dusted each other off, and proceeded amicably toward the Croom's Hill gate.

"Well, I feel better for all that," said Walter Barn. "But I still don't know what to do about Becky."

"If I were you, I'd wait upon the course of events. Let it ride—just a little longer."

15.

Out of Mourning

"What on earth have you been up to?" asked Clare, when Nigel had seen Walter Barn off on his bicycle.

"Fighting again. Quite friendly this time. Walt was determined to demonstrate his strength. He's a very pertinacious type."

"Perhaps he'll turn out a good painter, then. What did he want, apart from physical combat?"

Nigel told her about the conversation. From this, they drifted on to the subject of Dr. Piers, his family, and the two crimes. Clare listening with the calm attentiveness of a mere on a windless day, he reviewed the motives, the evidence, the crosshatching of lies and evasions with which more than one of the suspects had confused the pattern of the case.

"It all points to one person," Nigel concluded, telling her the name of this person. "I've no doubt in my own mind. I don't think Wright has, either, but he's got to eliminate the others and offer a case that will satisfy the Public Prosecutor. It takes time."

"And in the meanwhile?"

"Exactly. One can't expect this sort of killer to sit back on his laurels."

Clare came over in a swirl of black hair and flung herself against him. "Nigel. Darling. I wish you'd let this alone. I'm frightened. You must be in danger yourself."

"Yes. And I shall probably be in worse danger before we've finished."

"You're not going to—"

"If a scorpion won't come out of its hole—"

"You're too big to get into a scorpion's hole," said Clare, with a shaky laugh.

While they were having lunch, the telephone rang.

"It's Harold," said Clare when she had answered it. "He wants to see you. Tonight."

"Ask him to come—no, tell him I'll come round after dinner."

Clare gave him a long, meditative look; then, biting her lip, she returned to the telephone.

"Between 9:30 and 10," Nigel called after her.

At 9:40, Nigel was walking briskly beneath the power station. On the river to his left a dark shape slid downstream, its engines throbbing like a headache. By the light of a street lamp he could see, scrawled in chalk by some youthful misanthrope on the wall of the scrapyard facing him, the legend "I HATE MEN." Males, or just humanity in general, he wondered.

Ahead of him lay the narrow passage between corrugated-iron walls where Sharon Loudron had been strangled. The lamps the murderer had broken were repaired now; the passage did not look sinister, only squalid. "When the lamp is shattered," he murmured to himself, "the light in the dust lies dead." A burst of singing came from the "Cutty Sark" pub as he emerged from the passage onto Ballast Quay.

Nigel paused a moment to watch the port and starboard lights of the throbbing motor vessel swing slowly round as she made her turn northward into the reach. He could see, too, the bowsprit and rounded bows of the wrecked barge projecting toward him from behind the high wall that hid the quay she was moored at and Harold's house.

What with the noises of the river and the pub, it was impossible to be sure, but Nigel could not get rid of a strong impression that he was being followed. There was so much shadow along the waterside here, and in the wind that had strengthened a few hours ago some of the shadows seemed to move, to be blowing to and fro. Moving on, he found the door in the wall unlocked. He went in and rang the bell of Harold Loudron's front door.

Just after Nigel had left his own house, the telephone rang. Clare took up the receiver. A hoarse, muffled voice said, "Could I speak to Mr. Strangeways, please."

"I'm afraid he's just gone out. Who is it?"

"Rebecca Loudron. Is that Clare?"

"But, my dear, oughtn't you to be in bed? You don't sound at all yourself."

"Oh, I'm better, thank you. James told me not to get up, but he's gone out somewhere, so I've crept downstairs."

"Is it something urgent, then? You could get Nigel at Harold's house, if it is; he's gone along there."

"Well, it can probably wait till the morning. I must ring off now. Good night."

Replacing the receiver, Clare stood for a moment in thought. Then, throwing on a warm coat and a headscarf, she hurried out of the house.

"Hello. Good of you to come." Harold lowered his voice. "Graham's turned up. I don't think he'll be staying long, though."

Graham Loudron's presence was not at all what he had expected, nor, for that matter, as they went into the sitting room, did Nigel expect the transformation he found there. No dust, no disorder, no longer the air of neglect. Sprawling in a hammocklike armchair by the windows that overlooked the river, Graham tipped a hand at him. Nigel sensed a certain undercurrent excitement in the young man, which gave animation—even charm—to his usually inexpressive features. He remembered Rebecca—or was it James?—telling him that in their younger days Harold and Graham had rather paired off together.

"Becky and I have been doing our best to cheer Harold up," said Graham, while their host was outside fetching drinks. "He wouldn't come to stay at Number 6, so we drop in here from time to time."

"Your sister has been cleaning the place up, I see."

"Oh, yes, and cooking an occasional meal for him. Till yesterday, when you drove her into hysterics."

Nigel was prevented by Harold's return from commenting on this remarkable misrepresentation of yesterday's proceedings. As Harold poured out the drinks, after offering them in the hushed tones that he evidently thought suitable to a recently bereaved widower, Nigel studied him with attention. His City pallor had always been so marked that grief could hardly heighten it. Nor was the small, upright figure any less spruce; the temporary seediness and disorientation that overtake most husbands when their wives have died were notably absent from Harold's appearance, which was all the more notable considering how uxorious a husband he had been. If anything showed in him different, it was a withdrawn, almost wary look of the eyes, which had black rings under them.

"I haven't seen you since—" began Nigel, breaking the awkward silence. "I'm most terribly sorry about it all."

"Yes, it was bloody awful. If I could lay my hands on the person who killed her—"

Even tragedy could not rob Harold of his clichés.

Nigel plowed on. "I do hope you'll soon be feeling better —a bit better able to cope with things."

"Thank you. I've tried to carry on. My work in the City, you know—one has to keep one's finger on the pulse. Work is the only anodyne, though I can't say I'm feeling any beneficial effects from it as yet," Harold concluded, with a deprecatory and stilted little gesture startlingly reminiscent of his father.

Nigel caught a flicker of a smile on Graham's face. It was all the young man had contributed so far.

"Have you any idea how soon the police will have these matters cleared up?" Harold resumed.

"I'm afraid not. But they may be cleared up sooner than the police anticipate," said Nigel, his pale-blue eyes resting impassively upon Harold's.

"We were talking about Harold's alibi just before you came," said Graham, still exuding that aura of repressed excitement; it gave him, Nigel thought, a positively dangerous charm.

"I'm sure Strangeways doesn't want to—er—to talk shop," put in Harold, looking embarrassed.

"I bet he does."

"Which alibi?" Nigel asked.

"The trunk call he heard but didn't answer the night my father died. Tremendous bit of luck for you, wasn't it, Harold?"

"I don't know why you keep harping on that," replied Harold, with a kind of cautious resentfulness.

"Well, I ask you! Strangeways here has got it into his head that I killed Father and your wife: I've got no convincing alibis for either night; naturally I'm envious of your luck in having one."

"This is all extremely distasteful," said Harold stuffily.

"What did you ask Strangeways here to talk about, then?"

"Private matters."

"I stand rebuked."

Now it was Graham who uncannily reminded Nigel of Dr. Piers—the old man's suave and feline manner. Odd how he had left his stamp, in such different ways, upon his two younger children.

"Of course," continued Graham, "you could have faked that alibi. With your tape recorder."

"The police were perfectly well aware of that. The Inspector played over all my reels of tape, and—"

"All the reels he could find."

"Don't be ridiculous, my dear chap. The police turned this house upside down to see if I'd hidden any. Besides, I should have thought it was obvious, if I had faked up an alibi, as you put it, by leaving my tape recorder running in the hall, near the telephone, I'd have—"

"All this is beside the point," Nigel interrupted, in an impatient voice. He turned to Graham. "If you want to accuse your brother of the murder, why not come straight out with it?"

"My half brother. I've revealed to Harold the secret of my birth," said Graham sardonically.

"I don't know why you have to pick on me"—Harold's tone was almost sentimentally rueful—"we used to be such friends. When you were a little chap, first came to live with us, you and I were as thick as anything. I used to—"

"You used to love money, even then," Graham harshly broke in. "You encouraged me to pinch cash from Father and James, and gave me a percentage of it. Quite the businessman!"

"Oh, damn it! Look here, we were young then. Why rake up little peccadilloes like—"

"You've always been an expert in passing the buck and avoiding the blame, haven't you?"

Harold's face was whiter than ever under this goading.

"If you're suggesting that—"

"Well, you'd have been ruined if Father hadn't died so opportunely."

"This is absolutely intolerable!" Harold started up from his chair, trembling with anger. "And anyway," he lamely added, "it's damned bad form in front of a stranger—a guest of mine."

Graham began shaking with silent laughter. "Poor old Harold! True to type to the bitter end. 'His white collar remained starched when all around him wilted.' *Times* obituary."

"Won't you have another drink?" Harold addressed Nigel, ostentatiously ignoring his brother. Nigel watched him carefully as he poured it out. It was clear that Harold wished to be alone with Nigel, but Graham showed no signs of taking the hint. The three talked in a desultory way for nearly three quarters of an hour longer before Harold brought himself to say, "Graham, old boy, do trot along now, will you? It's getting late, and I want to have a private word with Strangeways."

"The dear old barge," said Graham, looking left out of the window. "What secrets she could tell! Why do you keep her still? Sentimental reasons?"

"She's going to the breaker's yard next month. Come on, Graham."

As Harold went to the door, Graham, rising from the window seat, gave Nigel a glance of urgent complicity and jerked his head in the direction of the quay. "See you very soon, I hope," he said.

Clare, staring through the window of the "Cutty Sark" bar, whose lights had just been put out to speed the unwillingly parting habitués, saw the figure of Graham Loudron stride briskly past the front of the pub.

"Closing time, please, Miss," said the barman.

Clare went out into the blowy night, tightening her headscarf. Nigel was still in Harold's house, presumably; should she go home now? Or go in and pick him up? She took a few steps homeward in her heelless shoes, which made no sound on the cobbles; then, changing her mind, she turned about and walked toward Harold's house, scrutinizing those on the opposite side of the street. One, with a small porch, seemed to be unoccupied. She glided into the porch and, resting her back against the door, prepared to wait.

"Graham really is an extraordinary chap. Sometimes I don't know what to make of him," Harold was saying.

Nigel let this unexceptionable proposition hang in the air for some moments before remarking, "I mustn't stay too long. What did you want to see me about?"

Harold Loudron, who had already been punishing the whisky bottle, poured himself another stiff dose.

"It's an extraordinary thing," he said, slurring his words a little. "I'd have thought Sharon's death would've broken me up altogether. But, fact is, sounds a fearfully caddish sort of thing to say, but fact is I've been feeling a new man—what's the word?—re—re—"

"Juvenated," Nigel supplied.

"That's it. Rejuvenated."

"Good for you."

"Whassat? Oh, I see. But you really do feel—don't feel I should be ashamed of feeling rejuvenated? Tell me the truth, old man. I can take it."

"No."

Harold's pale face was sweating profusely. "I don't mind telling you, between you and I, Sharon used to play me up."

"Did she?"

"You're damn right she did. Other men, you know," Harold confidentially muttered. "Keep it under your hat, old chap, don't want it to get around, de mortuis and all that, but

217

Sharon was a Grade A bitch. Couldn't help it, poor girl. Over-sexed. I've no doubt she picked up some fellow that night, and picked a wrong 'un, and that's how she—er—met her end."

"An interesting theory."

"You don't sound very enthusiastic. Who did murder the poor girl, then?"

"A person with a hopelessly deficient sense of reality," Nigel answered. Harold stared at him blankly for several moments, then resumed.

"What I was leading up to, she got them. Any man. She got *me*. Don't mind telling you she had me lashed to the wheel and steering any course she fancied. You may think I was infatuated with her."

"Well—"

"And you'd be damn right. But look at it from my point of view. She was so different from everything that my poor old father—and James and Becky—represented. You probably think me a very conventional sort of chap, but it's conventional chaps like me who fall hardest for girls like Sharon, every time. And she was such a marvelous girl to do things with," the widower enthusiastically continued. "Of course, she got bored with things quickly, but as long as they were new she was like a child, she got so excited with them. I know she found me a bit of an old stick-in-the-mud after a while. But she did *rely* on me, in a funny way, and that's why I simply couldn't boot her out or create at all when she started going off the rails. D'you get the idea?"

"Perfectly."

"I believe you do. Sympathetic chap, though I can't say I took to you at the start. Don't hit it off with intellectuals."

"You prefer boats."

"Every time, old man. What was I saying—oh, yes, now I really *loved* my wife; don't let there be any mistake about that. But it was a strain, keeping up with her and keeping down my feelings about—not to mince matters, about her affairs and so on and so forth. But this is the point, Strangeways: it was not till after her death that I realized what a strain it had been." Harold stared, sapiently as an owl, at his companion.

"Because the strain was no longer there?"

"Absolutely. You've put it in a nutshell. I woke up a morning or two ago, after the first shock had passed, and I suddenly felt as if a tremendous weight had been lifted off me, and I was free. I felt re—re—"

"Juvenated?"

"Don't be silly, old man. Never heard of it. I felt resilient. On top of the world. Sailing free. And all I ask is a tall ship and a star to steer her by."

Harold rambled on in this vein for a good while longer. At last Nigel managed to bring him to the point.

"Why did I ask you to come round? Let me think now. Oh, yes. How soon can I clear out of here?"

"Clear out?"

Harold explained, in a manner rather less prolix than his previous outpourings, that he had had an offer to join a party of three or four friends who proposed to sail a thirty-foot yawl round the world.

"They want to start in April or May, and I'd like to go with them. The police simply won't commit themselves to—trouble with them is they spend so much time asking me questions they've no breath left to answer one."

Nigel pointed out that, even if an arrest were made tomorrow, the legal proceedings might well drag on for several months.

"Legal proceedings?" asked Harold. "But why should I be involved in them?"

"You'd certainly be called to give evidence."

"But I know nothing about my father's death."

"There's the matter of your wife's murder," said Nigel,

gazing noncommittally at the pale, anxious face of Harold Loudron, who seemed to have talked himself into comparative sobriety.

"I'm hardly likely to forget that, old man," replied Harold, with a huffy attempt at dignity.

"You were going to chuck up your business altogether?"

"Why not? Actually the chap I was dining with the night poor Sharon was killed, he's quite keen to take it over. Anyway, I don't need to make money now; I shall be getting my share of Father's estate. Of course, I've had to borrow on it to recoup certain financial losses I'd sustained. But there'll be plenty left over for me to live on, now that Sharon—" he broke off, looking rather shamefaced, then firmly continued. "She did run through money, you know; sometimes she behaved as if I was made of it. But I couldn't refuse her anything."

"Anyway, you see yourself embarking on a new life?"

"I want to get away from everything—the City, Greenwich, this house. Its memories are too painful for me." Harold Loudron's moment of truth had passed; he was evidently about to launch forth on a maudlin and meaningless lament for the *temps perdu*. Nigel cut him short with, "Have you tried retracing the route you took from the restaurant that night? If you did it in the dark, you might be able to remember which turn you took off Tooley Street. Then the police could narrow down their inquiries."

"I suppose I might try that," said Harold gloomily. "But I doubt if anyone would have noticed me there. I seem to remember it was mostly warehouses."

"Well, that'd be a help."

"Oh, what does it matter, anyway?" Harold cried. "I shall never get it off my mind that if I hadn't been tight that night, I'd have been home in time to— Sharon would never have gone out."

"Well, it's time for me to be getting home too. Just on eleven. I really must be off."

16.

On the Mud

Nigel heard Harold lock the outer door behind him. He turned right and started walking homeward. The wind had risen: waves were slamming against the river wall, and a creaking and thudding could be heard from where Harold's barge was moored. As he came out opposite the "Cutty Sark's" darkened windows, he saw a figure sitting on the parapet above the river, in the angle made by the wall between Ballast Quay and Harold's house. There was a low whistle. Nigel stepped over the chain and went up to the solitary figure. Once again, he got a strong impression that he was being watched or followed.

"Thought you were never coming," said Graham Loudron.

"What do you want?"

"Ssh! Keep your voice down." Graham jerked his finger at the wall. "Don't want him to hear us."

"Look, it's damned late. Have you been hanging about here ever since?"

"More or less. I tipped you the wink inside. Didn't you get it?"

"Yes, but I can't understand—"

Graham's eyes glittered with excitement in the light of the street lamp at the end of the quay. "I found it. This afternoon. Hidden on the 'Sharon.' That reel of tape the police were looking for—at least, it must be that one. Come along. I'll show you."

Graham stepped off the parapet, over the gunwale of the "Sharon," onto her deck. After a few seconds' hesitation, Nigel followed him. They picked their way past the capstan, over several coils of rope and a tarpaulin, to the mainmast. It was dark enough here already, and at this moment the light went out in the windows of the room where Nigel and Harold had been sitting. The barge stirred uneasily at the onset of the waves that jostled her against the quayside; her moorings creaked; overhead the halyards were slapping and a block squeaked.

"Watch out here. Part of the decking's gone." Graham led the way along the starboard side of the vessel, hugging the bulwark and skirting a strip of darkness, four foot broad, which ran from the foot of the mast to the raised afterdeck of the barge. As he passed the end of this strip, Nigel looked down. He could just descry a jagged edge of planking, and below it, in the barge's hold, a sluggishly stirring, faintly gleaming mass. Mud, he thought; it must be the mud that has gradually seeped in.

Graham, bent double, entered the main hatch. Nigel followed him down the ladder into a pit of darkness that proved to be the barge's main cabin. Graham's electric torch lighted up for a few moments the mildewed pitch pine of the walls, a tattered old calendar still hanging from one of them, and at the forward end the jagged planking Nigel had seen from above.

"That bit of floor's gone," said Graham, extinguishing his torch. "Keep away from that end, or you'll fall into the bilge. Harold had a number of planks removed from here and the deck—they were rotten—but he never got round to replacing them. Are you armed?"

"Armed? Good lord, no. Why?"

"Well, I should think we could tackle Harold all right between us."

"But why should we have to tackle Harold?"

"You're very slow tonight. Didn't you hear me hinting about the tape and the barge? I thought I might get him rattled enough to give himself away. Like you tried to do with me yesterday. I wouldn't put it past him to guess that you and I'd go after the tape when we left."

"Oh, I see." In the blackness, Nigel could feel rather than see the excited young man's eyes probing in his direction. Graham went on to describe how he had given much thought to the question of the missing tape that constituted Harold's alibi for the night of Dr. Piers' murder. He remembered at last a loose panel, with a shallow cavity behind it, which Harold had once shown him in this very cabin.

"He's nailed it up, of course, after putting the tape in there. But I found it, all right, this afternoon."

"You've chosen a very dramatic way of revealing his secret," said Nigel equably.

"Oh, well, if you're not interested—" Graham's voice was positively pettish.

"But I am, I am. I suppose you did it this way so that you could crow over the police and myself. It's certainly one up to you. And it's very odd that the police didn't find this hiding place," Nigel added.

"They never thought of looking for the tape here."

"And you did?" Now that Nigel's eyes were growing accustomed to the darkness, he could see the shape of Graham Loudron sitting on the floor, his back against the bulkhead, hands in pockets. There was a loud thump, and the barge faintly shuddered.

"I say," Nigel whispered. "Could that be Harold jumping onto the deck?"

"Don't be nervous. It's only the rudder. It's a very heavy one, and the wheel's broken loose from its lashings, so the rudder bashes up against the quay wall when you get a steamer's wash coming in."

"Why do you suppose Harold hid the tape?"

"Well, isn't that obvious? If it was found, he'd have no alibi."

"But why *hide* it? Why not burn it—those tapes are highly inflammable—or just run the recorder backward and scrub it?"

"God knows why not. I'm no expert on Harold's mentality. All I can say is, there's a tape in there behind the panel. Look for yourself, if you don't believe me."

"Oh, I've no doubt there is. Now."

"What d'you mean, 'now'?"

"Well," Nigel calmly told him, "the police examined this barge from stem to stern some days ago. They found no tape. But let's see it, anyway."

"See for yourself." Graham shone the torch beam at the loose panel. Nigel moved over, withdrew the panel, and took out the reel of tape, which stood on end behind it.

"What did I tell you?" said Graham triumphantly.

"Oh, I didn't doubt there'd be a reel there. A reel you'd faked up, with a telephone bell ringing." Weighing the reel in his hand, he made a gesture as if to toss it into the bilge, then put it in his overcoat pocket. "You really are the most transparently foolish murderer I've ever come across."

Clare, at her post in the porch of the empty house, had seen Graham reappear from her right about five minutes after he had walked away. He must have gone down Lassell Street, cut across to Pelton Road, and returned to the waterside that way. She froze to immobility in the porch, which fortunately was in shadow from the street lamp, as he passed. He strolled, without any apparent attempt at concealment, onto Ballast Quay, where he moved out of the range of her vision; the sound of his footsteps ceased. He was evidently waiting for somebody, and that somebody could only be Nigel.

Some twenty minutes later, the outer door of Harold Loudron's house opened. Two voices said good night, and Nigel emerged. So unfurtive had Graham's movements been that, though she knew he was a double murderer—or at least Nigel believed him to be—she could not for a moment entertain the idea that Graham would try anything on, here, tonight. Then Clare remembered how Sharon had been strangled, at this time of night, in the dark passage only fifty yards from where she stood. She hurried silently after Nigel and was about to call out a warning to him when she heard his voice in amicable conversation with Graham. She paused for a moment in her tracks, the wind whipping her headscarf; Nigel surely knows what he is doing; I must let him play it his way, and not interfere.

Peering cautiously round the wall, she saw Nigel's back as he stepped from the quay into the bows of the wrecked barge. She stood, undecided. Knock at the "Cutty Sark" and tell them Nigel was closeted with a murderer on the derelict opposite their windows? Walk home, leaving Nigel to carry out, uninterrupted, whatever his mysterious plan was? Find a telephone and ring the police? After only the briefest hesitation, Clare moved to the river wall and soundlessly stepped onto the barge.

"And you're the stupidest, most amateur amateur detective," was Graham's schoolboyish retort. "Not even to come armed!"

"How do you know I'm not?"

Graham's torch flashed on, its beam holding Nigel steadily. "It doesn't much matter whether you are or not. I have a revolver, and I shall shoot if I see your hands going to your pockets." Graham allowed the torchlight to fall for an instant on the revolver he held in his other hand. "Move back to the edge of the floor. Now sit down. Of course, I intend to shoot you anyway, but I like the idea of making you sweat a bit first."

The torch beam struck against Nigel's eyes, and he closed them.

"Saying your prayers?" Graham jeered.

"What on earth will you get out of shooting me?" asked Nigel irritably.

"Pleasure."

"A revolver shot would certainly be heard—"

"I doubt it. Listen."

The old barge's tackle creaked and groaned, slapped and rattled in the gusty wind; every now and then the heavy rudder thumped hard enough to shiver its timbers. Booming sounds came from the hollow lighters off Lovell's Wharf as they pounded together.

"And even if it wasn't heard, you'd never get away long with a third murder."

Graham's toneless voice had an edge of excitement in it. "Don't you be so sure. When I shoot you, I shall tip your body over the edge there, just behind where you're sitting. You'll fall into the mud, which is quite deep—I've sounded it—and gradually suffocate, because I shan't shoot to kill you stone-dead. Your body will sink into the mud and disappear. It might never even be found."

"What a nasty little mind you have, my poor boy."

"Don't you dare patronize me!" Graham's voice came out in a sudden spirit of venom. "It's you who's got to crawl to me. I'll have you groveling before long."

"All right then. You've shot me and disposed of my body. Harold will give evidence you did not leave his house very long before I did. Other people must have spotted you hanging about here; you can't expect the luck you had when you strangled Sharon. What've you arranged for an alibi? No, I'll tell you. I bet you've made some childishly silly plan by which your brothers and sister will all come under suspicion, as you tried to do over Sharon's murder."

"Not so silly. You've underrated me from the start. That's the mistake that has brought you here tonight."

"I haven't underrated you at all. I saw, almost from the start, you were a particularly dangerous type—an incurable psychopath. In fact, I told Harold only just now that the murderer was a person with a hopelessly deficient sense of reality."

"Cut out the jargon," said Graham, in his stony voice. "I've enough sense of reality to get rid of you."

His eyes closed against the torch beam that mercilessly played upon them, Nigel became aware of the smells in the derelict barge—a smell of mud, a smell of the grain she had once carried and with which she was impregnated, a smell of pervasive rottenness from cankered timbers. Or it might have been the smell of Graham Loudron.

The young man was now boasting about his scheme. "Harold told me you were coming along here tonight. I arrived at his house first. I rang up from the hall, where he couldn't hear me—"

"Rang up whom?"

"Who do you think? Your mistress, or housekeeper, or whatever you call her."

"Clare Massinger?"

"Yes. Your ――― ―― ―― Clare Massinger." The vile words, enunciated in that dead, toneless voice, appalled Nigel.

"I pretended it was Rebecca speaking—it took Clare in completely—and found out you had left your house. I said James had gone out somewhere. When the police start to look for you tomorrow, they'll have all the same old suspects again: Harold—you were last heard of at his house; James out again, perhaps visiting a patient, perhaps not; Becky, who'd got out of bed to telephone your house, and had heard where you'd gone, and might have lain in wait for you along here; and, of course, myself. I never make the mistake of giving myself too definite an alibi."

"The mistake you make, my boy, is talking too much. While you've been chattering away about your cleverness, at least one person has come onto the deck and is listening—just up above my head there."

It almost worked. Graham's eyes switched upward; the torch beam wavered, but not long enough to allow Nigel to gather himself from his sitting position and make a leap.

"That was a feeble piece of bluff," Graham complacently remarked.

Clare had pulled her head back just in time to avoid the torch beam. She knew herself to be in a desperate quandary. If she called out for help, Graham would shoot Nigel at once. If she went for help, Nigel might well be killed before she returned with it. Besides, what could anyone do? Graham, at the side of the cabin, was protected by the decking above his head; it was Nigel, his face a white disk in the torchlight, who sat beneath the gaping hole where the deck timbers had been removed. The only way to get at Graham would be to shoot down at him diagonally from the forward end of that long rent in the deck, but Clare had nothing to shoot with. If Graham could only be enticed out from under the shelter of the decking, perhaps she could drop something on his head. Stealthily she crawled over the barge, groping for some heavy object. She encountered plenty of heavy objects, but they were all firmly fastened to the deck. There was the afterhatch; could she make her way down that and forward again into the main cabin without Graham's hearing her? No, not a hope; she did not even know that there was a way through, and she had no torch to find it if there was one.

Clare's mind went numb now. She slid face-down onto the

228

deck, weeping hopelessly. After a timeless pause of blank despair, she became aware that her right hand was touching a coil of rope. Carrying it, she crept back to the edge of the long rift in the deck. They were still talking. Thank God for that! Clare's cold fingers began to uncoil the rope.

Nigel was talking, not because he thought there was the least hope of rescue from his predicament but out of the mere animal instinct to prolong his life. To follow Graham, unarmed, into the barge had been a risk, of course, but he had gambled on its leading to a showdown; he'd won that bet, and it shouldn't have been so risky a bet for himself; Wright had assured him there was a tail on Graham Loudron. Graham must have shaken off this tail, or maybe some dumb plainclothes operative was standing about on the quay waiting for Graham and Nigel to reappear from the stinking bowels of the barge.

"You killed Sharon," said Nigel, "not because she knew something which would give you away but because she'd *told* us this something. It was sheer vindictiveness on your part, you vicious little monster."

"Talk on. You amuse me."

"She'd told me that she waited ten minutes in your room before you appeared, and that when you did you were 'madly above yourself,' in a state of strange excitement—just as you were tonight in Harold's house. You get a kick out of killing, don't you?"

"Mouth beginning to feel a bit dry yet?"

"And the next morning you gave yourself away, irrevocably, by your surprise and consternation when you found the body was not there in the bath. Well, it's lucky for your mother she didn't live to see what a bloodthirsty little maniac you've grown up into."

The torch beam shook. Nigel could imagine the expression on Graham's face.

"Leave my mother out of it, you —— ——!"

"Very well. We'll turn to your father. You'd found his diary. You kept that piece of it for insurance—it looked good as a confession of suicide—and showed it to me when you felt I was uncomfortably close on your heels. It was quite a bold stroke on your part."

"Thank you. May I have that in writing?"

"You'd been waiting for an opportunity to kill your father in such a way that it'd be taken for suicide. Also, you wanted to keep him in suspense for as long as possible—make him sweat it out."

"Like I'm doing to you now."

"Your chance came when you noticed Rebecca put a sleeping powder into his coffee that night. Would you care to carry on from there?"

"Oh, it was too easy. I went up and found him in bed, asleep. I ran a bath, took off his pajamas—I was wearing gloves, of course: burned them in the incinerator afterward—then I slit his wrists. That sort of woke him up. He recognized me, all right," Graham added, with an atrocious satisfaction, "before he croaked."

"You'd always wanted to do it that way, hadn't you?"

"What do you mean?"

"Make him bleed to death. Like your mother, who died of hemorrhages. 'Poetic justice' always appeals to the undeveloped, infantile mentality. Why, only yesterday you said to Rebecca, 'He seduced my mother, and then let her bl- bleeding well starve to death.' You never stutter. You just stopped yourself saying, 'let her bleed to death.' You can't get that out of your head. I wouldn't be surprised if this same penny-dreadful idea, quite as much as the notion of inculpating Rebecca, was what made you use her mother's stocking."

"I'd like to have killed her too—their mother."

"Well, you could dig her body up and spit on it. That'd be fun, wouldn't it, little boy?"

230

There was a hissing breath from Graham. Then he said, "You're trying to make me lose my temper, so that I come and hit you, and you grab my gun. Don't be puerile. You still don't know what you've been up against. I've outwitted you at every turn, and you might as well admit it."

How odd, thought Nigel, that in my last minutes on earth, I should be aware how the damp from these floorboards I'm sitting on is seeping through my coat, and feel quite resentful about it!

"You imagine yourself the cunning, heroic avenger," he said, conscious that an absurdly inappropriate lecturing tone was coming into his voice. "That's another typical delusion, like the delusion that you're going to get away with these murders."

"Perhaps I'm not. But, you see, I don't care," replied the young man, with dreadful, unmistakable sincerity. "That's why I'm so dangerous and why I've had all the luck so far—because I just didn't care what happened to me, once I'd made my father bleed to death."

"I asked you once if you hadn't got any ambition. You said you'd like to be a first-rate jazz pianist, but your face gave you away; you'd already achieved your ambition. Nevertheless, don't flatter yourself that you killed him to avenge your mother. That's a nice, convenient delusion. Makes you feel big, doesn't it, the idea of being a ruthless revenger?"

"Where will it hurt most to get the bullet?"

"The fact is, you're rotten with resentment. You smell of it. You kid yourself you did it as retribution for what your mother suffered. But you can't even be honest about that. You were getting your own back for what happened to you as a boy after she died; you couldn't take it, even then. Lots of boys have gone through as bad or worse and not turned into futile little self-pitying thugs. No, you're just out for yourself. You killed your father because of that, and because you wanted to get your hands on your share of his money—"

231

"That's a lie!" Graham almost screamed.

"—to bolster up your pitiful ego. You'd have cut your own mother's throat if it had suited your book."

The silence that followed was more than the cessation of speech; it seemed to eat its way outward like a pool of acid from the now just visible figure of Graham, corroding and corrupting the dank cabin against whose wall he stood. Nigel could talk no longer. He felt exhausted, exasperated, horribly soiled, too, rather than frightened. The barge creaked as another gust of wind struck it; overhead, a halyard chattered.

"I could break your nose with a bullet," said Graham at last, in an almost erotic murmur. "Or plug you in the pit of the stomach." The torch beam moved down. "Or smash your kneecap." The beam focused on Nigel's knees. "Go down on your knees."

"What?"

"I said I'd make you grovel to me. If you go down on your knees and beg me for mercy, I'll shoot you in the head. Otherwise, I'll put the bullet where it'll take you much longer to die."

"Judging by the way your hand is shaking, I doubt if you could hit anything but the cabin wall."

"Go on. Grovel."

Nigel began to get up from the floor. Now he was on hands and knees, and just about to flex his legs into a sprinter's starting position and hurl himself at Graham, who had come away from the side of the cabin and was standing only a few feet away. The floor felt slimy under Nigel's hands. His muscles were cramped; they hadn't the spring to launch him at his enemy. The thought flashed across his mind that in three seconds he would be paying for the trick he had played on James Loudron.

Clare had made a running knot and noose with one end of

the rope. She had taken a turn round a stanchion with the slack. Now, crouching at the side of the gap in the deck, she waited. She prayed for Graham to come out from beneath the shelter of the decking at the side of the cabin. She heard his threats, and saw the torch beam moving from Nigel's face, to his stomach, to his knees. And then, at last, Graham himself moved. He was standing almost directly beneath her.

With the gesture of one throwing a hoop in a fairground booth, Clare tossed the noose, which spread out and fell over Graham's head. The sound of its falling, the flash of it before his eyes, balked Graham's aim and at the same time startled him into pulling the trigger. The bullet flew higher than he had intended, and to the right. But, the instant before, Nigel had straightened up to make his desperate spring, so the bullet hit him in the left shoulder.

Clare saw its impact send him staggering backward, to fall from the edge of the broken floor into the hold. She hauled at the slack of the rope, made it fast, then jumped down through the gaping deck into the cabin. The noose had tightened round Graham's neck, and Clare's convulsive haul on the rope had lifted him off his feet. He dropped torch and revolver, to scrabble at the choking noose. He was stretching his toes, trying to reach the floor, a dangling, dancing puppet.

Sobbing, Clare groped about for the torch on the slimy floor. At last she found it. Mercifully, the bulb had not been broken by the fall. She ran to the edge of the flooring. The torch beam showed Nigel's body, face down in the mud; he was slowly sinking into it, and without a struggle. Clare jumped down. The mud, glistening like chocolate blancmange, received her; she managed to get to her feet, but the mud was still up to her thighs, and when she tried for a purchase on Nigel's shoulders, her feet slid on the slippery bottom of the barge.

After a violent effort, holding the torch between her teeth, Clare turned Nigel's body over so that his face, thick with

233

mud, was exposed. Tearing off her headscarf, she began to clear out the mud that plugged his nostrils. She did not know whether he was alive or dead—only that she must free him somehow from the viscous, porridgelike stuff that coated him all over. She was talking to him, or his corpse, in a loving, urgent murmur. "Wake up, darling," she heard herself saying. "It's Clare. You're all right. Wake up! Please."

The clogged eyelids fluttered. The eyes opened. "Put out that bloody torch, you bastard," Nigel mumbled.

"Oh, thank God! It's me, love." She pulled him upright against her body, but his legs had no strength in them, and it was almost impossible to prevent him buckling and collapsing into the mud again.

"I can't hold you up much longer," Clare despairingly said.

"Good old Clare." Nigel sighed comfortably, as if he was about to go to sleep. She gave him a violent shake.

"Ouch, that hurts, blast you, darling!"

At any rate, it woke Nigel up.

"Where did it hit you?"

"Shoulder," he said, wincing. "What do we do now?"

Clare shone her torch along the hold. As far as its light reached, it showed nothing but a level expanse of mud. The floor through which Clare had jumped was just within reach of her fingers; she could drag herself up into the cabin and run for help, but while she was getting it Nigel would sink down again into the ooze. And he was far too heavy for her to haul up, alone, with a rope. The deadly chill of the mud clasping her legs and thighs began to seep into her heart. Nigel opened his eyes a bit wider.

"Why not yell for help?" he inquired.

The extraordinary thing, Clare realized, was that in the stress and horror of the last few minutes, she simply had not thought of that.

She yelled, time and again, at the top of her voice, feeling her cries snatched away by the gusty wind, drowned by the rattle of halyards and the stunning thumps of the unlashed rudder, or never even penetrating out of this mausoleum of mud and rotting timbers. They were heard, however, at last, by Harold Loudron, who came running out of a door of his house, which gave direct onto the quay. All but spent, Clare heard him shout, and then the noise of feet running along the deck. Nigel's voice was raised to the rescuer now in a croak. "Look out! He's got a revolver!"

"It's all right, darling," said Clare. "He won't use it."

"Graham? He certainly will—unless he's escaped."

Lightheaded with relief, Clare almost giggled. "Don't fuss so. He can't escape."

"What on earth d'you mean?"

"I—he's—well, you see, I hanged him."

17.

Dr. Piers' Diary

Graham knows. Everything. What he hadn't guessed, I told him. He came into the study a couple of nights ago and said, "You're my real father, aren't you?" I admitted it. I asked him how he had found out. It seems he's been talking to some woman in Poplar or Millwall (what was he doing there, anyway?) who was a friend of Millie. That started him putting two and two together, for he'd somehow found out about those letters Millie wrote to me.

He accused me of murdering her. I told him this was nonsense. He proceeded to give me, in his cold way, a very highly colored account of his mother's last days. I did not let him see that every word was like a knife twisting in a wound. If only he had *felt* the horror of what he was relating, I should have broken down and implored him for forgiveness. But he was telling it all as a person tells a friend some malicious thing that has been said about the latter—with intent to discomfort, to note and enjoy the discomfiture. So my pride forbade me to indulge his curiosity and malice by breaking down under them.

Forbade me also to take refuge behind Janet. Poor upright,

possessive Janet; it is she who was the real villain of the piece, intercepting and hiding those letters Millie wrote me at the last. I could never forgive her for it.

And I was all the more implacable to Janet—I can confess it now—because I had an intuition, when the letters with my money orders for Millie began to be returned through the post with "Not known at this address" scrawled upon them, that Millie would be writing to me direct. Yes, I had a faint suspicion that Janet was hiding something from me; her behavior to me had changed; she never could dissemble. And for a while I let it pass, covertly relieved that I need not open up again the whole wretched, glorious affair of Millie.

But I said nothing of this to Graham. It would have been squalid beyond all words to use Janet's conduct as an excuse or palliative for my own.

Perhaps I should have denied at the start that I am Graham's father? I wish I *could* deny it. I hardly dare contemplate the sort of person I must be to have produced the person Graham is; Millie was a heart of gold; all Graham's dreadful traits must be inherited from me.

I was prepared to love him for Millie's sake, to show him every indulgence; but what a strain he has put on my good intentions. He'd only been here a few months when he started pilfering in the home. And then that shocking business for which he was sacked from his school; that should have opened my eyes to his real nature, but I still refused to believe that a child of Millie's could be irredeemably bad. I put it down to the hell he'd been through after she died.

Well, yes, and I have liked him too—for his independence, his intransigence, the momentary gleams of charm that remind me of Millie, above all for his quick wits, his brains. James and Becky are worthy characters, no doubt, but they bore me; Harold I find an almost meaningless nonentity. Graham at least has never bored me.

Now that my hours, as they say, are numbered (for I do

not make the mistake of not taking Graham seriously), I begin to see my life as a sort of inferior Greek tragedy, full of ifs and if-nots and heavy ironies. The *hamartia*, the fatal flaw in myself that caused me to seduce Millie—from this, everything has flowed. If I had not done so, Graham would not have been born, and Millie might still be alive. If Graham had not been born, there would have been no letters for Janet to intercept. If Janet had not then discovered about Millie, the last year of our marriage would not have been such as to erase all our previous life together and to alienate James and Becky from me; they have never forgiven me for their mother's death. And if Janet had not died when she did, I doubt if Becky would have taken up with that mountebank Barn, or Harold married a nymphomaniac; fundamentally, these were gestures made against me, gestures of would-be emancipation.

Yes, but wasn't my affair with Millie such a gesture? The last wild fling of a family man, a middle-aged doctor, against the cramping restrictions of home and profession?

No, it was not only that. It was more than an "affair"; I see it now, I knew it then, as the first time in my life I had acted purely on impulse, wholeheartedly, without calculation or self-regard. From the moment Millie came into my surgery, in the late autumn of 1939, I was possessed by her; I did not care what happened to me, my reputation, my family, so long as I had her love. The risks we took! They make my blood run cold now, but, like a soldier who does not care whether or no he is killed, I bore a charmed life. We were never found out.

Ah, a charmed life indeed. That young girl from the slums —what a flower she was! What passion and grace and sweet responsiveness! What a devotion behind it! No, I am not romanticizing her. That incredible summer, picking her up at our secret rendezvous, driving out to our pub in Kent, when the baby had started and I knew the blitzes would soon begin—a time of irresponsibility for me, of the desperate, utter happiness that one wrings out to the last drop only because one knows how transient it must be.

Since then, I have never lived, never really lived, only stayed alive.

And when I told her she must go out of London, for the baby's sake and her own, before the blitzes began, oh, the heart-rending docility and the absolute faith in me that she showed then! Some tears, but not a word of reproach. Not a hint (how many women could have resisted it?) that perhaps I was getting tired of her or using her own welfare as an excuse for ending something that endangered my career.

So she went away; and then she went on the streets and got ill and died—anything rather than be an encumbrance to me. Oh, God! There should be a God to reward her. And I tried to forget her, playing the little hero amongst the bombs and the conflagrations. I just wanted to be dead. A charmed life again, though. Only twenty years ago.

What would my other children think if they knew all this? Would they revise their opinions about the cynical, worldly old martinet they take their father to be? Probably not. Their imaginations are incapable of stretching beyond the point of seeing it as the squalid, clandestine infatuation of a man at the dangerous age for an enticing young bitch.

If Graham could convince me that he has a heart—not like his mother's; that would be too much to ask—but one capable of an infatuation for something outside himself, I would not mind so much. If he could be possessed by something, as I was possessed by her, and risk everything for it— something positive, not this cold and vicious obsession with getting his own back—then there might be hope for him, and if he killed me, I should not have died in vain. But this feeling for his mother he has worked up—I just don't believe in it. He's out for Number 1 every time; it's himself, not Millie, that makes him vindictive.

Of course, I've been blind. I've distorted my vision by trying to see Millie in him, re-create her through him. Otherwise, I'd have recognized the psychopath years ago. Too late now.

Lounging in that chair, his legs over the arm of it, watching me writhe in my very soul when he told me all about his mother's last days—how he enjoyed it, the young brute! And then the threats—not open, but devious, allusive, the torturer's cat-and-mouse game. Not blackmail, I'll give him that. No suggestion of your money or your reputation. I found the melodrama palling on me pretty quickly, and asked him point-blank, "Is your intention to murder me, then?" He pursed his little mouth in that calculating, savoring way, and replied, "You don't deserve to live, do you? You can't want to live, after what I've told you. Well, I don't think you have much longer to live—Father." Then he smiled at me and went out.

What am I to do? Too tired to write more now, let alone see my way straight. I'll write some more tomorrow perhaps. If I am alive tomorrow . . .

So there it is. He intends to kill me. And I must let him kill me. I've slept on it, and that is my conclusion. I owe it to him—or, rather, to her.

I hope, when the time comes (tonight? tomorrow? next week?), I shall have the resolution not to resist; life-and-death scuffles are so ignominious. But shall I? Interesting. Mind over matter; and in my experience matter wins every time.

It all depends how, I daresay. Poison? Enough lethal drugs in the dispensary to put down half my patients. No doubt he'd like to see me expire; justice must be seen to be done —an eye for an eye. But since he does not know that I intend to go like a lamb to the slaughter, he'd be afraid of my denouncing him *in extremis*.

What then? Bullet, knife, strangling, gas, blunt instrument, a strong push into the river? There are so many possibilities I must be on my guard not to guard against.

Knowing him, I know it will be something cold and cunning. Yes, and apt, the punishment fitting the crime; the emotionally retarded, immaturable sort of mind works in that sort of adolescent symbolism. Crude. The poetry of the primitive, the poetic justice of the child.

Oh, my child, our child.

Should I appeal to him? Not to his heart—he has none now, where I am concerned—but to his self-interest? It would be total humiliation; but worse, a humiliation in vain, for he is implacable. It's not merely what he said. It's how he said it, how he looked. I am not the best diagnostician in S.E. London for nothing; I have always known mortal illness when I saw it—a man's death first lifting up its little worm's head within him; and now I know the look of a man set upon another's death—the look that only his victim sees, and that so many victims fail to recognize.

Self-interest! He has only one self-interest. A monomania. To destroy me. Let him.

> Thou shalt not be killed, but needs't not strive
> Officiously to stay alive.

Yes, that's all very amusing and intrepid. But the morality of it? Do I consider it a good thing, in the interests of justice—personal justice as between him and me—to let him become, through my own passivity, a murderer? Ought I not to protect him from himself by protecting myself from him? A nice point in ethics.

If one believed in the soul, in eternal damnation, there would be no problem. But I do not.

If I loved him, love might tell me the right answer. But evidently I do not; it's what he represents for me—there's the bond, the beautiful, ingrown, paralyzing bond.

241

Anyway, how the devil should I protect myself against him? I can't wear armor all day and have every meal analyzed before I eat it.

How Janet would have reveled in this situation, with her Wee Free sense of sin and retribution! Cast thy haggis upon the waters, and so on. No, I should not be mocking at poor Janet; after all, I'm half Scottish myself. And she did her best; brought me all that money and gave me children and made an excellent housekeeper.

Let me face it; there's an ineradicable streak of cheapness in me. Men at the point of death shouldn't indulge their levity. I wonder what they'll do with the money when I'm dead. James will save it, Harold squander it; Becky will marry that worthless little buffoon; and Graham?—how would he use it? They should each get thirty thousand pounds after death duties are paid, and that's not counting my life-insurance policies—another eight thousand pounds to split up among them. Unless . . .

Good God, yes, that's it! Forestall him. If I died before he could kill me—why didn't that occur to me?—it would solve the whole problem. Justice would be done without making him a murderer. The high old Roman way out of difficulties. Fall on one's sword—only I haven't got a sword, and if I had I'm so light I should probably bounce off the point. Petronius, then. The hedonist's method. Euthanasia. Yes, that's the answer.

But don't think of it in terms of expiation. It is simply to save him—I mean to pacify her shade. Expiation is a meaningless concept socially, however necessary it may be for the individual's peace of mind.

Nothing, *nothing* can redress what happened to Millie. The squalor, the hemorrhages, the appeals I never answered. Her despair, her death, for me they blot out forty years of good work. Crowds will flock to my funeral. They'll eulogize the good physician. They'll not know I was dead years before they put me in the ground.

Tired, tired. Can't write much more. Wonder what Strangeways and Miss Massinger made of it all at dinner last night. I must do it soon. But I'm too tired to kill myself tonight. I suspect it may need more resolution than I'd thought.

Millie, Millie. First seen sitting on that wooden bench in a row of patients. Heart-shaped face. Slender, golden—a daffodil, common and unique. The sweetness. The trust, the absolute trust. Betrayed. An old man's quavering, mawkish sentimentality. How Graham would jeer at it!

Nevertheless, Millie my only love, those brief months of ours were the one time when, outside my work, I have lived fully, positively, with all of myself, because I was totally involved in you. If that was an illusion, it's worth a lifetime of sanity.

But I sent you away—from the best, least selfish of motives—but it meant slowly waking up—no, slowly returning into the sleep of habit, convention, self-regard. So I dwindled back to "normal," shrank back again within the limits of what life had made me and people expected of me.

It was your nature, my love, to accept and to forgive. If you were alive, I would not even have to ask your forgiveness. But you are dead, and myself I cannot forgive. . . .